I0619875

The Ink Weave

A Collection of Short Stories

Fatima Razi

Published by

Cover by Fatima Razi
Illustrated by Fatima Razi

First Published and printed by Authorhouse UK, 10/25/2014.
ISBN: 978-1-4969-9276-5(sc)
ISBN: 978-1-4969-9277-2(e)
1st Edition

Published with Inktribe on Amazon/Kindle © 2023 Fatima Razi.
2nd Edition

DEDICATION

For Javed.
Because you are the only romance in my life.

CONTENTS

ACKNOWLEDGMENTS

Writing a book is a slow, lonely and sometimes emotionally draining experience. But my short stories are fun, fast and such a blast to write. None of these would be here without my friends and family. So to those who read them, those who brought me coffee, and those who inspired the women here, I thank you.

And none of this would be possible without my mentor and boss Mahe Zehra Husain, who inspired me to just do it. To put myself out there again and not be afraid. So thank you MZ for this book.

CATCHING THE BULL'S EYE

Two days ago, my life was simple.

Two days ago, I didn't have to be handcuffed to the backseat of a muscle car.

Two days ago, I wasn't the victim.

"You might as well stop glaring at me sweetheart, I have thick skin."

"To go with your head?" I shot back sweetly, batting my eyes at the back of his big thick head.

To be kidnapped is one thing. To be kidnapped and subjected to this kind of manhandling is another. Although I don't want to, I have to add here that my kidnapper works for my father. Only my father would know who to send.

My kidnapper happens to be six feet four inches of hard muscle. To say the man is built like a truck would be a lie. Because this is no man. My father wouldn't send a man to do this job. No. He sent The Bull.

Meet Hyde Bullwark aka The Bull.

In my father's line of work, I got to see thugs, FBI Agents, politicians and mob bosses; sometimes all in one. And then sometimes you got to see the demons.

The Bull was six feet four inches of inhuman muscle. Even in his finely tailored black pants, and the open-neck black collared shirt, he's more than a man. With long goblin-like ears that are frighteningly elegant compared to the two, eight-inch, red, rough horns growing back along his hairline and tipping up towards the end, Hyde Bullwark is a sight one never forgets. Like the devil's right-hand man, he's the seraph of trouble that stays with you for life well after he's gone.

And then they humanize him with a tiny single gold ring in his left ear. As if that would take away the wide toothy mouth showing canines that could tear bone with a single bite.

My father knew not to send a man to find his daughter.

"You're a sweet kid."

My foot shot out and smacked solidly into the back of his driver's seat, but futilely. There was only a minute jerk of his eyebrow otherwise, he was immovable. Truth was I was aiming for his head, but from my angle, I missed.

He merely reached out and turned up the radio and the 'Kings of Leon' began to sing louder. It didn't help that the monster had great taste in music. Outside my window, the dusty expanse of our misplaced road trip did nothing to ease my nerves.

When I'd gone to college I'd thought my life would be my own. When I'd told my father I was getting married to a nice man, he'd given his blessing, but even then I'd felt a sort of acquiescence. As if he was humoring me. Now I knew why. The man had made me crazy in the first two years of our marriage. He couldn't understand my sensibilities and I realized he couldn't keep up.

A girl who grew up with a demon babysitter was bound to have issues. My father realized my special talent for kicking ass and being stubborn on my third birthday when I refused to share my tricycle with my playmates. So he'd allowed me to spread my wings and fly as far away from the roost as possible; in my little false paradise, I was far away from my father's world, and master of my own destiny.

Well, destiny came to bite me in the ass in the shape of Hyde Bullwark.

"Is this the dreaded silent treatment?"

I resisted the need to spit on him. It seemed my father had probably given him a dossier on me, which meant he probably knew the kind of underwear I wore as well. My father was thorough if nothing else. My silent spells were famous, to say the least.

"Look kid, I know it must be tough."

"Is this the part where you try to relate and offer parental guidance because trust me, it'll fall on deaf ears?"

There was a muted snicker from the driver's seat as he slowed for an intersection. "I know a lot falls on deaf ears with you babe."

"Don't call me babe!"

From what little I knew of him since he'd dragged me out of bed and carried me on his shoulder, I should have probably not demanded anything. The guy didn't react well to orders. I wondered how my father worked with him. Whatever I told him to do; he'd do the complete opposite.

"Whatever you say, babe."

See what I mean?

"I bet nothing gets past YOUR ears," I retorted childishly. I knew it was immature to try and shoot him down, but I was pissed as hell at being hauled like cargo. It didn't take a genius for me to figure out that I wasn't going anywhere else but where he wanted to take me. Not only did he overpower me with sheer muscle, but the guy was fast. Faster than I was and I've had my glory days.

"I've heard all the Dumbo jokes."

"A demon who knows Disney; a wonder of wonders."

"I did have a childhood."

"Have you heard the ones where they say big ears don't necessarily mean big__"

"Yes," he snapped, cutting me off, blood-red eyes glaring back into mine from the rearview mirror. "I have."

I couldn't help but quirk an eyebrow at him. "A demon with sensibilities. Oh, how quaint. Does that mean I can't say 'fuck' without making you flinch?"

"I'll just take it as an invitation, babe."

Instant heat rushed under my skin and I swallowed the unwelcome flush of embarrassment. The last thing I needed was for him to come on to me. My father would see his head roll if he so much as touched me wrong, but that didn't mean he couldn't have a death wish.

"Relax sweetheart, I don't fuck the merchandize."

Hackles predictably raised, I squawked indignantly before straining forward to glare at him. "Who are you calling merchandize you ugly troll?!"

Twisting his head around, he flashed me the widest, most intimidating smirk, complete with fangs. "Resorting to name-calling already?"

"You haven't used my name once since you took me hostage!"

"Now that's harsh, I'd say it was more of a waylay."

"Don't play word bingo with me you overgrown Chihuahua!"

"Lay off the ears!" He growled and the car nearly vibrated with his irritation.

It would have been wise of me to quit while I was ahead, but then I've never been very wise. If I'd been wise I would have gone and settled on Mars to get away from my father. "What's the matter Bully, don't have an EAR for humor?"

The thick fingers seemed to tighten on the steering wheel almost like they were imagining my fragile little neck between them. I was about to

open my mouth and throw another barb at him when he lifted his right
hand off the wheel and slid it back towards me between the front seats.

Shrieking at the large groping fingers around my stomach, I jerked back
against the seat, slapping and kicking at his questing hand as the long arm
allowed him enough slack to manhandle me. "Get your hands off me!"
Screaming and spitting, I was short of biting him, but decided against it
considering the hairless arms looked too thick to damage; my teeth were
human. "Don't you dare touch me!" And then when the seat belt clicked
into the buckle, holding me plastered against the backseat I realized he only
meant to secure me further. But then I could have sworn he coped a feel
while trying to find the belt.

"If you move another muscle," he warned in a low gravely snarl, "I will
rope you like a cow and gag you for the rest of the trip."

I didn't much appreciate being called cattle neither did I want to be
gagged so giving into wisdom, I fell silent. It was only the sound of the
radio and my own calming breaths that hung in the car for a long while.

It was only because he was bigger than me. If he'd been human, I could
have so taken him.

I hated my father.

"So you're my father's new guard dog."

His head whipped around to stare at me when I finally found my voice.

At the incredulous girth of his eyes, I couldn't help but grin back at him.
"What? You said if I moved another muscle. I didn't move at all."

"Your mouth's a damned muscle."

I didn't like the connotation, but that was probably my own gutter brain
and not his intention so I let it slide. "You didn't specify."

"Let me make myself clear then," he grated out through clenched teeth.
"I will truss you like a damned turkey if you do anything else besides
breathe and blink. Are we clear?"

It was a chore not to dissolve in giggles. "There's just one problem."

Shaking his head, he kept his eyes on the road as the car raced down the
empty, dusty road. "What?"

"I'm human. What if I gota hold my pee? Are you sure you want to get
your interior changed?"

He would be banging his head on the steering wheel if we weren't
driving 240 miles per hour.

"What I do with your father is not your concern."

Snickering, I decided that my mouth could get into enough trouble; I
didn't need to move at all. "I suppose; my father has been rather deprived
since my mother died."

The belt was the only thing that kept me from catapulting out of my
seat, through the windshield and out onto the asphalt.

His door sprang open and my eyes nearly popped out of my head when he climbed out. "You know what kid, he didn't say you had to be talking when I brought you in."

And to my horror, he opened the back door and climbed in intending to actually tie and gag me.

To say I reacted badly would be an understatement.

Even though I couldn't manage much with one hand bound to the seat frame, I kicked and screamed as the bulk of his muscle came down over my torso and his wicked leer blurred my vision. FYI, I don't hit like a girl, but whatever my thrashing frame hit, the guy only grunted in annoyance as I was un-cuffed and thrown on my stomach to be 'trussed like a damned turkey'.

And then everything around me exploded.

With my world twisting off its access, the screech of metal and shriek of glass drowned out any protests I might have had. The creature that had been holding me down was now wrapped around me like a cocoon. One big hand was cradling my head against a hard pectoral, the other wrapped snuggling around my left butt cheek as everything around me twisted and rolled and rolled before coming to a slow groaning stop.

The hard jut of his prominent cheekbones pressed against my head, his legs wrapped around mine, I forgot that I should probably kick his ass for groping me. My breath was harsh, painful against his throat, every bone in my body jarred, every muscle and tendon stretched in protest, every hair follicle standing on end. Then I saw the metal frame of the car wrapped around us like a metal blanket, the seats ripped and broken as we lay somewhere between the gearbox and the back seat.

Someone had rolled the gorgeous blue Shelby into a pretzel. And we were still inside.

"Babe?"

Mouth parting on a ragged breath, I clutched the soft cotton of his shirt in my fists. "Don't," I half croaked, half coughed, "call me..."

The puff of chuckling breath wafted across my temple and he lifted his head far enough to meet my eyes. "Obstinate woman."

"Coming from a Troll, that's a compliment," I gasped. "Oh god, I can't move."

"Maybe because we're rolled like a burrito." I felt more than saw his back muscle flexing as he tested the shell around us. "Hold still."

Burying my face back against his chest, I let him extend one arm up slowly as he bent the metal top of our poor car with his bare hands and tore an opening. There was a moment I marveled at the play of muscle in his biceps but then he deftly rolled himself on the bottom and then his hands landed on my ass, hauling me further up the stretch of his body.

"Hey!" Eyes widening, I glared down into vermillion eyes when they came directly under mine.

7

The demon underneath me seemed to simmer with irritation. "Don't flatter yourself, sweetheart; it's better than having you trying to crawl all the way up. Now shut up and reach."

Before I could tell him what he could do with his help, I was thrust up toward the opening. It took me time to climb out of the junk and it was only when I stood next to the shell I'd crawled out of that I realized what had happened.

Something had hit the muscle car from behind and thrown us at least twenty feet off the road. I would have run for freedom but I was still staring at the blue oval shape of twisted metal that used to be a Mustang.

Hyde landed in the dust beside me with a resounding thud, the ground nearly shaking underneath his weight. It was then that I realized that had Hyde not been in the back already wrapped around me, I wouldn't have been discernible from the metallic wreck we'd climbed out of. And then I saw the cuts and bruises on his arms and legs, the faint trail of red on his forehead. Like an idiot, I stared up at him in horror.

The red eyes blinked at me for a second, an eyebrow hiking up in question as he dusted himself. "It's okay."

"Okay!?" I shrieked as the first waves of panic and shock crashed over me. "HOW is this okay?!" I pointed to the twisted metal pretzel. "This is NOT okay!"

Holding up both hands as if in surrender to my panic attack, he spoke calmly, almost tenderly. "Alright, I realize that you're in shock."

"Shock!" I knew I was repeating everything he said, unable to catch even a thread of his calm and I'm not the kind of person to lose it easily. "This doesn't begin to define shock! Someone crashed into us and disappeared into thin air. You're bleeding and I'm about to have a heart attack. Define how this is alright!"

The unflappable creature seemed to draw a slow breath, running a weary hand through his slicked raven hair, fingers slipping over the rough red horns that seemed even starker in the sunlight than his ears.

Then his ears twitched. Almost like a cat's.

I had meant to laugh but he was already reaching for me. "Hold on to me."

"What!?" My shriek melted into a choked breath as he swung me onto his back and the first gunshot was fired.

Then he was running.

I've ridden horses before. I've ridden amusement park rides. I've even ridden one of the best species of men. The man that shall not be named anyway, but I would take any roller coaster over piggy-backing on Hyde's back. It makes me wonder what the damned cowboys thought was so cool about riding a raging bull. Or in this case a running bull.

My thighs were bruised, my arms were bruised, and I'd knocked my head into his a few times. He wasn't only thick-skinned like I'd thought. His head was as hard as a rock. It felt like years that he sprinted at inhuman speeds through the dusty landscape, but it was only twenty minutes. And even though he was layered with a fine sweat, he didn't look winded. Now I realized how he was so damned fast.

This guy was all muscle.

And he was slowing. Then stopping.

And then he was falling.

Muffling my yelp against his throat, I was just in time to slip out from under him as he collapsed.

In the middle of nowhere.

"Perfect." I lay there on the ground, flat on my back as I stared up at the cloudless sky. "Just perfect." Turning my head I looked at the thing heaped beside me and wondered what side of the bed I'd woken up on. I must have done something horrible to end up here. He, on the other hand, was still lying there on his face in the dust. "Fucking perfect."

Propping my elbow on the ground, I slowly rolled to my side and crawled over to his big stupid carcass. What was the point of saving my hide if he was only going to fall over dead in the end? Then I realized that he wasn't dead. In fact, given the amount of blood making red mud on the ground, it could very well be that if he wasn't dead, he would be.

The guy who saved my life was going to be lying in a pool of blood. And all because my stupid father wanted his daughter to come back to the roost. It was so damned unfair. There was no way I was getting his death on my hands.

Rolling him on his back, I was relieved to see that even though he was bleeding, the gash on his forehead wasn't as big as my imagination had made it. For a moment I wondered if tearing my shirt to make a bandage was cliché. But there was a problem. In the movies, the heroine cut her shirt with her teeth and tore it into neat little bandages. Not only did my hero resemble a villain, but there was no way in hell I could cut my expensive t-shirt into anything with my teeth.

Then I reasoned. He was a thug. Thugs all carry some kind of weapon. And lo and behold, I found the knife in his belt. The fact that I stopped to admire the rather yummy peak of his abs is nothing. I mean he is an overgrown Chihuahua. So not my speed. Either way, I managed to cut off his sleeves up to his elbows and tied them to make one very black bandana slash bandage.

I was gloating and admiring my work when the scarlet eyes opened, focused and darkened with disappointment. I couldn't help the tight smile. "Yes tubby, I'm still alive. Thanks to you."

Grunting, he sat up too fast for me to react and all too soon we found ourselves nose to nose. To say I was surprised would be stretching it.

Because the troll I'd been shanghaied by this morning was not the same guy who was staring into my eyes now.

Although hot around the collar, I noticed his features were bold with a strong, straight high-bridged nose, a powerful chin, and high, harshly carved cheekbones. And eyes that were the darkest hues of red – piercing and intense. The kind of eyes that froze a woman to the spot whenever he directed his attention on her and sent grown men scurrying into crevices. I realized that if I stuck my tongue out I could taste him and the thought shocked me into immobility.

Almost as startled as I was at our proximity, his vermillion eyes were suddenly unsure. And the misplaced emotion on the monster was oddly endearing. "You didn't run away," he mumbled incredulously.

And just like that, my pride decided to assert itself. "Hey! I'm not completely unscrupulous. The only reason I tried to get away before was because you kidnapped me from my bed."

"You make me sound like a cradle snatcher."

"If the shoe fits." Pulling away from the discomfiting notion of his breath on my face, I wrinkled my nose and rose to my feet and dusted my poor designer jeans.

"What the hell happened to my shirt?"

Blinking down at him, I saw him sit there, with his legs sprawled out in front of him like a petulant child, his mouth hanging open as he stared at the jagged edges of his black sleeves.

"You were bleeding."

Eyes snapping up, he stared at me as if he wasn't the one with the horns on his head.

I merely shrugged. "What? Did you think I was going to cut my perfectly good and healthy t-shirt?" With a snort, I stretched the crick in my back and walked a few paces away. "So, which way are we going?"

"I used to think your father liked me."

Turning my head, I frowned at him. "Is this where you tell me how you regret saving my life, blah blah woof woof?"

"That or I could just tell you the truth."

"Which is?"

"I get paid."

Fury burning in my gut, I reached out to kick him in the shin, but the demon had already rolled to his feet and now towered a good foot above me. I hated how God made all the male species bigger. It's degrading. And unfair as hell. "Maybe I shoulda left you bleeding in the dirt!" Stomping my foot I turned and started walking.

"Babe?"

And I kept walking. I would have continued walking had he not chosen to stay silent. Because it was the realization that he might actually let me walk away that made me stop. Looking over my shoulder, I glared at him. "Are you coming?"

"No."

Whipping around, I planted my hands on my waist and scowled. "Listen you ungrateful troll, just because you rescued me from a crushed car doesn't mean that this isn't your fault, to begin with! You started this!"

"Yeah, sweetheart." His mouth parted into a leer, mocking and vile. "But there is only one problem with your request."

"What!?"

He lifted one tanned arm and pointed behind him. "The nearest town is that way."

I will admit it. I had one fiery urge to be buried alive there, but then the self-satisfied gleam in his red eyes breathed courage back into my limbs and I stalked toward him. And for a moment, just one solitary, satisfying moment, he thought I was coming straight at him. So it gave me infinite happiness to walk past him and keep walking. This time I knew he was following me.

*

"You want me to what!?"

"Book us a room and get a key, I'll meet you at your window."

I gawked up at the man as he stood beside the drain pipe. He was pretty fast I could give him that. And strong, I had seen the evidence. But he was looking increasingly pale and decidedly wobbly. To expect him to climb into a second-story window would be a disaster. But then having a demon walk into an old Inn would be suicidal. Demons weren't trusted. Hell, a lot of folks still thought they were the stuff of legends.

And I realize that it's downright ironic and comical to be worried about my ex-kidnapper turned savior now damsel in distress. I mean, let's face it, there was no way in hell I was going back to my father in a body bag. Or to explain why I'd killed his best man. Demon. Whatever. I couldn't let him die.

Letting out a slow breath I nodded. "Fine. I'll try and get something on the ground floor."

"You're most kind." His tone, although, didn't indicate he was grateful at all.

Ignoring the need to bite him, I relented that it was a thought that was linked less and less with how much I hated his arrogant male complex. I walked through the front door of the rickety Inn and was instantly hit with the smell of tobacco and old shoes. That was the trouble with this country. Everything smelled of cowboys. Hoping that my overly bright smile didn't scare away the innkeeper, I approached the desk and rang the little bell.

The beady-eyed man turned to me with narrowed eyes.

In the ten minutes it took to procure a room for myself, I was propositioned twice, offered a job and free room and board if I decided to sleep with him. After having said no on all accounts and threatening to break his nose with my fist he finally noticed the shiny hundred-dollar bills that Hyde had given me and led me to the room in the back. On the ground floor.

Getting him out of my room was a feat on its own and I tried to catch the sleazy man's fingers in the doorframe but the little bugger was pretty fast. Maneuvering Hyde through the window was another. Although he had managed to throw his leg inside, he decided to fall asleep on me while the rest of him was still outside. The inhuman sprint for our lives had probably taken most of his energy. Cursing the aching muscles I would have in the morning, I finally managed to haul his big ass inside and let him fall into a heap on the floor. He could sleep there for all I cared. I wasn't his nurse.

The hot water in the shower beckoned me.

It was nearly dawn when the bed dipped and the springs began to scream in protest. When the fingers wrapped around my waist, I came up screeching, but the hand slid up my side and curled around my mouth before I woke the neighbors.

"Christ," he hissed against my ear, his teeth grazing the shell so I couldn't help the shiver that skated down my spine. I chalked it up to fear when he finally spoke. "It's just me."

Grabbing his fingers firmly with my own, I dragged his big hand away from my jaw and glared over my shoulder into his glowing red eyes. "It's never just you. What the hell are you doing groping me in the dark?"

"If I was groping you, babe, I'd have gone for the breasts."

As heat slowly flooded my cheeks, I wriggled away from him far enough to realize that he'd taken ninety percent of the bed. Either I could fall off the side, or let his shoulders and legs rest against mine. The floor actually seemed more welcoming. "You're a pig."

"You really need to make up your mind."

It was pointless to reply to him, it would only be an encouragement, so I cursed my father for having sent this creature after me and settled on my side, resigned to letting his arm press into the length of my back.

Then his knuckles slid against the curve of my ass and I spun around with a glare. "You did that on purpose."

Even in the dark, I could see the flash of white fangs as he chuckled. "You picked the room with one bed."

"The double bed was on the second floor and the damned manager offered to share it with me."

"Should I go break his face?"

I had been prepared for another barb, something like how the sleepy old manager was all that would hit on me, but the very serious, very pragmatic question he threw back at me, suddenly stole all sanity from my brain. Why the hell did that sound so nice coming from his mouth? I wanted to ask him if he would do that for me? But I knew the answer, so I asked the question I wasn't sure about.

"Because my father pays you to."

"No." He answered matter-of-factly. "Because I am meant to protect you."

Shifting onto my back, I craned my head to look into his face, the moonlight doing odd and eerie things to the fangs and sharp slants and slopes there. "Really?"

The head turned; the red horns were almost black in the monochrome light of the moon. He really was a nice-looking troll.

"No. Not really."

"Asshole." Scowling at the twinkle of mirth in those fathomless eyes, I shuffled back onto my side, slapping my pillow into perfect shape and refused to turn around even when he stopped laughing and spoke my name.

I was almost convinced that I wasn't sleeping next to a monster when one strong arm looped around my waist and I slid back against the hard warmth of his chest and thighs. "Hey!" Stiffening immediately, I grabbed his hand in an effort to dislodge it from where it was comfortably splayed against my stomach, nearly encompassing the soft belly completely with his large palm and long fingers.

"There's not enough room, relax."

"Get your hands…"

"Shhhhh babe," the husky breath whispered against the back of my neck and my pulse skittered off its kilter. "Nothing's going to happen to you while I'm here," he promised against my ear softly with a gentleness that was uncommon for his power and size. "Just sleep."

And almost like every nerve in my body seemed to turn into him, my body relaxed and the fingers of sleep pulled my eyes shut.

*

Morning found me in his arms. Not spooned together as we'd fallen asleep, but full-on embracing in the streaming sunlight. He was on his back, one of his thick hands curled into his pillow, the other resting easily into the small of my back as I lay there sprawled on top of him like a protective blanket. My legs were tangled in his thicker ones, one hand laying over the slightly faster beat of his heart, the other embarrassingly enough jammed into one of the front pockets of his jeans. It was that damned hand that was the root of all my troubles.

Because somehow I'd managed to get it wedged in tight and on his back, there was no slack for me to pull it out. It was also the reason I'd come awake, because of lack of circulation it had fallen asleep. If I flexed my fingers, they'd be touching him in places that I was sure wouldn't be appropriate. If I tried to pull it out, he'd wake up and find my hands down his pants. Either way, I realized. I was fucked.

And then I totally forgot about waking up. Because yesterday while he'd been accosting me and carrying me around like a sack of flour, I'd seen that he had a beautiful body. But here in the soft light of the morning sun on his face I noticed that underneath all the fangs and horns, he was gorgeous. High prominent cheekbones, square firm jaw, sharp proud nose and wide wicked mouth didn't seem as intimidating now that it was relaxed in sleep.

The insane urge to kiss him was nearly overpowering. I blame him for the whimper that escaped my mouth when his tongue slid out to wet his bottom lip and the red eyes slowly opened. Maybe I stared too long. Maybe I'd laid there through the whole morning, but now he was waking up and my hand was still wedged into his pants. I had to do something. There was no way in hell I'd ever be able to live this down. So as quickly as I could before he came back to earth, I shifted my torso and let his hand slip further down onto my ass rather than my back and watched his eyes find their focus and then widen. The mouth I'd found totally irresistible parted on a startled breath. "Shit."

"I told you this was a bad idea."

His fingers flexed on the round flesh of my ass to reaffirm where it was before he swallowed thickly. The sudden bob of his Adam's apple was rather enticing. Maybe the previous day's insanity and the morning magic were making me horny. Maybe he was endorphin-induced male ambrosia in the morning because I had no explanation for why I suddenly thought he was so damned cute.

"Who accosted who in their sleep?"

"No idea." I was pretty sure it was me, but I couldn't very well tell him that. "Hand still on my ass by the way."

I could have sworn there was another squeeze before the warmth of his palm slid away and then to my absolute horror, he extended both arms up over his head and stretched like a big cat. With his body rolling underneath mine like a porn-induced fantasy, I decided that if I didn't get away from him in the next ten seconds, I'd never leave that bed with my clothes on. So throwing all caution to the winds, I yanked my hand out of his pants and rolled off him in one quick move and rose to my feet. "I get the bathroom first."

And then I gave myself the coldest shower I'd ever had.

What was it with women and big strong demons?

It was indecent! I was a sick, sick woman.

When I emerged, the tall demon was standing in front of the bureau mirror examining his stubble and the cut on his forehead. I had a rather tempting mental image of walking up to him and wrapping my arms around him from behind. I didn't know if he would mind or not, but I was pretty sure that my father would have his head on a plate. Besides the usual male groping most women become accustomed to, he had been keeping his distance. Sort of. Truth was, that line had blurred a long time ago.

His eyes met mine in the mirror and darkened with a question.

Dressed in my previous clothes, I didn't feel any cleaner, but beggars couldn't be choosers. "Bathroom's free."

My breath froze in my lungs for a moment when he turned and walked towards me, a predatory gleam in his eye. If he chose this moment to throw all caution to the wind, I realized I would go down happy. But when he walked past me to the bathroom it struck me that he was merely enjoying my predicament and paying me back for yesterday.

Petty, self-serving, sexy asshole!

Deciding that it would serve him right to think I'd run away, I went down to arrange for some breakfast. I didn't know what he ate, but the wad of bills he'd handed me yesterday was still in my jeans so I walked downstairs and begrudgingly asked the sleazy old man for some breakfast. The little dining room filled with people as I waited. Chattering and ignoring the oddly bedraggled woman between them.

The street outside was busy with old trucks and dusty people going on with their day. I wondered what it would be like to disappear into a little town like this. Where it didn't matter that stock prices were plummeting. Where no one bothered about advertising. Where angels and demons didn't have to be two sides of the same coin. Living with my father and his world of glitz glamour and intrigue, I'd always longed for this simplicity. I'd always wanted to disappear.

Now I had bullets flying around me and possible killers on my heels while I tried to make it back to my father. Of course, there was one very big problem still upstairs in my room.

There was a hiss of whispers and the distinct sound of male boots on the hardwood floor behind me. When all heads turned in unison, I realized that my big problem was no longer upstairs. With a groan, I let my head drop into my hands as the chair scraped against the floor before he sat down.

I didn't have to look up to realize he'd just blown our cover.

"That was a stupid thing to do."

Lifting angry green eyes I took in his shaved and showered form only to flounder at the prospect that even with his cut-off sleeves and wrinkled clothes, he appeared completely dignified. That's a lot to say for a guy with horns and dog ears. Safe to say he'd found himself a baseball cap somewhere, it barely fit his head, but it was enough to cover the horns and his ears. Everyone was staring because without the sharp reminder of his demon heritage, he appeared to be just a tall, good-looking, broad man with a body most women killed for and men died to get.

Any anger I might have mustered sifted out like smoke as I stared at him in horror. I needed to see the horns. The horns reminded me that he was untouchable. Without the horns and the fangs, he was no longer a troll. He was a very masculine and sexy man.

"Babe."

Blinking out of my stupor, I managed a half-mast glare. "Why couldn't you stay up, I was bringing breakfast."

"There was no secret message in the bathroom mirror." He leered at me and I wondered if he was hinting at the fact that he would have liked the intimacy of foggy bathroom mirrors. But I was sure it was just my overactive imagination and hormones.

"Where'd you get the hat?"

"I ransacked a room on the first floor."

Mouth dropping open, I missed the Inn Manager walking up to us until two plates were smacked down in front of us.

"Who's your friend sweets?"

I would have told old sleazy what I thought of his prying, but Hyde lifted deadly scarlet eyes to the man and I could have sworn there was a growl under his breath. "Take a hike, she's mine."

The little old man didn't waste a single moment in darting away. When The Bull turned back to his breakfast and noticed my stunned expression he rolled his eyes. "Don't let it go to your head."

"That was unnecessary."

"Eat your breakfast."

There were times his infinite hotness wasn't as apparent as I would have liked. He could piss me off with only one well-placed cutdown. And it didn't help that he treated me like a child. Maybe that's what I was to him. A responsibility.

Maybe I was suffering from Stockholm Syndrome.

Yeah. That was probably it. He wasn't hot. I had tunnel vision.

"So are you going to tell me who tried to kill us?"

"No."

The demon only grunted when my booted toe smacked into his shin. The red eyes skirted up deliberately and sharpened with warning. I merely held his gaze until he let out a disappointed little sigh. "Do you have any idea why your father wants you back?"

"Because he's tired of bossing you around?"

"He never gets tired of bossing me around."

I remembered the rather lascivious comment I'd made about their working relationship and my mouth twitched with laughter.

His scowl meant he remembered as well. "Fuck this, no money is worth this." Even though I could hear the dismissal in his voice, I took into account that he'd already devoured his breakfast and his eyes were amused.

Snickering under my breath, I grabbed the toast and jumped out after him, trailing behind him as he paid the manager and stepped out into the morning sun.

As we walked down the road in companionable silence, I realized it didn't matter where we were going. Somewhere along the road, I learned to trust him. Trust him to keep me safe. But then he had made the promise as well. He would keep me safe. Nothing could harm me while he was around. And even though I was the most independent of women there was something about this guy. It made me want to be protected. It was stupid, juvenile and everything against my feminist independent notions.

"Do you care at all?"

The question caught me off-guard. "About my father?"

"About why he wants you back?"

"Do I have a choice in the matter?"

He stopped so fast that I nearly walked into him. Blinking up at him, I watched him squint down at me, his eyes darker under the shade of the baseball cap. "If I said yes, would you still go with me?"

Why didn't he say go back to my father? Why did he have to look down at me that way and ask me to go with him? It was unfair. Swallowing thickly, I rallied all my courage and tried for an unaffected shrug. "Probably not."

It was a bald-faced lie and immediately his mouth quirked up at the corners. I should have just kept my mouth shut. Rolling my eyes at his cocky half-smirk, I brought my foot down to step away from him, but one powerful hand wrapped around my wrist and I was yanked out of the sunny street and into the alley against the side of the building.

I probably should have screamed. I probably should have kicked. I should have done everything but let him spin me into his arm and smack me into the wall, the bulk of his weight pressing me there, one hand curled around my hip, the other flattened beside my head on the wall.

I should have done something besides gasping in what could only be an invitation and tilting my head back for him.

So you can imagine my mortification when his lips brushed my forehead as his chest rumbled with a soft growl. "Dammit, black SUV, three o'clock."

Oh. So he wasn't overcome with lust and love for me. He'd merely been shielding me from our pursuers. The thought that I wasn't in any eminent danger was overshadowed by irrational disappointment. It took a gargantuan effort not to let the discontent show in my voice. "The Inn?"

"Too risky," he whispered against my temple, eyes on the passing vehicle. His hand slid down my arm to curl around my wrist and soon he was pulling me deeper into the alley. "Come on, we need to find a car and some decent cover." I wanted to point out to him that there was a rather tall wall on the other end but I knew not to question him. He always had a plan.

At the blockade, he shifted his body and crouched low and then to my shock he shot up and jumped agilely onto the top of the walk, squatting there like Spiderman, his muscular legs bent. With one large hand, he held the girth of the brick and reached the other out to me.

I was starting to get seriously ticked off by his need to spoil me with his knight-in-shining-armor attitude. Maybe it was me. I'd given him the wrong impression. Maybe the only way to get my head on straight was if I got my own act together. What happened in the alley was proof enough. I needed to remind him I wasn't some simpering little girl he was returning to her father.

So with a deep breath, I took a few steps back.

His eyebrow shot up in humor. Was I running?

But I wasn't running. Not away from him anyway.

Bracing my foot against the ground, I took off in a dead run for the wall and jumped. If he hadn't been holding the wall, he might have fallen as I scrambled up the bricks, my sneakers finding just the right leverage and then I was up and over landing on the other side in a neat crouch.

My smile was triumphant as he dropped down beside me. "Show off."

"You started it."

"I merely wanted to offer you a hand."

"Oh sure. That wasn't shameless self-pimping. I believe you."

His mouth twitched with a smile as we walked side by side toward a beat-up old truck. "Get in."

The heap didn't look like it had run in decades. "This is our escape?"

"Inconspicuous. Get in," he repeated with a deliberate warning.

With a dejected sigh, I opened the creaking door and slid inside. If something hit us in this old Junker without its safety checks, I doubted a hoard of Hyde's brothers could save me.

The car came alive under Hyde's careful manipulation and soon we were rumbling out of town, with him looking completely at home in the dusty old truck. I stayed low, eyes darting back to the rearview mirror constantly.

A tiny cell phone landed in my lap and I blinked up at him. "You swiped someone's phone?"

"I'm shameless, yes. Call your father."

I would have taken it in better light had he told me to call the executioner. "No." I tossed the phone back at him.

Catching it with one hand, he let out a slow breath. Wasn't I just a constant disappointment to him?

"What the hell happened anyway?"

"Are you trying to be my friend?"

"This is going to be a very long ride Princess, so we might as well."

"I can't be friends with you," I explained calmly. Of course, it wouldn't do any good to tell him it was because I was crushing on him now.

His sigh was sad and defeated. "Don't I scare you at all?"

He was exasperating at times. Laughing, I shook my head. "Yeah Tubby, your long ears are the stuff of nightmares."

His grunt was irritated. "I haven't eaten enough people to deserve this."

"Give it up Hyde. I think we're past the point where you can scare me into doing anything for you?"

"How do I get you to do anything for me?"

"You could seduce me."

The words were out of my mouth before I could smother them.

Damn my sharp tongue. Father said it would get me into trouble.

The demon was uncharacteristically silent as he stared ahead to the road.

We'd come a long way since I'd been bound in the back of his car which was now a metal pretzel. Trying to make light of the situation I grinned at him. "Relax big guy. I was joking. The last thing I want on my conscience is to have my father break your bones."

"Your father won't touch me."

My grin faded like a wilting leaf at the blunt warning. Suddenly the fact that there was nothing but his own restraint holding him back was disconcerting. My father was a formidable man. If Hyde didn't answer to him or if he didn't care, the stakes had just gone up.

I was about to ask him when the little cell phone began to ring. Startled by the sharp interruption I watched the little device vibrate in his lap before he fished it out and answered. "Yeah?" It gave me a few moments to study his profile as he listened to whoever was on the other end. "Yeah," he agreed simply into the phone.

The phone call was obviously expected, but something had come undone in our little blue truck.

"Twenty minutes," Hyde spoke into the phone before he rolled down the window and unceremoniously tossed it outside. He was already pushing the old truck to its limit. I didn't even hear the thing smash into a rock.

The silence was stifling. I wanted to tell him he was a big ugly troll. I wanted him to harp about my stubbornness. His silent treatment was a lot more painful than my own.

"Are you going to ignore me now?" I asked, unable to help myself; I crossed my arms and glared at him. "Is that your new strategy, because I gota tell you it sucks."

"Shut up Amila."

My name on his lips suddenly cut like razor blades all over my skin. The sound of it caught me off-guard. I thought maybe he didn't know my name. To speak it with such conviction was staggering. Even if he hadn't demanded my silence, I wouldn't have been able to form a complete sentence anyway.

"There's a chopper coming for you."

Shocked out of my stupor I gawked at him. "What?"

"It's not safe anymore on the road for you. I asked them to come to pick you up."

"I hate flying!"

"I know that; your father told me, but circumstances are unavoidable. You're taking the bird."

I didn't like how he said 'you' instead of 'we'. "Would it be bad humor if I made Dumbo jokes now?"

"No, coz I ain't flying."

My fears were confirmed; I couldn't help the bubbling panic. Panic that he was going to hand me off to someone else. Panic that I might never see him again. Panic that it mattered whether I saw him again or not. I was out of my mind. This was stupid and ridiculous on so many accounts. I didn't know what to say to him. I wanted to rant, rave, and demand that he finish his job himself. I wanted to ask him if he was abandoning me. I needed to know if he'd felt anything while he'd held me in his arms all night?

"What happened to 'it's a long ride and being friends'?"

"You don't want to be my friend."

"Is that what you're all pissy about!? It was a joke."

"Let it go Amila."

"STOP calling me Amila."

Flashing red eyes snapped to me, sending twin chills of fear and excitement down my spine. "What the hell do you want from me?"

Good question. But I had no answer for him now so I evaded. "Is this because I said you should seduce me? I thought you had a sense of humor you big ugly troll!"

"I do. And it amuses me that a little slip of a girl thinks she can be my friend."

He might as well have slapped me. For a moment I was silent and the only sound in the car was that of the protesting tires being pushed to their limit. I couldn't help it. I shook my head sadly. "For a big bad demon Hyde, you sure are a coward."

"Better a coward than getting freezer burn."

That was more like a well-placed sock in the gut. All my life I'd been called the ice princess. Now I knew that he probably knew every little weakness. Everything he could use to twist and hurt me. I should have gotten angry and although my blood boiled, my pride screeching for retribution, the moisture in my eyes was sadness.

He didn't say anything after that. I hated him too much to say anything to him.

Not until I saw the black chopper in the distance, the round crest on the side a sharp reminder of where I was going. As the truck ambled closer, I couldn't stop the words as they bubbled out of me. "My father is calling me back because it's my turn to take over the family business. Because my dead half-demon mother didn't give him a son. He got stuck with me." Turning my head, I saw the muscle working in his jaw. "Do you know what he said to me when I told him I was going to marry Frank? He didn't say 'good luck daughter'. He didn't say 'I love you, sweetheart, be happy'. He said 'I'll wait.' He knew I was going to fail at being human even before I started. I guess he was right. What you are, you can never change. I'm sorry that you're just like him."

My door fell open under my weight even before the truck had rolled to a stop and then I was my father's daughter as I walked across the dusty ground towards the snarling black helicopter.

But I was also the woman who wanted to be more than what destiny demanded.

My hand on the metal rail of the four stairs, I wondered if I should turn around and look at him one last time. Because after I climbed into the bird, I would never see him again. The woman was allowed the weakness, but the chair my father vacated would not.

The craving to turn around was nearly blinding but I would have climbed in had I not heard his voice.

"Babe."

Like a puzzle piece sliding into place, I turned to reach for him. His arms wrapped around me like bands of steel, his mouth coming down hard on mine. And I was lost.

If I'd imagined his kiss to be hot, the heat of his lips against mine was scalding. The unspoken hunger and forbidden desire was a burning that started where his mouth met mine but spread through me until I was clinging to him. Desperate to let him soothe the screaming fire in my veins. The hard planes of his body did nothing but mold the soft curves of mine to it. To think I'd waited all my life to find this only to lose it forever.

I wanted to cry, let the tears mingle into our kiss. To douse the longing that burned there, but he gave me no room for anything but to kiss him back. His lips were as devouring as they were with his words, his promises, his threats. They swallowed all restraint and hesitation from every cell in my body, one wide hand holding the back of my head in its palm, the other wrapped around my waist to hold me up against him, fingers fisted into the back of my t-shirt.

If my father's people around us stared in shock, I never noticed.

I let my hands run up the sharp rough slants of his face to push away the baseball cap so I could touch him better. My tongue tangling with his, I let my fingers explore the duality of sensations; the rough hard bone of the horns, the soft silk of his raven hair. Then my fingers skimmed over the long line of his elf-like ears and his mouth slanted on mine and stole me from myself.

I've been kissed a lot in my life, but I knew that this would be the last kiss I'd remember.

And then he was releasing me, his hands sliding up to my shoulders, grasping there and tenderly pushing me away, but his mouth lingered on mine, gentling the kiss until I wanted to scream and hold him in place. His lips parted from mine and shared one last, longing breath with me before he stepped too far away for me to touch.

The vermillion eyes were already saying goodbye long before he turned and walked away.

Letting my eyes slide shut, I let them guide me into the black chopper and to the life, and I'd been running away from since I was three.

*

He watched her with confused eyes. For two weeks, he'd been asking and the girl had been evasive. He'd run out of questions. He'd thought she'd finally be happy. He couldn't, for the life of him understand why The Bull had failed. He'd never counted on this outcome.

The familiar green eyes lifted and an eyebrow quirked. "Will you please just say whatever it is that's cooking in that wicked old head of yours?"

The old man leaned back into the couch while his daughter sat behind his desk, fixing his accounts. "I resent that." Her head tilted curiously and Murphy grinned at her. "I'm not that old."

Rolling her eyes the beautiful young woman went back to her numbers. "Amila?"

"No father I'm not in the mood to share my woes with you."

"I cannot understand why you are unhappy."

And that was the wrong thing to say, he realized the moment her eyes flashed with fire. "You don't?" Her hands smacked onto his mahogany desktop and she rose to her feet like an accelerating hurricane. "You don't know! You honestly don't know! You decrepit, old, selfish man! You have no idea why I'm not happy!?"

Eyebrow raised in a slight arch, he tilted his head in a suspicious expression that might have been saying 'no shit'. He didn't know what they called it these days. But he was thoroughly lost. "I've been trying everything to find an answer to that I believe."

"You screwed me over, you nasty, old man!"

"I?!"

"You sent me off with Frank with that glint in your eye. Yeah, you know which one. The 'I'm smarter than you little baby and I'm just humoring your spoilt little ways when in reality I'm just waiting for you to fail' look!"

Murphy resisted the need to smile at her. Like her mother, if he tried to reason with her while she was headed to the crest of her anger, he'd get dragged along for the wild ride. So he bit back the chuckle at the poignantly familiar sight of his daughter having a hissy fit just like his wife used to. It was a good thing he was well-equipped. "My daughter?" He looked at her with what he hoped was honest shock. "Fail?"

Blinking at him in bewilderment, she seemed to go around in circles in her head before falling back into the swivel chair as she had done when she was four and defeated. "Oh stop it. You're just humoring me now. I know you."

This time he allowed the affectionate laugh. "You are, most obstinate, my daughter."

"Don't play holier than thou with me father. You knew I'd never be happy," she lamented with a disgusted twist of her mouth.

His snort was equally displeased. "Not with that spineless little boy, Frank. Of course not! Why do you think I sent Hyde!"

Her head snapped up in alarm, mouth comically hanging open. "What?"

The older man shrugged. "I don't feel much remorse for trying to intervene. Although I doubt Hyde knew he was being sent to you on a silver platter, I had such high hopes for him." he shook his head sadly. "Such a shame."

"Whoa!" On her feet now, she lifted a hand towards him to almost physically hold him from speaking. "Whoa. Hold up." Her smile had a touch of insanity. "I must have stepped off into the twilight zone there for a moment because I swear it sounded to me like you sent Hyde on an incognito matchmaking spree. With me!"

His eyes were impassive. Although her eyes pleaded with him to deny it and spare her the meltdown, Murphy spoke clearly, "I did."

Her manic smile elongated into abject shock, eyes abnormally wide, mouth round. "No," she breathed disbelievingly.

"Yes."

Her shock melted into a shriek. "No!"

Murphy rolled his eyes. "This is pointless."

"You wanted me to like him?!"

"Why else would I send him to bring you to me?" He rose with a frustrated breath. "I swear I have always allowed you to make your own decisions. To choose your own path. Find your purpose, but you take this independence thing too far Amila. Wasting yourself in that wilderness because you don't want to admit Frank was a pansy is incredibly stubborn not to mention idiotic! You have a home and a life; you're not a rejected

23

child or a jilted lover. You're my daughter," his voice raised a notch. "And no daughter of mine lives with a 'Frank'."

For a moment, his daughter seemed to sway as if she was caught between hugging him and yelling at him. But then her mouth quirked up in a winsome smile. "You wanted me to like him? You planned this?"

"I only orchestrated it as an order because you never do as you're told. I should have known you'd foil that too." His sigh was defeated, affectionately tired. "Do you realize how hard it is being your conniving father?"

"I'm beginning to realize that," she chuckled low under her breath, shaking her head in amazement.

Instantly Murphy's ears perked up. There was a sad sort of hope in her voice. And then he began to notice the subtle differences. Ever since she'd returned he'd thought she was unhappy, when now that he looked closer he realized it wasn't unhappiness, it was longing. What he thought was bitterness, had actually been regret. And where he'd seen reluctance, he now realized that it had been helplessness.

She wasn't sad about being back, she was sad about being back without The Bull.

For the first time in his life, he had actually managed to get through to his daughter. This would mean Hyde had been the perfect choice. Of course! How could he be so stupid? He was never wrong!

"Amila?"

"Yes, father?"

"What the hell are you still doing here?"

The young woman lifted her head, her pretty, green eyes shining with a new soft glow of faith. Then she ran around his desk and threw her arms around him tightly before dashing out of his office.

Yes, Murphy finally sighed in relief as he walked to his desk. She was just like her mother.

It was comical standing in the hallway with two black-suited men flanking me from both sides. I didn't even want to comprehend what he would think when he finally opened the door. If at all he was in there.

"Yo! Flotsam and Jetsam?"

The two bodyguards blinked at me in bewilderment as if I'd spoken to someone else.

"Don't tell me." I frowned up at them. "The little mermaid? Ursula?"

Their stares were blank.

"No wonder I ran away." I sighed. "I think you boys should stay out here."

"Our instructions were…"

Turning my scathing green eyes on them, I scowled. "Did I stutter? That wasn't a request, or is it that you don't trust The Bull to keep me safe?"

The sudden flare of horror and unease was grotesquely appealing.

I was a very bad human being. I blame my mother's side of the family.

Then the door swung open with a hefty yank and I met the furious red eyes of the demon we all feared and loved. "What!" He roared, his razor in his hand, one-half of his face covered in foam. His ears twitched irritably.

I don't know what it is. Maybe I'm just wired wrong, but I had merry visions of sitting on his bathroom armoire shaving him neatly while he stood between my parted knees. Naked.

I might have been smiling stupidly and for quite some time because Hyde had indeed realized just who had come knocking on his door. "How the hell did you find me?"

His bark finally snapped me back from my daydream and I blinked up at him like a floundering fish out of water. "Huh?"

The corner of his wide mouth lifted up at the corner for a moment, scarlet eyes flashing with amusement. "Amila?"

I finally found enough cognizance to frown at him. "Are we seriously going to have this conversation in the hallway where these two hobbyhorses can hear?"

The two men fidgeted uneasily beside me.

Hyde lifted cocky, deliberate eyes to them and with a triumphant, nearly predatory smirk, he swept his hand into his home. Inviting me inside. "Mi casa, es su casa."

There was something possessive in the way he stared down at the two men itching to follow me inside; I had to roll my eyes. Males were no different no matter what the species.

"Tell me how you found me."

I would have never willingly stepped into the kind of neighborhood he lived in. Even with my half-demon lineage and the two bodyguards, my father had assigned me. I would be too afraid.

The dirty concrete steps leading up to his apartment had been no indication of what lay beyond the browning door that might have been white at one time.

But once inside I realized I had stepped into another world.

There was no other way to describe it.

I'd climbed the stairs to hell and stepped into heaven.

His apartment comprised the entire top floor of the dilapidated building. But there was nothing dilapidated about his living quarters. In one great big wall-less expanse was his living room and kitchen with only a tall black marble counter to separate them. Across the room before the opaque white windows and two steps up was a huge king-size bed in wrought iron. Everything else in the apartment was warm earthy tones of brown, blue, and green with a splash of an odd red and orange somewhere.

The place screamed Hyde and belied the nature of The Bull. Tall bookshelves, endless rows of CDs, littered magazines, and paintings artfully placed. It was like a centerfold out of the living edition of Gentlemen Quarterly.

"Fuck this, I'm going to shave."

Satisfied with my scrutiny of the private life of the demon I'd fallen for, I finally lifted my eyes to him and smiled coyly. "Need help?" Maybe I was lucky.

His jaw hardened before he pointed emphatically to the masculine, black couch by the fireplace. "Sit."

"Woof." I saluted his retreating back and grinned when his feet paused for a heartbeat then with a mutter he disappeared through a door that I assumed led to the bathroom.

But I didn't sit. Trailing around his private world, I let my fingers run over the man he was. I'd met the demon. I wanted to know the man who had kissed me goodbye. The man who would now have to accept me in his life.

I touched everything. The books, the CDs, the bed sheets, the shirts that hung in the closet. The stray cufflinks sharpened the image in my mind. Hide in something more than the ratty jeans and black wife beater. A tux. A tie.

"Do you ever do as you're told?"

I was examining his night table and the big Rolex watch when he came up behind me.

Over my shoulder, I took in his well-worn blue jeans and the predictable white wife beater. But I had to admit the muscle in his shoulders and arm deserved to be aired out. They were fine.

Noticing the blunt interest in my wandering gaze, he tossed the towel he'd been dabbing on his freshly shaven jaw and stalked straight for me. "Honestly woman, you're wearing on my patience. I'm going to get straight answers from you, or so help me…" His growl tailed off menacingly and it took every ounce of my self-control not to let my mouth twitch with a smile. He didn't scare me and I had a feeling he wouldn't be too happy about it. Also, I didn't think it'd be conducive to my mission.

Getting Hyde in my arms.

Since he'd crowded me against the edge of the bed, I happily sank into the mattress as he stood baring down at me like the angry bull he was associated with. "You make it sound like you didn't want to see me again."

If surprise overrode fury, Hyde didn't show it. He merely glared down at me, arms crossed. Immovable. "If I wanted to see you, I'd have seen you."

If I hadn't been acquainted with his man's evasive male posturing I would have been wounded by his words. Rolling my eyes, I leaned back on my hands and delighted in the flick of his gaze over my languid frame. "If you didn't want to see me Hyde you would have tossed me out on my ass the moment I walked in."

"Good idea." He reached out as if to grab me by the scruff of my neck.

He expected me to bolt, but I sat up, my head nearly level with his torso and it was endearing when he took a cautious step back. Actually, it was comical to find that I could intimidate the larger demon. It was an odd rush of power. "Cut it out, Hyde."

"Stop pushing me Amila," he ground out between clenched teeth. "I know why you're here. Nothing's changed." I had no idea what he was implying but then he continued. "Just because you've taken over doesn't make me YOUR goddamn lapdog."

And that was when realization dawned on me. Why he hadn't resisted my intrusion. Why I was still in one piece. The epiphany sucked every last ounce of confidence I'd mustered to come and see him. It drained what little surety I had in his feelings for me.

I was a fool.

He'd come for me before because of my father. Duty.

He was now tolerating me because of the same duty.

How could I have been so damned blind?

"You think I'm flexing my muscle because I'm your boss now."

"Why else would you be here?"

"Bastard," I whispered under my breath, eyes on everything but him. Turning, I rolled across the king-sized bed and came up on my feet on the other side. There was a flash of surprise in those vermillion eyes but I was already rallying my courage to walk.

"Wait."

"Fuck off," I snarled as I marched across the hardwood floor of his living room and headed straight for the front door and Flotsam and Jetsam outside.

The big hand wrapped around my wrist and I swung around with every ounce of anger and rejection bubbling in my belly.

The fist cracked against the rock of his jaw before it was twisted behind me.

I would have bruises later I was sure.

"Let me go!"

Holding both my fists in the expanse of his hands, he pinned them behind me against my lower back and dragged me up off my feet to press against the hard muscle of his chest. Trapping me there, squirming in his firm grip as I resisted the urge to spit in his face.

An involuntary smile darkened his face, his eyes lightening with humor the more I struggled. "Now this brings back memories. I forgot it's dangerous to have you walking around freely."

"Let me go you overgrown Chihuahua!"

Laughing at my spitting anger, he dragged me further up off my feet so I had no leverage whatsoever for an escape.

Then his front door blew open as my two bodyguards flew into the apartment.

For just a moment, we all watched each other in a strange tableau of wary anticipation.

Finally, Hyde's red eyes flared and narrowed on the two guards. "Get out."

Oh dear, I knew that tone. That was the same tone I'd seen him use on the lecherous Innkeeper when he said 'she's mine'. The memory of it warmed me from the inside, despite how this wasn't similar.

Then the steady growl began to grow in his chest. The two men seemed to tremble under the sudden vibration in the air, the wild glint in his demon eyes, the horns fiery red as Hyde opened his mouth and snarled with an almost feral warning.

It was sick and twisted.

Because I wanted to throw him down and ravish him.

The two guards felt quite differently. They took one look at the fangs and fled outside.

The door snapped uselessly back against its now broken lock and finally left me at the mercy of the pissed-off demon. I didn't blame them at all.

Hyde's growling had diminished marginally but his eyes were still trained on the broken door almost as if he could see the two men beyond.

Men! Rolling my eyes, I cleared my throat.

Reluctantly he drew his eyes away from the boundaries of his home and frowned at me. "I hope you're satisfied, woman. You reduce me into a territorial, brainless animal when you're in the same room."

Why did it sound so much like a confession? I was afraid to hope. "Is that supposed to make me feel better?"

"I should hope so."

"Well it doesn't," I glared and squirmed against the solid feel of him. "Will you please put me down?"

"Will you try to hit me again?"

"Probably."

"Shouldn't be so bad; you do hit like a girl."

Anger catching fire, I snorted incredulously through my nose as my knee angled to jerk up between his legs. However, almost as if the freak anticipated my move, he let out a husky laugh against my temple, tightened his hold on me and threw me against the weight of the nearest wall.

When my head hit the wall with an emphatic crack, I saw stars. On the other hand, maybe it was because the hard planes of his body were stretched along mine in the same strange fit we always made. "I swear sometimes I think you get off on holding me down, you big-eared freak."

His warm minty breath chuckled against the rise of my cheekbone. "Tell me why you came here."

I wanted to die first. "Is this some strange pissing contest?"

"It would satisfy my ego, yes."

"It didn't satisfy your ego to smooch the boss's daughter in front of his men that day?"

"This is different."

The sudden somber lilt of his rasping confession snapped my eyes open in alarm. There was an odd weight in his words suddenly. Something had changed. "What are you saying?"

The unshakable intensity of his gaze held me immobile, all thoughts of sex and gratification pushed further back. At first, I thought he wouldn't speak, and then with a defeated shudder of his shoulders, his mouth pressed firmly against my brow in a reverent kiss. "It didn't matter then. It only matters now."

The implications were suddenly too jarring. Struggling against the grip he had on my hands, I drew my head away to coax him to look at me. "Hyde…"

"Babe," Lifting his head away from mine, he sighed and met my eyes and again the depth of the emotion there assaulted me. "If I had seduced you then and you had given in, we would never have been sure why."

My mouth parted with a startled breath. "What…"

One hand wrapping around both my wrists, stubbornly refusing to relinquish his position of power, he slid one hand out from behind me and held my jaw, his fingers stroking there gently. Madly. I wanted to laugh at his need to control me. Silly monster. There was no need to control where we were going. But maybe he knew that.

"I always knew your father was up to something and you wouldn't tell me what the hell went wrong with you both. I respect the conniving old bastard, but I didn't really know how low he'd stoop until you finally told me when you stepped out of the damned truck." His sigh was resigned. "And then I knew why he sent me."

"But you let me go!" I accused him, eyes wide at what he was hinting.

"I let you go so I could keep you babe. So there was no doubt in either of our minds."

My mouth dropped open. "You mean you walked off with that dramatic kiss so you could prove something!" New life charged my bones as I struggled hard against him. "You asshole! You made me wait all this time so you could prove to yourself that I wasn't suffering from Stockholm Syndrome!?"

"Stop." The growl reverberated through every marrow in my body as his hips angled up in a blunt warning.

Hissing partly with the sharp stab of pleasure mixing with my already seething blood, I stilled against him. "Let go of me, you big testosterone-driven BULLY!"

"I imagined this going better," he muttered to himself with a shake of his head.

"LEMME GO!"

Scathing red eyes narrowed on mine and his body pushed me hard into the concrete my breath whooshing out of me in a gasp, all fight leaving my body as the lightheadedness that followed. I was annoying how well he knew to calm me down.

"You!" He hissed viciously against the heat of my mouth. "It was YOU who had to see proof. You, you spoiled little tycoon." I would have bristled but the downward spiral that had started the moment he touched me was dragging me further into the maddening abyss of the freak chemistry he and I shared. My breath harsh, eyes shut; it took every ounce of my willpower to keep from rutting against him as he spoke. "You were the one who had to see it Amila. You were so damned willing to play that tragic heroine. The martyr being led to the damned gallows. It suits YOUR pride to dramatize our purpose. Like your fight with your father. Your apparent running away. The man you married. The fight you put up against me. The truth is sweetheart," he purred and my muscles coiled for absolution as his hips ground harder against mine, "you want to be held down babe. YOU get off on it and your damned father knew it! That's why he sent me. Because I could throw you down and make you mine no matter how much you pretended."

With a cry of triumphant defeat, I arched in his arms. "Oh god, Hyde!"

"Say the damned words and put us out of our misery already."

Vision blurred by the haze of desire singing through my veins and the simple freedom of having someone who could match every blaze of heat there, I met my demon eyes. The anticipation there was gut-wrenching. Demanded obedience. Absolution. "I...," his eyes glinted at the shuttered pause, his tongue darting out to wet his bottom lip almost as if he could taste it.

"I win."

For a breath, he stared down at me incredulously.

Then he threw his head back, roaring with laughter as I smiled triumphantly up at him. His hand slid up into my hair, the expanse of his palm holding my fragile cranium affectionately, his gaze returned to mine still dancing with mirth. "Stubborn bitch."

"Dog-eared troll," I shot back, breath still harsh and panting, body melting and molding against his as he finally released my wrist, and rested his hand beside my head, his other coiling around my waist firmly.

"Shut up and kiss me, babe."

"Don't call mUMPH!"

And we loved happily ever after – until I screamed again.
Flotsam and Jetsam found us on the living room rug.
They quit the next day.

THE END

THE QUEEN OF FLAMES

Alexandra Windmere sat on her throne trying to remind herself that she was queen. For ten years she'd been schooled and prepared to play this role. She'd forgone her dreams, her youth and her passions so that she could be here today. Her parent's death had decimated the adolescent hopes for love, poetry and adventure. In their place had been lessons, etiquette and politics.

No.

They hadn't bred a queen. They had bred a king.

"And his bull has scr__"

"Ahem."

He shot a frightened glance at the intimidating armored Captain beside her. "Begging your pardon your highness," he amended, "defiled my cows! Now he demands he has a share in the offspring!"

Part of being a monarch meant she presided over the court. One of her least favorite things to do. Much to the chagrin of her cousins would think it grand to command other people's lives and tell them what was right and wrong. But Alexandra was bored out of her mind.

Stifling a yawn, she tried to sit up straighter on the throne that was fit for her deceased father who had been a large man. Large in all directions, she recalled affectionately. But she couldn't indulge in one of her daydreams right now; she had to solve the case of the defiled cows. Four hours of helping people solve problems had slid her down into the wooden throne, her legs almost sprawled straight out, chin precariously held on her fist. Dragging in a weary breath she focused on the villager holding his hat in his hand and gazing up at her with imploring, hopeful eyes.

"How many calves have your cows borne?"

Her voice echoed through her vast throne room. The ministers had stayed characteristically silent. Either they agreed with everything she said, Alexandra figured, or they were leaving her to her own demise.

The villager blinked at her in confusion. "Seven your highness."

"And how many of them are male?"

"Er...three I believe," he offered reluctantly.

"Well since the perpetrator was his bull, you will give him the male calves and keep the females."

The villager opened his mouth to protest then frowned as if considering her decision. "Well, I suppose that's fair enough. My calves will grow into more cows."

"Great!" She grinned enthusiastically and rubbed her hands in anticipation. "Are we done?" She turned hopeful eyes to the stiff man standing beside her throne.

Her Captain of the Guard twisted an eyebrow at her blithe display before nodding at her indistinctly. For now, he implied.

Resisting the urge to roll her eyes, Alexandra rolled to her feet instead and bit back the groan her stiff back demanded. Wouldn't do well for the Queen's image to be walking like the Hunchback of Notre Dame, she reasoned. Smiling pleasantly to her ministers, she stepped off the platform, picked up the gold hem of her heavy gown off the floor and walked out of the hall in relief.

Outside, on the way to her retiring room, she let her shoulders droop, slid one fist back to brace against her lower spine and bit her lip. "Next time Gareth, remind me to get a cushion for my royal behind."

"Next time My Queen, if you didn't slide like a drooping violet, you'd fare better."

Tossing him a castigating glower over her shoulder, the young queen stumbled into the familiar and comfortable confines of her retiring room, the Captain closing the ornate double doors behind him. Before he'd turned around, Alexandra had kicked off her shoes, picked up her skirts and collapsed into a helpless heap in the chaise in front of the window. The Captain sighed at the picture she presented.

In the gold of her gown and the sunlight that touched her tumbling flaxen hair, his Queen poignantly reminded him of his deceased King.

Although where he differed in stature, King Raminas had sprawled exactly like his daughter after a hard day's work. "Must you sit like that?"

The delicate face twisted into a grimace and she slid another inch lower in her seat.

Shaking his head, Gareth let it slide. She was allowed her rebellious notions behind closed doors. "I hope you remember. You have to attend the Prime Minister's Son's wedding tonight. You're hosting the reception."

Her grimace morphed into a full-fledged scowl. "Damn it Gareth, I'm going to have to prance around like an idiot while every hopeful dangles himself like a lost puppy under my nose in dreams of becoming my Lord and Master!"

"The Court has been generous in allowing you the freedom to choose at your leisure."

"Bah!" The woman grumbled and slid out of her perch to walk towards the fireplace where her parent's pictures were mounted. "I will marry when I'm good and ready."

"But Your Highness…"

With a tired sigh, she turned her honey-colored gaze to the man who made it all worthwhile. "Must you call me that Gareth? We are alone now."

The Captain frowned. "I suggest you get used to it."

She crossed her arms and turned to him squarely. "Gareth, you've been my playmate, caretaker and confidante. I believe you've earned the right to call me Alexa."

"And I believe the sooner you get used to being My Queen the better."

Rolling her eyes at his stiff and proper rant, she turned back to the smiling faces of her parents. The tall, broad flaxen-haired King sprawled on his throne, his fist resting against his temple, a smile of contentment clear on his face. But those who looked closely would see the mischief and life in his animated green eyes. Beside him stood a petite, mahogany-haired woman with eyes like rum. Like a fairy princess, she stood straight and regal in layers of pink chiffon and rubies. Two unlikely rulers with short little destinies, Alexa lamented. Oh, how she missed them at times like these.

Times when there was so little softness in her life. Times when she wanted to be more than a queen. When she wanted to be a woman. A daughter. A friend. It was sad how she could miss Gareth while he stood in the same room as she did.

And then she felt the gentle hand on her shoulder.

Spinning around, she launched herself into his arms before he could stop her. Burying her face against his cloaked shoulder she held him as she had when he'd been a knight; sent to relay the news of her parent's death.

For one brief moment, Gareth allowed himself to hold the tiny woman with the weight of their kingdom on her shoulders. Touching his mouth to her golden head he smiled. "You're doing a fine job, Alexa."

She reveled in the simple loyalty and love she felt for this man who had been her father, her mother, her brother, and her sister. Her everything. "I still miss them," she whispered, her forehead resting against his chest, drawing strength from him.

His fingers were brief but they passed soothingly over her hair once before he had stepped away to look into her eyes, his hands firm on her shoulder. "And you will miss them always."

She smiled up at him, her demons laid to rest in his fierce loyalty and unconditional support. "What would I do without you Gareth?"

"I shudder to think Your Majesty."

She groaned at the title. "I knew it was too good to last long." She waved an imperial hand at him. "Go now, Captain. I'll shed my ugly skin and dole up like a doll so you can play Pick-The-Perfect-Suitor at the Wedding reception."

His teeth flashed at her wickedly. "I already have a list."

Her shoe hit the closing door and her Captain's snort of muffled laughter echoed around her.

*

Her feet were killing her.

She longed to step out of the death-trap heels and rest her feet. She ached to let them roll back to their natural position, her back screaming for respite, but Gareth had been true to his word. His 'list' had kept her on the floor for nearly three hours with every Duke, Earl and Prince who had yet you tie the noose.

Her mouth curled at the inward joke. The knot even, she amended mentally. Almost guiltily lest her Captain or her tutor Madam Arabella heard her.

"Are you having any fun, Your Highness?"

Crashing back to the world she'd been ignoring, her body automatically following the motions of the dance, she blinked up into the dark eyes of the sharp-nosed Duke. "What?"

The man smiled, as if secretly pleased at her lack of focus. The idiot probably thought she was enthralled with him. She wouldn't have bothered with his company but he was Councilman Theodore's son. It wouldn't have been good politics to refuse him. The truth was she wanted the damned waltz to end so she could ease her parched throat and pained feet.

"Some." Smiling faintly at him, she lifted her distracted gaze around the crowd that swayed to the beautiful melody of the violins. How she would have liked to stand before the stage and listen to the musicians. Alexa had been deemed tone-deaf by Madam Arabella. The talented Burmese woman could dance, sing and act all at once. She was versed in seven languages, knew how to do accounts, and was a scholar of history as well as an excellent seamstress. Next to her, Alexa felt like a mole.

But Madam Arabella had introduced her to the world of music and Alexa had been bewitched.

"Isn't that right?"

Cursing herself for drifting off again, Alexa looked up at him with a polite little smile. "I wouldn't know. Derek, could you kindly walk me to a chair, I believe all this spinning and the Champaign is making me a tad dizzy."

He stared at her like she'd asked him to cut off his hand and feed it to her.

When he stayed rooted to the spot like an insipid statue, she brought down her foot to leave him there on the dance floor alone and incite the wrath of who knows who, but she was through with being propositioned tonight.

"May I?"

The gruff, authoritative voice nearly made her weak kneed with relief.

The young Duke glared daggers at the tall Captain, dropped her like a hot potato and stalked off in search of better prospects. Sliding into the older man's arms, Alexa lifted her weary eyes to his laughing ones. "Is this what I'm reduced to? Last born Princes with not a cent to their name offering themselves on a silver platter borrowed from someone else?"

The Captain cracked one of his rare smiles. "Not your type?"

She sighed with respite when Gareth spun her around the dance floor towards the back doors to the gardens. It was just as well that he was her guardian or his monopolizing of her time and his attachment to her might not be taken well in their gentile setting. "If only I knew my type Gareth."

"Tall, dark, and handsome?"

"I'd go for short, pale and unsightly if he only had a brain."

"Sometimes I worry that that woman has taught you too much."

He'd lead them to a pretty little stone bench that provided a glittering view of the beautiful ballroom with the beautiful untouchable people. Maybe that was her problem, Gareth wondered. She was entirely too approachable. Completely at home with the servants as she was with her crown jewels. Maybe he was to blame for her 'bare bones' approach to her rule. She personally spoke to her people; she demanded to be included in everything and spent hours poring over books so she could know why the farmer couldn't make enough cheese to sell into the local market when he had more than enough cows to do it. What was he doing wrong?

And then she'd revamped his milk production by redistributing his human resource and setting a reasonable price for his product.

Gareth wanted to bow to her on more than one occasion. And not just to piss her off.

The Queen sat on the stone bench, reaching under her skirts to pull off her shoes as she buried her toes into the soft grass. "Madam Arabella cannot be thanked enough for everything she's done for me. Without her, I'd have turned out like my Cousin Nina Nine Inch Nails."

Gareth shook his head. "Sometimes I fail to understand what you are talking about."

"That's alright Gareth." She smiled prettily at him. "Sometimes, so do I."

"Good, because the Council has decided on a suitor."

The blood drained from her face and Gareth concluded she even fainted like a queen.

The maids were fanning her as she slowly came to. "Oh, my lord."

"Your Majesty! Oh, I am so happy to see you awake!"

Groaning at the sound of her chambermaid's sing-song voice, Alexa reminded herself that she couldn't strangle the poor woman; she had a beautiful voice. Lifting one hand before she'd be smothered with concerned hands helping her, she held them back. "Give me a moment. I had the ugliest nightmare. I dreamed I was dressed like a fairy princess and someone told me I was being married to the Ogre."

Gareth stood there, arms crossed, waiting for her to become coherent. When those caramel eyes lifted to his, he only looked back resolutely.

Her mouth dropped open almost comically. "No."

His raised eyebrow was confirmation enough.

She was on her feet in a flash. "Absolutely not!"

The maids cowered away. Madam Arabella was sitting on the side of the bed, her hands in her lap, her back straight as always. She turned to the Captain as if in a silent 'I-told-you-so'.

Gareth let out an exhausted breath. "Your Highness, please be reasonable."

"What am I?" The Queen sputtered. "Some sort of royal chattel?"

Those raven eyes hardened instantly. He was displeased even if he could understand.

It was Madam Arabella who spoke, her hawk-like eyes trained on the three maids staring in horror at the outburst. "Out!" She commanded and like obedient little puppies off they went.

As soon as the door was closed, Gareth scowled. "Do you really think, that I approve?"

"You seem to!"

Shaking his head, he turned to the ridged woman. "Would you kindly explain this to her?"

Madam Arabella turned her glittering green eyes to the Captain and met his gaze apathetically. "Why should I; you are doing a smashing job of botching this up."

"Are you jesting Madam?"

"Does it appear that I'm pulling your proverbial leg, Captain Gareth Van Buren?"

Alexa's eyes darted between her two caretakers while they glowered at one another intensely. "Oh, now I've seen everything." She touched her temples trying to make the sudden headache go away.

"What?" Gareth snapped at her.

"You're flirting while I'm having a nervous breakdown."

"Alexa!" Madam Arabella must have displayed ten shades of pink. She sure as hell blushed like a maiden for a woman of the world, Alexa noticed.

"Don't." Glaring at her Tutor, the woman walked straight to her closet and dug into the back for the secret stash of sherry she kept there.

When she turned with the bottle, the disapproval was mounting on Gareth's face. "This is hardly the time…"

"I think this is a perfect time," Alexa announced regally and flopped onto the settee as she poured herself a goblet. "I'm about to be bartered like cattle, I believe a little drink would hit just the right spot." She raised the toast to the two uncomfortable people. "Carry on with the flirting. It's quaint."

Gareth snatched the bottle away from her, but she'd already poured herself a hefty portion and downed it. "You're being unreasonable. They have allowed you to rule these past two years when you know that they had demanded a union before your coronation. I do not believe we need to incite their wrath for this any longer."

"That's easy for you to say, you're not being forced into a marriage!"

"For god's sake woman, when then?" Gareth lost his temper, his raven eyes flashing, the dark hair escaping from his perfect ponytail. "We can no longer shelter you with claims of your innocence, you are a woman grown. Twenty-five years Alexa! You know you have to marry sooner or later."

"I would prefer later," she said, her nose in the air.

"This IS later!" Turning back to the older woman he growled. "Dammit Arabella, talk to her! You know this is needed."

The woman rolled her eyes and rose with a soft hiss of her breath. Exasperated. "All you men are alike," she muttered under her breath and sat down daintily on the settee where their queen sat with her head in her hands. Putting a gentle hand on her shoulder Arabella softened her voice as she did on those rare occasions. "Alexandra, did you not know that being Queen would require you to take this step, willingly or unwillingly?"

Her whole being rebelling against the archaic and unwelcome notion, Alexa lifted her eyes to the woman who taught her what it was like to be free. And now she was asking for a price for her lessons. "What of Keats? What of sonnets and Midsummer's nights? What of them Madam Arabella?"

She touched the young queen's hair, a smidgen of sad sympathy in her green eyes. Alexa wanted to scream. "Sweetheart," she whispered achingly. "They are dreams for people who do not bear the burdens of a kingdom."

Jumping to her feet, Alexa wrenched the golden crown that sat on her head and tossed it on her bed. "Then maybe I don't WANT to be queen."

"Alexa!" Gareth stared at her in horror.

Deflating, the young woman ran a hand over her disheveled hair. "Oh, I don't mean that, it's just." She pleaded with the two desperately. "There is so much of my Kingdom I have not seen. You both know that bringing in a King would undermine everything that I've done for my people!"

"We will make him see our way of thought," Gareth provided but his heart was not in it.

"You do not lie so well Gareth." Alexa met his gaze unflinchingly and wouldn't let him look away. "You know I am right. You know why the council pushes for this. You know it is not the results they have problems with, it is my methods."

"They have allowed you free reign."

"So they could choke me with this new chain now!" She began to pace. Everything she'd studied for. Everything she'd even built would be fruitless. "Dammit Gareth," she growled like a man. Like a King. "I will not have some self-serving old farts run my kingdom for me, no matter what puppeteer they purchase for me!"

The Captain let out a lamenting sigh. "Then what do you suggest My Queen?"

"I need more time."

"You have none."

Her honeyed gaze now cut into his like a tiger's eye. "Buy me time. I will go away. An extended vacation. Something for my health. Until we find a solution. And there is a solution for this Gareth. I refuse to bow down before six stubborn old men who are too afraid of change."

Running a frustrated hand through his hair, Gareth turned to Arabella in hopes of having her reason with their headstrong queen, but one look at her resolute face made him groan. "Oh, you cannot possibly agree with her."

"And why can I not possibly?" She rose from her perch fluidly, her green eyes demanding an answer to her challenge. Sometimes Gareth wondered if she realized he battled himself not to rise to it.

"Be reasonable Madam."

"I believe you are reasonable enough for the both of us." The older woman came to stand beside their determined queen. A touch of bite in her tone. "The Queen has been working much too hard. The news of her forced engagement has taxed her. Although she has agreed to their terms, I will need her to retire to the Summer Villa."

"No," Alexa spoke firmly. "Not the Villa. If they are to give me any peace of mind, I will need a better hiding place. Better yet, a more opportune disguise. Something that will allow me the freedom to look at options." She held Gareth's cautious gaze without question. "I will reside at your Manor in Caerleon as a guest." She pushed on despite the Captain's disapproving glare. "A commoner."

"Out of the question."

Stepping up to him, she touched his jaw tenderly. "I make a vow Captain. If by the end of my 'vacation,' we are unable to come up with a solution. I will return and marry whomever the Councilmen choose. Willingly."

One foot tapping spasmodically, everything warred in him to refuse. It was futile. The council was absolute. Their good King had wanted the checks and balances in place; he hadn't realized how troublesome they might be for his daughter in the future. The council would never waver and change their mind. There was no solution.

But the damned green eyes were still flashing with challenge. Meeting them helplessly, Gareth let out the breath he'd been holding. "Fine. But she goes with you."

"I don't think…"

Madam Arabella placed a hand on the woman's arm, her gaze fixed on the Captain's. A silent agreement seemed to linger there. Agreement – and acceptance. "Do as he says, Alexa." Turning to their troubled Queen, she softened her eyes. "Let it be for now. You have won. Come." She ushered her towards the door. "We must go back to the ballroom as if nothing has been agreed upon. We will not speak of this again. We leave tomorrow."

"But…" How could she just drop everything and leave? She wanted this, but so soon? She wasn't ready!

Madam Arabella smiled wickedly at her charge. "Do you trust us at all child?"

Alexa didn't dare deny it.

*

She stood amongst the wisps of white gold, the scissors snipping away the final strand that completed her goal.

Gliding her eyes back to meet her own in the mirror she met the new person.

Gone were her years. The subtle curves and the royal curls.

Where Queen Alexandra Windmere had stepped into the mirror. A young lad of barely sixteen stepped out in brown soft leather breeches and a white cotton poet's shirt. With the yard of white cotton wrapped around her chest, she was for once glad that there wasn't much to conceal.

For all practical purposes, she was now a distant cousin of Gareth's, twice removed.

Her mouth widened into an adventurous grin. Madam Arabella could cook up the most fantastic stories.

With her head lighter, Alexa tilted her head calculatingly. Without her sooty kohl and rouge, she appeared pale and common. With her flaxen hair cropped short around her nape, she delighted in how it fell around her face in jagged wisps that transformed her usually feminine features to boyish youth.

Arabella would have a cow, Alexa snickered.

It was early. Too early for even the maids to be up. The sun hadn't started to burn up the horizon to start their traveling day. Even though Arabella and Gareth had assured her that they would take care of everything, Alexa had been unable to sleep. So she spent the time gathering what she needed, delighted she still fit into her adolescent clothes. A time when it had been plain old fun to be a tomboy. Before she discovered men. Before she discovered breasts and the differences it was associated with. Arabella would be livid about the hair. It had taken years to grow out, but to Alexa cutting her long golden tresses was a necessary evil.

Thankful that she'd had enough presence of mind to grab a cloak and bring down the hood before her chamber door creaked open and Gareth stepped in. Frowning at the lamplight, he turned to where she stood beside the bed. "You didn't sleep."

"I couldn't."

He sighed. "And you say you trust us." An eyebrow arched at the very prepared traveling bag and her state of dress. "Do I want to know?"

Her smile was sheepish. "I would appreciate it if you don't."

Nodding in accord, he picked up her bag, but then seemed to pause as if reconsidering it.

"You cannot change your mind now Gareth."

He peered at her over his shoulder. "I wasn't My Queen."

She frowned up at him. "What is it then?"

"I think I'll miss you."

Her mouth widened into a gorgeously happy smile. "You think?"

"I know."

His arms wrapped around her when she stepped against him. His mouth planting one gruff kiss against the crown of her head, he stepped away. "What's in this bag anyway?"

"Just some essentials."

"Arabella already packed for you."

"These are things Arabella would have overlooked."

Again the Captain paused outside her door. "Why does it feel like I'm sending you into more trouble than you are already in?"

Kissing his cheek, she tucked her hand into the hook of his elbow.

"Captain Gareth Van Buren. You worry too much. Now, where's my chariot."

"No chariot. You're riding."

"Do I at least get my own mount?"

They whispered between themselves through the darkened hallways of the castle; Gareth leading them with memory rather than a candle.

"I wouldn't put you on an unfamiliar horse no matter how dire the situation."

His protection filled her heart with warmth. Knowing he was with her, Alexa vowed she could move mountains. She gazed at him affectionately, roughly gauging where his head should be as he lead her towards the courtyards in the back and to the stables beyond.

"When you get to my Manor, make sure you have Felix send me word."

"Is your brother as grumpy as you are?"

"Ahem. No."

"Ah, then we shall get along splendidly."

"Felix only oversees the manor's upkeep. He doesn't live there. And I would appreciate it if you would stay away from him."

Stay away from Gareth's brother? Whatever for? But Gareth went on speaking.

"I've already arranged everything. Arabella will handle the rest. Felix should stay out of your way just fine and let you ladies rest until I can come to see you. If I leave immediately they will get suspicious."

What was wrong with Felix anyway?

"Make sure you stay out of the village. Caerleon's a small town, if someone saw you there, the council will get suspicious. For all practical purposes, you might as well be in the Summer Villa, they don't care much. They don't want to handle an emotional queen. They are already making preparations for your wedding and other legal matters; I don't believe they will have time to worry about your emotional tantrums."

Why didn't Felix stay at the manor?

"Your Majesty, are you listening to me?"

Blinking out of her thoughts she smiled reassuringly at him. "I know you've got everything prepared Gareth. I trust you implicitly."

"Yeah," he grumbled gruffly. "Can I say that I do not like this harebrained idea of yours?"

"You may not."

He scowled as they stopped beside the two horses, Arabella already cloaked and mounted. Beside them stood one of Gareth's Knights, Fawlks. The aging knight smiled a crooked smile as the Queen was helped up into the stirrups of her mare. Gareth held the reigns and met the older man's eyes with a warning. "Watch them Fawlks."

"Don't you worry none, My Lord. I will be their shadow. No harm will come to them."

Squeezing Alexa's hand he walked around the gray mare to the silent woman in the green robes. "Ride hard."

The hood turned down, her face invisible. Alexa could feel that their eyes had met from the sudden stillness of Gareth's frame. She was about to tease them about it when Arabella leaned down with deliberate slowness. Her chin peeked out of her hood and she captured Gareth's lips with her own, her hand curling into his raven hair.

Mouth gaping like a fish, Alexa gasped at the rather blunt sensuality of their kiss, Gareth's own hand sliding up to curl into Arabella's scarlet hair before she pulled away with one last aching nibble of his bottom lip.

Stepping away as if nothing had happened, he met the wide astonished eyes of his queen and slapped the rump of her horse before she could comment.

And then the wind had her.

"You and Gareth!?"

"Alexa…"

"You and GARETH!?"

"Alexa please," Arabella hissed as they sat by the campfire, the old knight keeping watch. "And will you take off the awful cloak?"

"It's cold."

"Oh, for god's sake!"

The young woman chuckled. "You're starting to even sound like him." Poking the fire, the disguised queen leaned forward, the firelight casting shadows across her face, the warmth chasing away the fatigue of the horse ride. "So how long have you been going behind my back?"

The older woman pressed her fingers into her temple as if the answer alone gave her a headache. "Really Child, I don't think you are in any position to give me a third degree."

"Why not?"

"Because I know you are hiding more than your inappropriate attire beneath that cloak."

Alexa glowered at her, more upset at being found out rather than Arabella's tone. "And you Madam are changing the subject." Standing from her perch, she walked the few steps and warmed her hands with the flames. "I still cannot believe that I didn't see it."

"You were not looking for it, I believe."

"I think myself very perceptive."

Arabella chuckled low under her breath. "Sometimes My Queen, you don't see past the end of your nose."

"Is that a barb?"

Her green eyes were laughing. "Probably."

"Hmph. Just because I'm not wearing the crown doesn't mean you can be impertinent. Now," she rubbed her hands and turned her full attention back to her evasive Tutor. "You will tell me how long this has been going on."

"What exactly?"

"Do not play games with me Madam."

With a sigh, Arabella cast a glance towards the knight who seemed to be engrossed with keeping watch, but she knew better. Those men. They heard everything. She didn't want to get into her relationship with Gareth right at this moment, but she also knew their curious queen would not let it rest. She'd been patient through the hours of traveling until nightfall when they had to make camp. They'd hardly stopped for more than a few minutes. She knew Alexa's questions would have to be answered sooner or later. And her Queen mostly preferred sooner. "I never taught you to be so nosey."

"I did that on my own." Crossing her arms and her tone implying that no more evasions were allowed, she waited silently.

And so Arabella told her of the stormy night that he'd brought her to the Queen's aid. How Arabella had been thrown off the bridge by the bandits. How the knight had rescued her and decided to give her shelter. She spoke of how he'd held her so tightly on the horse and Alexa couldn't help but smile at the unnatural glimmer in her Tutor's eyes. But there was an underlying sadness to her when she spoke of Gareth. Alexa knew her proper Captain well.

"And you finally spoke of your affections to him?"

The woman didn't immediately speak, but when she did, her voice wasn't as unsteady as Alexa had thought it would be. "His knightly vows came first."

Alexa's mouth dropped open. "Are you kidding me!?"

"Do I jest often?"

"Never enough." The young woman frowned in confusion. "But that's the stupidest reason I've ever heard in my life!"

Arabella's smile was sympathetic. "You have much to learn about men Queen Alexandra."

"Hmph," waving off the thought with one hand, Alexa picked up the little thermos and poured herself another cup of hot steaming tea. "And so that goodbye kiss was what?"

For once her able Tutor had no quick reply. When she spoke her voice was weary. "One last reminder, but the man only sees his kingdom and his allegiances."

"In other words: me."

Green eyes snapped up in alarm. "I would never imply such a thing."

Alexa's smile was understanding. "I know. But it is me, isn't it? He won't leave my side."

"Would he have to leave your side to be with me?"

"You distract him."

"At every opportunity," the older woman purred softly, mouth tilting up into a wicked smirk.

Shaking her head, Alexa sat back down on the blanket spread on the ground and sipped her tea. "I see that you both are rather hopeless at it."

"Most people are hopeless at the hands of love."

Grinning into the flames Alexa realized that everyone could afford to be helpless but the Queen. A queen always found a way. It was almost part of the job description.

"Oh Alexa, what are you plotting? Please do not make it harder than it already is."

Innocent caramel eyes blinked at her Tutor. "Whatever do you mean?"

The green eyes were admonishing. "You mean to play cupid."

"And when I mean to do something, I do it." Squeezing her hand, Alexa put the cup down. "Let us rest now. I mean to get to Caerleon and have all my questions answered."

"Why I am uncomfortable with that notion?" Arabella lamented, and then watched the young woman carefully make her way around their little camp, taking a fresh cup of tea to the Knight and talking with him as if he was an Earl. She noticed the way, she stood with her arms behind her, clasped beneath the cloak, eyes bright and attentive, mouth moving excitedly and sighed. The petite queen could dress like a þag lady and she would draw attention. There was something about this woman that would make peasants and royalty fall over themselves to please her. She commanded respect and admiration. Arabella had no idea how Gareth expected her to keep her hidden until the time came.

Gareth had been plain.

This time was only to allow Alexa her last few moments of peace and freedom. The council would be immovable. The only way Gareth could see to help ease his queen's trouble was to introduce her new suitor in a less pressurizing environment. Maybe there was a chance the boy could convince her. Maybe this wouldn't have to be such a great sacrifice for the beautiful, headstrong queen.

Maybe.

*

"Are you mad!?"

Alexa sighed deeply and turned to the silent knight riding ahead of her. "Fawlks, is it really all that bad?"

The poor old knight trembled with horror at being caught between the two women. "I…well Your Highness…that is…" It was disconcerting. His Queen, the vibrant little woman, was garbed in faded old leather and worn cotton under her thick cloak, her hair cropped short. As far as he was concerned, she could be dressed in potato sacs he wouldn't be able to tell which was better. It was one of the things his deceased wife cursed him for.

Taking pity on the rambling man, she turned back to her irate Tutor. "Oh come on Arabella," she pleaded, her body angled towards the infuriated woman in the green cloak. "When you get over the shock, you'll realize that it's the perfect disguise."

"A BOY!?"

"I can tell you're still in shock," Alexa muttered and sullenly went back to leading her mare down the mountain road.

Shock wasn't what Arabella would have called it. She was aghast. If Alexa was determined to play this role, she knew it would be next to impossible to introduce her to her suitor. Their entire preparation would be shot to hell. There was no way they would be able to explain to the Prince why his bride was prancing around looking, for all practical purposes, like a pubescent little boy. "And you did not even think to consult me!"

"I thought we agreed that I would go in disguise!"

"Dammit Alexa, I was thinking more along the lines of a hat! But that hair!"

Her hand drifted up self-consciously. "What's wrong with it?" Alexa glared at her teacher.

"It seems as if you were attacked by a pair of rabid scissors!"

"Oh, you're just being a wet nurse. This is the perfect disguise. I look nothing like myself. No one will know I'm in Caerleon, I can move around as I please and not a soul will take notice."

That's exactly what bothered Arabella. The Prince would run screaming and everything would be ruined. "I do not approve Alexa."

"Well then it's a good thing the Queen approves," she provided helpfully. "And I suggest you start calling me Alex. I figure the name should be close to my own so that I know you're calling me. Imagine calling me something like Ivan or Philippe or something. I'd think you're speaking to someone else."

"Gareth is going to be furious."

"Gareth can get over it," Alexa rolled her eyes before turning her attention to the uncomfortable knight. "How much farther to the Manor?"

"Just beyond that hill."

"Good. Last one there is a monkey's uncle."

Arabella's mouth opened to protest, but the Queen had dug her heels into the side of her mare and shot off like a lightning bolt. She snarled at the startled old man, "Well don't just sit there, after her!"

The lands around Caerleon were beautiful. Although the Manor sat a little off the village, their approach was set in the path that cut them down the middle. On the right was the beautiful red brick house with sloping roofs and rich burgundy windows and doors. On the left sat the small little Village of Caerleon. The cathedral stood high in the central plaza. And lush green hills surrounded everything. Gareth was the owner and master of little land, but what land he owned was breathtaking.

For a woman who hadn't had time to step out of the confines of her castle and was unable to walk the streets of her villages without starting a stampede, she relied on her Knights and the Ministers to keep their lands. Many of the Ministers had been Knights. Many of them had kept their titles. Earls, Dukes, and everything in between and beyond. She wondered if maybe Gareth would one day like to be promoted. Everyone did. She didn't know how she'd get through anything without him. The trouble at the borders, the occasional riots and insurgency. Battle plan, strategy. She relied on him for so much.

Sighing, she turned back to the peaceful landscape around her. The Earl of Flamehart. She smiled at the memory of when her father had given Gareth the title. He'd been a young knight then. She remembered there was an interesting story that came with his title. She wondered if Arabella knew of it.

Turning Stormy, her mare, towards the Manor she rode up the stone path and grinned at the low fence and gate that surrounded the manor. Sliding her hand over the galloping mare's neck she spoke close to her ear. "Think you can take it?"

Stormy answered with a sharp whiny and a nod of her head. Alexa once again wondered how the horse could understand. But then she'd practically grown on this beast.

Stormy picked up speed and leaped over the fence effortlessly, her hooves clattering against the cobblestone as they galloped up to the house.

And then disaster struck.

Alexa had learned to ride when she'd learned to shoot. Now she could ride and shoot. But that didn't mean that the occasional bout of clumsiness didn't take her. Although she knew and no one would believe her, the mare had seen the black stallion standing peacefully in front of the door and screeched to a halt without so much as a warning.

Alexa flew out of her saddle and landed straight into the rosebushes screaming like a banshee.

"Damnation!"

Muffling her shriek, the young woman tried not to struggle as the thorns bit skin through her flimsy clothes, her hands already starched, back aching. But the curses weren't coming from her mouth.

If she had planned to scream at the sight of the man that stalked up to her purposefully, the shock of seeing him stole her breath.

Wild red hair like blood was tied at the nape, a few strands flying about his face. The sharp upturned nose and the chin disappeared into a rakish goatee that wound around his upper lip. But it wasn't the wild hair or the rakish features. It was the burning red eyes under sooty eyelashes that froze the blood in her veins.

"Are you out of your mind!?" He barked at her and she jumped, receiving more scratches for her trouble. But Alexa was just glad she hadn't whimpered. Queens did not whimper.

When he reached out to her, Alexa shrank back. With an exasperated sigh that was oddly familiar, he planted his hands on his hips over his low-slung pants. "For a boy who leaped over my damned fence at breakneck speed and tackled my rosebushes, I hope you're not shy."

Her mouth dropped open in surprise. He couldn't tell. She resisted the urge to laugh with joy and jump up and down because the damned thorns were still digging into every part of her she could name. And some she couldn't. While she was rejoicing that her disguise was perfect, he had reached out this time too swiftly for her to protest and grabbed her by her forearm surprisingly firmly and hauled her out in a single heave.

Stumbling, she grabbed his shoulder to steady herself and realized how tall he was. And then she remembered her fear. Jumping away from him, she stared like a blithering idiot into those devil eyes and gulped.

His lips stretched into a thin smile. "Boo."

With a squeak, Alexa streaked straight for her horse. She'd only gotten as far as to grab the reigns when Fawlks and Arabella's horses halted beside her. The knight was out of his saddle before anyone could utter a word and started examining Alexa from head to toe. "Are you alright My Queen," he whispered reverently.

"Fawlks," she hissed low under her breath. "Don't call me that!"

"Oh, but if something had happened to you, Lord Gareth would have had my head on a plate! Hell and damnation you are harmed!"

"I cannot believe you would do something so irresponsible Al__"

"Alex!" The Queen glared at her two companions pointedly. "Why do you keep repeating my name over and over again? I know I am Alex." Batting Fawlks spasmodic hands away she snarled at him. "Stop poking me! I'm fine!"

"Quite the impertinent baggage isn't he?"

Alexa instantly fell silent. Although she did step behind the old knight to peer at the strange man garbed in black. He stood beside Arabella's horse and extended his hand to her. "The Lady Arabella I presume?"

"You presume correctly," Arabella announced although not without the withering glance she cast toward Alexa. Placing her hand in his she let him guide her off her horse, his hands lingering around her waist a moment longer than necessary, so she glared at him. "And you are?"

The man swept away his cloak and bent low in an elaborate and rather dramatic bow. "Felix Van Buren, Earl of Flamehart at your service."

Alexa's eyes widened. THIS was Gareth's brother?

Fawlks cleared his throat and stepped forward to shake the man's hand as the introductions were made. Felix's eyes stayed on the hoodless Arabella and instantly Alexa didn't like him. She wondered if he was a man of loose character. Maybe that was why Gareth kept him away from his Manor. So until Gareth was here, she promised, she'd keep an eye on Arabella so that the slithering devil didn't get his claws in her. Heathen.

"I was told to expect two ladies." The red eyes turned to Alexa who was still hidden behind Fawlks like a cowering fool.

With color rushing up to her cheeks she stepped around the knight rather regally and crossed her arms in a defensive stance. "Yeah well, you got me instead. Alex Windmere," she stated with apparent authority and masculine confidence as she extended her hand to his as Fawlks had.

The hand was decidedly harder, the pads of his thumbs rough and Alexa had to stifle the yelp as he gave her hand a tight squeeze. Yanking it away she saw the humor in his eyes and glared right back.

Felix Flamehart watched the boy glare back at him haughtily. There was too much hot air in his adolescent bones, he concluded. "Why the change in plan?" He turned to the woman with stunning green eyes. Now here was the kind of guest he wouldn't mind having. Such supple mocha curves, sharp scathing green eyes cut right into his gut. Magnificent woman. Certainly a stranger to their lands. He would have to thank Gareth for sending her his way.

Arabella didn't miss the blunt appraisal in those vermillion eyes. She winced at the very feminine stab of pain at the thought that she would have loved to have Gareth look at her that way. "My sister couldn't travel. She twisted her ankle. Alex hadn't been out of the estate for quite some time. I thought the travel might do him good. I hope you don't mind." She knew Gareth didn't get along with his younger brother. That he had foregone his family as he did everything else for his kingdom and that Felix had received the title by default. She also knew that Felix's unnatural red eyes warranted many stories around the coast and Gareth wanted to wash his hands clean of it. And so Felix had been asked to find his own accommodation. But for their Queen's predicament, Gareth had asked for his assistance. As much as he didn't approve of his brother and his habits, Gareth trusted blood above all else.

But not enough to tell him their Queen stood in his courtyard under the guise of a boy.

And not enough to tell him the teacher was the woman in love with him.

"Mind Madam?" Felix flashed a roguish grin at the beautiful woman. "I wouldn't have minded if you brought your whole family with you to vacation at my humble abode. I assure you, the pleasure is all mine."

Alexa stepped forward before she could stop herself. "Stop flirting with Arabella!"

Felix startled at the sharp command. Offended at the boy's attitude and his apparent protective streak towards the woman, Felix crossed his arms and regarded the whelp down his nose. "And what do you know about flirting little one?"

Alexa had half a mind to tell him exactly who she was, but Arabella had already grabbed her wrist. "Alex for god's sake, this isn't the time."

"I agree My Lady," Felix took her hand in an apparently friendly gesture but Alexa could see the foggy desire in his red eyes. "Pardon my manners. I was distracted by a flying elf." His barb was meant to be teasing but it only incited more of Alexa's wrath. "Let me welcome you to Flamehart Manor." And then her horror he put two fingers into his mouth and whistled shrilly.

Like obedient dogs, two servants came stumbling out of the front door. The footman and the butler, from what Alexa could gather from their attire. Racing to their side, their bags had been unstrapped from the horses and rushed into the house within a few seconds. Even Arabella was thrown by the sudden flurry of movement.

The Devil only grinned wickedly and pulled them into the house which reminded Alexa of the bowels of hell.

Stormy stood gazing at the black stallion like a besotted fool.

Arabella sat in the chair, her hand braced against her forehead, elbow resting on the arm of the chair, legs stretched straight ahead in an uncharacteristic sprawl. "Please, Your Highness. Let it go."

"I will have his head on a plate!" She paced the little rug like a caged lion. Still wearing her traveling clothes, albeit without the cloth that had been tired around her chest, she fumed and snarled, her breath wild. "How dare he!"

With a groan, Arabella came out of her chair. "Come now, Alexa. We've been traveling for two days. I am tired and hungry. Let us just go down to dinner."

"No." Alexa crossed her arms stubbornly. "He was hitting on you! On his brother's__"

"For god's sake Alexa, he does not know!" Arabella snapped, her green eyes flashing intolerantly. "Will you please let it go?"

"But Gareth…"

"Gareth does not want me!"

The stark declaration doused some of the flames in Alexa's heart. For a moment she stood there facing the woman who had shaped how she grew up. The woman to whom she owed so much. She wanted nothing more than for the two most important people in her world to be together. It was cruel to keep them apart for obligations. Especially since she wanted the union as much as they did. She wanted to smack Gareth upside the head and command him to fall in love with the woman who, Alexa knew deep down inside, would make him very happy.

As if realizing what she'd revealed, Arabella's spine stiffened and the passion died in her voice. "I don't believe I can lay out any clothes for you that I have brought with you. Let me find you something appropriate from what you have brought." Walking to the chest of drawers Arabella busied herself with rifling through Alexa's old clothes.

Alexa was still lost in thought, he eyes fixed on the beautiful rolling grassland from her window and the lake beyond. From her window, she could see all the way across the village. And like Rapunzel in her tower, she suddenly felt very alone.

"My Queen?"

Looking over her should she saw Arabella frowning at her as she put the soft brown pants and crème colored silk shirt on the bed. Alexa couldn't help the sad smile. "I want one of us to marry for love Arabella or all the poetry and stories you told me will be lost forever."

The crystal green of her eyes melted, but she looked away. "Haven't you noticed Your Highness? The most beautiful poetry and prose speak of tragedy and unrequited love." Then she was gone in a swirl of her gown.

Alexa spent a long time at the window before she dressed. Gareth would have to break his damn vows and complete this love story. Alexa promised herself that by the end of this forced vacation, whether she had to marry or not, Arabella and Gareth would come to their damned senses.

*

She had reached for the bottle of wine before she realized what she was doing.

From his seat at the head of the table, Felix barked to the server. "Watch it, man! We do not serve children under my roof!"

In horror, Alexa watched the goblet being lifted away, the wine bottle being transported back toward her host. Eyes tightened into narrow slits she glowered at the red-haired devil who lounged in his seat. Maybe she should have thought out this young boy's disguise after all. But then she caught the smug half-smile on Arabella's eyes and the flicker of a smile on Fawlks'. Scowling she picked up the cup of water and took a hefty gulp, muttering all the curses she'd ever heard Gareth use.

"So My Lady, what would you like to see first?" Felix spoke as they ate their dinner.

"The cathedral," Alexa piped up, popping a black olive into her mouth. It was only the horrified wideness of Arabella's eyes and Fawlks' choking breath that made her realize she'd answered to 'My Lady'. She winced. Okay so maybe this 'being a boy' business was going to take more work. Clearing her throat, she thickened her voice. "Arabella would like to see the Cathedral I'm sure. She's religious."

She wanted to say 'nun'. But that would be too absurd considering the dip of Arabella's necklines and the tantalizing rouge she always wore on her lips.

At that moment the woman in question was gripping the table to keep from hyperventilating.

Felix regarded the boy as he sat in the chair to his right. With his eyes on his plate, Felix could have sworn Alex saw everything. He hadn't liked the protective streak on this boy and now Felix wondered if he was going to be a rather large pain. There hadn't been a moment alone in the woman's presence and it was not for lack of trying. Even though the boy's outright lie didn't deter him, Felix realized that he would have to put a little more effort into distracting the pungent little lad. "And you Master Alex, what is it that you would like to see?"

Slumping lower in her seat, Alexa was suddenly very uncomfortable under the heat of his gaze. Pushing the food around the plate with her fork, she wondered if ignoring him would make him talk to someone else, but then she was worried he'd pick Arabella again. She wished Fawlks would do more than watch everything with amusement. What Alexa wanted to see desperately was the village. But she was afraid to ask. Knowing Felix, he'd find someone to take her while he wooed Arabella behind her back. Lifting her caramel gaze, she fixed him with one of her patented imperious lifts of her chin. "The Manor. Gareth spoke highly of it. I wish to see his home."

The blunt tilt of his regal face made the Flamehart blood boil. "With all due respect Master Alex," his fluid voice dripped with venom. "This is as much my house as it is my brother's. In fact, more so mine since Gareth hasn't had the time or the inclination to see to its upkeep."

Arabella groaned under her breath as she saw the Queen visibly bristle at the man's tone. Alexa bordered on hero worship where Gareth was concerned. She knew the young woman would now find an enemy in their host and it would only make things harder. She'd already sent word to Gareth of what had happened. She hoped he would come prepared with the Prince so that their situation could be salvaged.

If Alexa didn't order Felix Flamehart to be taken to the gallows before that.

"Gareth inherited every spec of this land for his service to the king!" Alexa shot back at the odious man, resisting the urge to upturn her cup of water in his lap.

"And then he left it to rot while he served him!"

"You have no right to malign his service to his kingdom!"

"And you have no right to order me around in my home!"

"I can order you around as long as you inhabit Odyria!"

"Alex!" Arabella gasped. She pleaded silently with the prickly Queen. This wasn't going to help. They had to stay in Felix's care for some time. It wouldn't do well to upset their host and be tossed out on their behinds. Turning appealing eyes to the Earl, Arabella tried to smile. "I apologize for my nephew's outburst. His parents spoil him so. Alex," her green eyes were desperate as they turned to the seething Queen, "apologize at once."

"He needs pistol whipping Madam."

The final nail smacked into the proverbial coffin, Alexa rose out of her set, her napkin hitting the plate with a resounding 'thwack'. "Arabella, you may eat your fill. Then I want you in my chambers so we can exchange some wise words before I do something rash." Turning to the silent knight, she narrowed her eyes in a silent 'watch her'.

The older woman swallowed her groan. "Yes."

With one last scathing glower in Felix's direction, Alexa marched out.

Fawlks went on munching on his beef steak. "My compliments to the chef."

Felix watched the emotions play on the woman's face. Why could the damned scarp of a boy command this woman? The little heathen probably ran the whole house mad. The tyrant had stolen the warm color of Arabella's cheeks. "I apologize. He's a spoiled little beast, but I should have demonstrated some maturity." Picking up her hand he gently touched his mouth to her knuckles, his eyes darkening as she met his gaze. "Please accept my apology."

With a wavering smile, Arabella withdrew her hand, the raven eyes still haunting her; especially since the man's voice reminded her of them. "I fear I am not usually so sensitive. I do so love Alex. I wish you would not antagonize him so."

"For your peace of mind My Lady, I promise to play nice." He grinned wickedly. "I'll even try to be polite. Would you both like to see my house tomorrow?"

This time her smile was genuine. "We would."

Fawlks cleared his throat and suddenly everything was back to business. Arabella sighed inwardly. Oh, how these Flamehart boys could play.

The tour had gone by almost uneventfully. True to his word, Felix had been cordial while Alexa stayed mute. After their heated discussion, the perturbed Queen had conceded to her teacher's advice and decided to stay silent. Her purpose here wasn't to explore or make friends with the self-appointed Earl. She had to get away from her role-play towards finding a solution. So she walked through the halls a footstep behind Arabella as Felix spoke of the buttresses and the carvings and paintings.

Fawlks had already set out for the Capital. Soon Gareth would come. Alexa wished Gareth could be here now. Displaced from her home in a house and town that was foreign to her, the Queen felt lonelier than ever. As much as she loved her Tutor, Alexa missed the ease with which she could speak with Gareth about any and everything. She wanted to write to him, but she was worried someone would discover it was her. No. She trusted him. She would wait.

"Library."

Her head snapped out of the clouds and she realized Felix had been talking to her. Blinking up into those unnatural eyes, she wrinkled her brow in question.

"Arabella tells me you like to read little elf."

She doused the irritation at the realization that Arabella had been revealing her likes and dislikes to their host as she took in the expanse of the library. It really was beautiful. For a moment, she smiled taking in the thick and thin, varying spines of the countless volumes on the shelves.

"We have books on every subject."

"Farming?" Alexa quipped as she stepped away from their touring group to slide her fingers over the shelves.

Felix blinked at her in surprise. What did a spoiled little rich brat know about farming? Maybe he was just being a wiseass. "Name an author."

She glanced at him confidently over her shoulder. "Igor Garvoisky."

If the man was surprised at the accurate name, he didn't show it. Merely flicked open the lapels of his black coat, the gold-trimmed collar opening around his throat before climbing up a sliding ladder. "Which one?"

Arms crossed she resisted the urge to smirk. Even Arabella couldn't contain her smile, a touch of pride there. "The Mating cycle of the bull." The ladder wobbled and startled crimson eyes gaped down at her. The smirk mushroomed across her mouth, caramel eyes dancing with mirth. "Or maybe you only have his notes on stud farming."

Arabella's laughter exploded out of her, fingers pressed against her lips, she turned and fled the library.

Instant fury built in Felix's veins, but there was also a touch of admiration. There was more to this boy than mere tyranny. Maybe the little genius wasn't pampered. Maybe he was just a know-it-all. Gauging the distance carefully, Felix leaped off the ladder.

He delighted in the widening of those beguiling honey-colored eyes as the boy squeaked and took a wide step away. And Felix's smirk shamed his.

Hating her feminine sensibilities she wished she could clock him with a fist and wipe that smirk off his face. Instead, Alexa hardened her gaze, feet set apart in her black long boots. "You have neither. What a pity. Next time, you can visit my library. I bet you'll find some volumes on humility. Who knows, even you might learn some." With one last wiggle of her eyebrow, she turned on her heel and followed the ebbing laughter in the hallway. "Arabella, would you like a walk in his lordship's gardens?" Linking her arm through the older woman's the Queen smiled sweetly at the stunned man. "Coming your lordship?"

The rest of the tour went by with more humility than before. No longer did Felix mouth off about the furniture and the Ming Vases. In fact, when Arabella asked about something, he offered a curt, accurate reply before moving on.

"Really My Queen, must you embarrass him so?"

"With the size of his ego Arabella, he can afford some." Alex was reclining in the bathtub while Arabella was on a footstool. It had already been three days. There was so little time to actually find any privacy anymore. Felix was everywhere.

"If you keep this up, he will get suspicious."

Sinking deeper into the bubbles, Alexa closed her eyes, a smile playing over her mouth. "There is something infinitely delightful in seeing him stumble."

Arabella nearly choked on her breath. No. Her green eyes took in the playful little smile, the flutter of her eyelashes and the hint of pink under her skin. No, Arabella lamented inwardly. Gareth had to arrive with the Prince soon. Things were getting more complicated than they had originally planned. Because now it was imperative that Felix never discover who this young boy was.

*

As much as Alexa had thought she'd enjoy the freedom, she was confined. Arabella wouldn't allow them a trip to the village. The Queen was smothered and Gareth had not arrived yet. Arabella was lost in her books lately and usually, Alexa would have joined in, but the wayward Queen was too far from home and any peace of mind. She'd been up most of the nights trying to figure out how to get out of marrying. But there was no solution she could think of. No amount of blackmail could make them change the rules for her.

She'd already proved to be a good statesman. She'd demonstrated clear-headedness and fairness. She'd discussed and decided on battle strategy, what more did they want from her?

She put aside Arabella's warning and wandered out of the Manor.

The short walk down the stone path finally lead her to the archway with the gaping gates.

Beyond them, the little village throbbed with life. Women carried earthen jars on their heads, and the men pulled carts of produce as the market bustled with the busy morning. Keeping the hood low over her head, Alexa stepped into the throng of people and instantly smiled.

Her people.

It was no great mystery that she was well-liked among her subjects.

There was nothing like it in the world. It made her feel proud to serve them.

With life going on around her at its own unique pace that didn't match the one she was used to in the castle, Alexa smiled at the woman who wanted her to buy apples. She shook her head politely at the man who displayed the finest Egyptian cotton. She whirled out of the way as a wayward carriage tried to avoid a pothole.

By the time she made it to the town square she was out of breath and grinning like a fool.

"You there! Boy!"

Smile fading, the Queen winced. Maybe her mirth lasted too long.

Turning slowly towards the owner of the voice she saw the thick burling man struggling with a small cart having hit a pothole in an alley entering into the square. "How's about a hand lad?" The man wiped the sweat off his brow. "For a few silver?"

The wooden cart was loaded with flour. Alexa knew it would require more than a hand, but the poor fellow looked to be in a lot of distress. "You couldn't have picked a poorer fellow sir."

His laugh was boisterous and contagious. "Ah lad, maybe you'll build some muscle. Come now," he motioned to the buried wheel, "I will lift the barrow and all ye have to do is push."

That didn't sound so tough.

Rolling up her sleeves, Alexa stepped behind the stuck wheelbarrow and planted her hands firmly on the sacks of flour. "How's here?"

The man bent down and grabbed the spoke of the wheel firmly. "On three?"

"On three," she offered him a mock salute.

With a nod, the man flexed his muscles. "One. Two."

Alexa braced her feet against the ground and grit her teeth.

"THREE!"

Putting all her weight against the flour she grunted as the cart shifted, lurched forward an inch and then dropped back.

Gasping at her sheer miscalculation of its weight, she stared at the man. "This is impossible! We need more men."

"Bah! I cannot afford more men. Put your back into it!"

"Sir you give me too much credit already." She assessed the situation and there was only one solution. "My name is Alex."

The big dirty hand stuck out at her promptly. "Razool."

"Well, Razool. It seems we will have to unload first."

"Are ya mad!?" The man exploded, black beady eyes spitting flames. "Do ye know how long that would take? I will miss the crowds at the market!"

With a sigh, she held up her hands in an appeasing gesture. "And how long have you been struggling with his already?"

The man seemed to be thrown for a loop. Muttering under his breath, Alexa almost missed the very sheepish, "Bout half an hour."

Judgingly by the number of sacks he'd stacked, Alexa figured he got greedy in the first place and tried to take too many at once. "I can promise you we can unload and reload in twenty minutes or you keep the silver."

He eyed the wee lad with mistrusting eyes before nodding. "Deal."

She nodded and slid her arms around the first sac while he reached for another and they began to unload. "Have you heard about the story of the ant who was building a hill?"

"Huh?" Sweat already trickling down his forehead, he peered at the boy as they slowly but steadily emptied the cart.

"Well," Alexa began in a patient tone, happily distracting him from the task and keeping herself from showing the strain. Even though she wasn't a weakling, the heavy lifting wasn't the kind of strenuous work she was used to. "There was this worker ant who had promised the queen he would single-handedly construct the anthill. The queen told him it was too big a job for one little ant, but the ant was determined. And so he set out, gathering little specs of dirt and began stacking them slowly and steadily. But he hadn't realized how long it would take."

Razool had stopped peering at the boy oddly but was now listening raptly as the sacs were finished unloading, her story never faltering. Moving in place to push the cart free Alexa continued. "And soon enough he realized that if he carried two specs rather than one he could finish faster. So he carried two specs. When I say lift." She nodded at him and the man positioned himself beside the wheel. "But still the ant feared he would be there for months so the ant decided to stack four specs. LIFT!"

The cart popped free and rolled forward. Bracing it with a rock, Razool returned to where they'd placed the flour sacs. "Then what happened?"

"Well, he soon discovered that he could lift ten times his weight, exactly like his ancestors had claimed. Ecstatic, the ant made excellent progress." Alexa grunted as she reloaded the sacs back onto the cart her arms screaming for respite, but she wasn't one to back out of a challenge. "The other workers watched him work and marveled at the brave ant that was indeed making the anthill all by himself. The queen would surely reward him. She might even give him his own anthill where he could start his own family. They cheered. They cheered and cheered as the ant walked to and fro between the growing anthill and the barren earth." For just a moment, Alexa grabbed the edge of the cart and caught her breath, her hair drenched under the hood, her back screaming in pain. Being a boy was seriously taxing on her now.

"And then what happened?"

She noticed Razool's rapt attention. He let her stand back and she watched him move the remaining sacs alone, without complaining as if in a trance. "Encouraged by his accomplishment the little ant decided one extra spec couldn't hurt and so, on his next round, he brought eleven specs back with him."

"What happened?"

Now that the cart was free, she grinned at him cheekily. "He got squished."

Razool watched her with stunned awe. Then he threw back his head and burst out laughing; a deep bellyaching laugh coming from him as he put one hand on his fat stomach and slapped his thigh. Joining in his discovery, she chuckled and rubbed her arms. "I reckon he got stuck in a pothole."

"Could be," Alexa agreed victoriously. "Next time stack in moderation."

"Don't you worry, lad. I will remember this lesson." He dug into his pocket and fished out three silvers. "Two for your win and one for yer excellent storytellin' skills. Ye oughta be in business Alex."

Alexa didn't want to embarrass the man so she took the money with a smile and an elaborate bow. "Be careful now."

"I will. Be off with you lad. Bet yer mama's worried sick." With a wink and a snort under his bushy mustache. "See ya around."

And then he dragged the cart away, his shoulders still shaking.

Alexa looked down at the three copper pieces in her hand. In the glow of the morning sun, she smiled. Why was it that she was the happiest amongst her people? She sighed as the sudden weight of her decisions returned. The council wanted her to return to being an arm ornament of a strong king. But what did some stranger know about her people? How could he understand what these men and women stood for? What they did all day. How they lived and cared for their family?

Fist snapping closed she lifted her eyes to the cathedral where the children ran out wearing choir clothes. Walking inside she watched the simplicity of how it was decorated. Were the prayers the same regardless of the place? She noticed the old woman sitting in the pews, silent, contented and in deep prayer.

Prayer was the same even if you did it in the wide open sky. So she lifted her eyes to the heavens and wished for aid. She wished for her miracle. She wished for her destiny.

On her way out, she dropped her silver into the poor box.

Her return to the Manor was slower than when she had left. The sun was now overhead but her thoughts were still jumbled and unclear. Her mission, still murky.

She made her way around the house to the stables. She figured a ride around the estate would do her good. But the moment she stepped into the stables, she froze.

There stood Felix in dark pants and nothing else. His skin was vibrant like his loosely tired hair and eyes. He was a stark contrast against the black stallion that fidgeted before him. The horse kept tossing his head to the side.

"Shhh Midnight, what's wrong with you boy?"

The head tossed again with a rather furious snort.

For a moment Alexa leaned against the door to the stables as the man tried to calm his horse.

The horse was as restless as the man was.

It was only when she lifted her eyes to spot her mare that she realized what was going on.

Her first instinct was to go forward and smack the stupid female for falling for the raven stallion with the prickly disposition. But then she saw the way the creature cast doe-eyed glances at the horse; the recipient in turn itching to go to her. Muffling her giggles, Alexa wondered if there was something wrong with this countryside. Maybe it was the season. Love seemed to be around everywhere. Unrequited or otherwise.

"AWO!"

Head snapping around she watched in alarm as Felix stepped back holding his nose where the stallion had hit him while tossing his head. Rolling her eyes, Alexa pushed away from the door frame and walked towards him. "You're misunderstanding his request grotesquely."

The red-topped head swiveled around at the stately voice. Touching the slight trickle of blood from his nose, he threw a fiery glare at her. "Here to laugh at my pain boy?"

"Stop calling me boy," she grunted and pointed to the overturned tub. "Sit down and put your head back before you bleed to death."

"Now see here…"

With a frustrated little moan, she held up her hands. "Sit down and put your head back before your bleed to death…please."

Felix blinked at the sudden change in the boy. He'd always noticed that the boy had a touch of femininity that he would probably have a hard time growing out of. Although his attitude made up for him what he lacked in stature, there would always be softness to Alex. Maybe that's why he was always too gruff.

Conceding to the 'please', the Earl of Flamehart sat down on the metal tub and slid his head back as instructed.

Alexa reached out tentatively to touch the black stallion's head and instantly he stilled. She met those dark eyes and chuckled. "Oh you're like your master, aren't you?" She whispered. "Softening up to the family." Beside them, stormy called out to her. Turning to the antsy mare, Alexa grinned. "I'm bringing him, you brazen hussy." Opening the door she led the black stallion towards her Mare.

"Hey!" Felix was on his feet when he noticed the movement. "What in the devil's name are you doing?"

"Sometimes you people don't see things past the end of your nose," she quoted from memory and gestured to the two horses nuzzling each other.

Felix stood there dumbfounded. "Well, I'll be damned."

Crossing her arms smugly she watched the animals whiny and nod to each other in happiness.

"Your mare's in heat!?"

There goes the romance, Alexa sighed. "No."

"Then why the hell is Midnight acting like a lovesick puppy?"

"Maybe because he IS a lovesick puppy."

Felix frowned at her. "Come now Elf, don't tell me you have some idiotic notions about love and romance. Didn't Gareth sit down with you and explain how it is?"

Curiosity and ire mixing with gall at his arrogance, she planted one fist on her hip and regarded him with interest. "No. Perhaps you will enlighten me." Maybe it would have been better to just go back to the manor.

His teeth gleamed in the morning light. "Have you never had a woman, then?"

The notion made her want to rediscover her breakfast, but she wisely kept that to herself. "No."

"Ah." He nodded as if everything finally made sense to him. "Well, then I see the problem."

An eyebrow arched. "I have a problem?"

"Well sure," running a hand through his already tousled hair, he walked towards the happy couple and petted his stallion, standing a hair's breadth away from her.

For just a moment the smell of morning, pine trees and man filled her senses and she let her eyes slide shut. Holy hell, he smelled good. Not of horses and hay at all like she expected.

"Alex?"

Eyes snapping open in horror, Alexa took a step away from him and wrinkled her nose in disgust. What the hell was she doing sniffing the man? It was a new kind of wrong, she decided. Maybe they shouldn't be discussing her problem at all. Maybe she shouldn't be alone with this man. He was nothing like Gareth and much too smooth for her. "I don't have a problem," she stated gratingly.

"Oh come now, my boy. To not know the touch of a woman. To never feel her bosom and richness of her flesh." The wicked flash of his teeth made her gape at him. "There's nothing like it."

"Oh my god!" Embarrassment melting into fury, she pointed a very emphatic finger in his face. "If you come near Arabella again, I will personally shoot you!" Turning on her heel she marched towards the door.

"Aww, don't be like that Elf. We were just getting along." His hand caught around her wrist. Since she was a lot smaller than him, when he didn't move she was slingshot back against him. With a squawk of alarm, she tilted her head back to demand her release immediately, but she got the first up close and personal look at his devil eyes.

They weren't frightening at all, she realized. In fact, from her new proximity, they were like glittering rubies.

My, but they were pretty.

Imperceptibly she softened in his arms and Felix stiffened.

For an insane moment, Felix thought the lad was going to kiss him. And then another thought occurred to him as he felt a shudder go through him. He named it for dread.

Maybe the boy hadn't had any women for a reason.

Alexa was suddenly released.

Disoriented for a moment she frowned at the man who held up a hand, his breath short, eyes impossibly wide. "What? What's wrong?"

"You...why didn't you...by the gods, I am a fool!"

Stamping and cursing like a mad elephant he paraded around the length of the stable. Even the horses watched him for signs of insanity.

When he had more control over himself, he stopped in front of her and placed his hands on her shoulders. "I understand. I understand how this must be difficult for you to see me with her." Alexa was completely lost as he looked down at her with forced sympathy. "They sheltered you back home, didn't you? Never let you really express yourself?"

"Huh?" Her face twisted with confusion. What the hell was he babbling about?

"But it's okay. I understand. You know my Uncle had a gander once." Her eyebrows hiked up in alarm. "He just never liked any of his geese. He couldn't understand him until he saw him with his neighbor's gander one morning."

And if she hadn't known as much about farming and done extensive research on how cows mate so she could figure out their milk production, Alexa would still have been staring up at him in bewilderment. But when the dots connected in her head, the laughter rocked out of her in shrieks of mirth.

When the boy nearly collapsed in on himself in helpless laughter, Felix dropped his hands and watched the frail body fall into the hay. At first, Felix watched him roll and quake with laughter, a trembling finger pointing to him. But whenever the boy seemed about to stop, one look at Felix's face would set him off again. Damn all his maybes. The laughter was answer enough. His epiphany had been wrong. And this boy was just plain evil.

Confusion gave way to fury. Felix reached out and grabbed the whelp's shoulder before hauling him to his feet. "Maybe it's time for some lessons in manners."

Her legs were still rubbery with laughter, Alexa let him drag her out of the stable, her hands clutched around his arm, peals of laughter still fluttering out of her when she recalled how he had tried to appear like he understood her plight. It was only when she saw the lake's edge that her mirth vanished. He wouldn't. "What the hell are you doing?"

"Cooling you off."

Her body locked in panic but he was much stronger than her. "Don't you dare!" She struggled in his grip and cursed her feminine structure. "Unhand me Flamehart! HELP! ARABELLA!"

"Stop screaming like a girl Master Alex. It is unbecoming on a knave."

The lake loomed closer. "NO! Felix, you don't understand!"

"Oh, I understand perfectly Master Alex. If someone had done this to you sooner, your Aunt wouldn't be so tortured by you."

Eyes wide, Alexa only had the time to draw one squeaky breath before she was tossed into the icy water.

The shock nearly made her swallow water, but then she wrapped her arms around herself and let herself sink a few feet. The water was cold as she had suspected. She had to clamp down on her teeth to keep them from chattering. Above the flickering surface of the water, she saw the man standing there at the edge his hands on his hips as he waited for her to surface. She turned and kicked deeper.

Felix stood there grinning. He anticipated the sputtering and gasping look on the boy's face. Oh, how he would delight in his embarrassment and discomfort. Make fun of him, did he? Gareth should know better than to let know-it-all tyrants like him run free.

Yes, Felix chuckled inwardly. He would delight in the look on his face when he emerged.

His smile faded.

If he emerged.

And then the dread pooled in his belly. Without another thought, he dove in.

Swimming under he spun around trying to locate the boy, but there was only more blue in all directions. Holy mother of Maker. Felix's heart sank. Twisting around he swam deeper under watching the murky blue become darker. When his lungs screamed for respite, even though his heart hammered and demanded he look again, he kicked up to the surface. Gasping, he drew another breath and dove back under, going deeper, but without results.

The panic warred with horror and fear until Felix didn't want to breathe.

Bursting up through the surface, he panted and caught his breath, nerves singing in horror at what he had done. How could he be so careless! He should have asked if the boy could swim! He should have never tried to teach him anything and now he had murdered an innocent confused little...

"Looking for something?"

He nearly went under again. Jerking around he stared at the bank where the apparition sat. Cross-legged. Alive. And cheeky as hell.

"You little runt!" Guilt exploding into rage, he knifed towards the water's edge. "WHEN I GET MY HANDS ON YOU!"

Laughing and running, Alexa held up one hand in victory. "IF you get your hands on me!"

Damn, but the boy could run.

Wet, dripping and chilled Alexa had never felt more alive.

Ascending a hill, she knew that even though he was a ways off, Felix would catch her. But the flag made her halt in her advance. Mouth widening in joy, she held up one hand to call out to them, and then she saw the smoke. "Oh my god!"

The body slammed into her from behind, but Felix looked up when he realized she wasn't struggling. His gasp was ragged against her ear. "Arabella!"

There was only one thought in her mind. Someone had told them where she was.

And then she saw the streak of white burst free from the smoke and head east. Her hands clutched Felix before he could sprint towards his burning home. "NO!" She drew him back.

His red eyes were burning with anger. "Are you mad? Let me go!"

"No, look!" She pointed to the rider holding a large bundle in front of him. Riding at breakneck speed.

"What the hell..."

"It's Gareth." Her mind shifted gears. "We have to go."

"What!?" He gaped at her command. "This is my home, who the hell dares..."

She grabbed his arms and met his eyes squarely. "Listen to me Felix, there's too many of them. Do you really think that Gareth would be running away if he could take them?"

Her breath held, she silently warred with those crimson eyes, until they dulled. "Gareth's too much of a hero."

"Yes." She grinned widely at him and he found himself smiling back. "They won't bother with the house if it's empty."

"But there's a hole in the west wing."

"Come on, Felix, we can't stay."

"A HOLE!"

She rolled her eyes at his fixation with the manor. Grabbing his hand she pulled him towards the stables. "We'll fix it. What's to the east?"

"The port town of Dhak." The man sounded distracted, pouting at being commanded.

"Then that's where we're going." She sprinted into the stables and opened Stormy's gate. The moment the saddle strapped in place the horse alerted to her keeper's anxiety. Swinging up onto it, she turned to speak when the old cloak smacked into her face.

Felix shrugged into his shirt before mounting Midnight. "I would rather not be responsible for you freezing to death."

"Oh yeah. You sound destroyed," she countered, dropping the hood over her head and leading the horse out. "Ten gold coins say I get there before you."

The grin on Felix's face was feral. "You're on."

Alexa smirked, kicked Stormy forward and let the adrenaline sing in her veins.

Felix realized that as long as the boy was around, something kept happening.

*

The sun was setting by the time they entered Dhak.

Dismounting his horse, Felix looked around the dark shadows that always clung there. Beside him, Alex's feet hit the ground as he cooed softly at his mare. "Be still my sweet, he won because he cheated."

The Earl frowned at the lad. "I will pretend I didn't hear that." Shaking his head at the bubble the boy seemed to exist in; Felix scanned the usual dark alleys and reprobates that dotted the late hours of the seedy port town. He was worried about how his house was faring. But he was uncharacteristically concerned for the woman his brother had made off with. Something about Arabella's stiff spine made him want to soften the woman. Although, the image of her curled into Gareth's chest as they rode away burned in his mind.

"You know glaring at the shadows won't make them go away."

Felix didn't bother replying to his barb. "Stay close," he instructed and lead his horse through the town.

Alexa stuck her tongue out at the back of his head and pulled the mare to follow. "Sometimes he does sound all grumpy like Gareth," she whispered to Stormy who seemed to nod.

A hand snapped back and Alexa went deathly still as it splayed against her stomach.

Her breath stuck in her throat she suddenly felt lightheaded. *Oh please god*, she prayed. *Don't let me faint now!*

"Do not speak a word."

She couldn't if her life depended on it. Because if his hand had been an inch higher she would have had a lot more explaining to do.

And then the red and green blur hurtled into Felix without warning.

"Oh, Felix!"

Oh, Felix? Alexa frowned and then her eyes nearly popped out of her head when she noticed the blur had been a rather curvaceous woman who was now very much attached to the Earl's lips. Mouth parting in shock, she resisted the urge to reach forward and smack him, but the woman was already drawing back, although not without a satisfied lick of her bottom lip.

Disgusted beyond reason, Alexa crossed her arms and glared daggers at the woman. Just the flare of her hips and the ample bosom spilling over her bodice confirmed it. She was a woman of profession. The first thing she'd do when she got back would be to put these women to better use. Like maybe laundry!

The sensuous, long-lashed woman seemed to notice her and then did a double take. "Felix, why in heaven's name are you dragging her along with you while coming to see me?"

And the rug was swept out from under her feet. The caramel eyes widened in desperate plea as Felix turned to frown at Alexa in confusion, a touch of rouge still on his mouth. "Her? This is Alex Windmere. He is vacationing with his Aunt from the capital. Which brings me to my joy at seeing you Sherry. I need your help in looking for my brother."

The dark sultry gaze darkened and Alexa felt the fist wrap tightly around her windpipe. The woman opened her mouth to protest then raised an eyebrow as the woman traveling with her Felix shook her head desperately over his shoulder. She narrowed her gaze with a silent promise to get answers later before smiling indulgently at the Earl. "Oh, so it is business that brings you to my doorstep. I caught your scent a mile away."

The man snorted but smiled affectionately at the beautiful Tavern Mistress "More like your boys alerted you to my arrival. I know you have your claws in all that goes on in this town Sherry. You must help me find my brother."

Linking her arm through his she led him through the streets to the warmth emanating from the Tavern windows. "He rode in about an hour before you. He had a woman with him." She smirked at the now-silent Alexa, who stood behind the Earl, her eyes on the ground. "Seems you brothers are up to no good as always."

"Where is he?"

"Nursing that bullet wound I gather."

Alexa gasped, all caution thrown to the wind. "He's hurt?!"

Sherry nodded. "Yes, but he'll live. No one sews wounds like my Penelope."

"Is she the one with the mole on her…"

"Yes, you bad boy." Sherry purred and planted another lingering kiss on his grinning mouth. "You remember all of them don't you?"

Alexa only felt mildly irritated with just how much of a lecherous scoundrel this man was. How the brothers differed, she sighed inwardly. Turning to the woman before she could start sucking on his bottom lip she raised her chin. "Take me to him."

"Oh, you may not command me here 'Alex'."

The younger woman had the decency to wince. "I apologize, My Lady. Please, take me to him."

The Tavern Mistress regarded her for a moment. "When he's not screaming for my Penelope," she provided gleefully. Delighted at her pun. "You can wait in the parlor with the other woman. Stay and talk with me a while Felix."

The Earl watched the young lad quickly tie his mare to the trough and dart into the building. He sighed. "Later maybe Sherry. I need to keep an eye on that boy. He brings trouble."

"You don't know the half of it," Sherry muttered under her breath as they went inside.

"Hell!" Gareth cried out, his breath wheezing as the petite woman hurled herself against him, her arms wrapped around his neck, her face buried into his chest. With a groan, he slid his good arm around her and held her tightly, missing the thick mass of gold that had previously adorned her pretty little head. Arabella had already relayed the turn of events and if he hadn't been reeling with the pain, he would have lost hair for it. But they hadn't gotten the time.

Blinking back tears she knew would give her away, Alexa held the man tightly, just drawing strength from him. The past week had been taxing and having him beside her finally seemed to break all the restraints she'd been forced to hold.

Her Captain seemed to sense the need for reassurance from his Queen and sighed into her fragrant hair. "It is okay, Your Highness," he whispered soothingly. "All will be well. I'm here now."

Pulling away, her eyes glistening with tears she swallowed thickly, trying to glower at him effectively, but failing. "Don't call me…"

He raised an eyebrow. "Would you prefer Alex then?"

Lifting her nose imperiously she stepped away. "I shall."

He held back a smile and then met the glistening green eyes. Yes, he supposed. He had probably given her quite a scare when he'd slid off his horse, the blood everywhere. It was a good thing Sherry had recognized him, which he realized had only made those green eyes worry more. Now when he was on his feet and without blood, he realized he wanted to reassure her as well. *Damn you, Bella*, he cursed vehemently in his heart. *Why now?*

Sherry was the first to pick up on the tension that thickened in the room. "Now then, maybe I can get you men some drink while I find something to clean up this here girl." She touched Arabella's arm gently, the Knight's blood drying on her pretty blue dress. "Come with me, child."

Gareth raised his eyes to the red-haired man who watched him silently and nodded. "Yes, I suppose we have time for a drink and a change of clothes. But we cannot stay long."

"We'll see Flamehart."

"I am Flamehart," Felix snapped. "I think it's appropriate to remember HE abandoned us."

"How dare you!" All Alexa could see was red, but Sherry grabbed her arm rather firmly.

"Oh no, you don't. Let the men work this out, you are coming with me." Sherry hissed against her ear and added, "If you know what's good for you."

Alexa remained rooted to the spot and Gareth sighed. "Go with her Alex."

The Queen in her warred to defend her Captain, but she wasn't Queen here. Not right now. Scowling with frustration, she wrenched her arm loose from the woman's grip and marched towards the room Gareth had emerged from. "Fine."

"Alex?"

"What?" She snapped at Sherry unnecessarily, still piqued by Felix's outburst.

The woman smirked. "We are going that way," she chuckled and pointed to a door covered with colorful beads. Alexa stuck her nose in the air and stalked away.

While Arabella changed mutely behind the screen, Sherry demanded answers. But she wasn't prepared for them.

"Oh, my Lord! The Queen!" The woman fell into a lopsided curtsy. "Your Highness! I didn't know!"

Alexa winced. "And you could not have known." She touched the woman's shoulder gently. "Please get up, you're making me uncomfortable."

"But you're the Queen!" The sultry eyes were suddenly huge.

Alexa couldn't help but smile. "No one's curtsied to me in a week. Please rise."

On wobbly feet, she rose and fumbled with the hem of her dress. "If there's anything I can do…"

"You can." Alexa watched Arabella step out and blinked at the gorgeous green chiffon the woman had been loaned. If Arabella had been exotic before, now the lack of her defiance softening her features and hair tumbling around her shoulders; she was breathtaking. Alexa grinned inwardly and anticipated the look on Gareth's face. She didn't envy the man. "You can keep my secret and provide us a safe place to catch our bearing."

The Tavern Mistress' eyes twinkled with mischief. "If it's hiding you need My Queen, you best ask Felix. No one knows these parts better than does."

Alexa warmed to the woman, but it still plagued her. "Would you like to do something else?"

"Oh anything for you, Your Highness."

"No," she shook her head, holding the taller woman's rough hands. "I mean is there anything you would like to do apart from this Sherry. Besides it. Can I help you? You do not have to do this anymore."

The voluptuous woman's smile was surprisingly tender. "Ah, My Queen. Of all my girls that work here, we are a necessary evil."

"I did not mean to imply…"

"Yes, you did." She laughed. "When love is hard to come by Your Highness, we sometimes provide the peace they need."

Alexa didn't approve neither did she understand, but they had been here since before time. So she let it go. For now.

More so because she had more pressing matters.

Arabella was still silent. Her brow darkened. "You can do me one other favor, Sherry." She nodded at the woman who had suddenly lost her fire. "Find her some nourishment; I am going to have a word with a certain stubborn idiot." Muttering about delusional old men, she marched out determinedly.

Felix watched in rapt fascination as Alex dragged Gareth away by his arm. As an adolescent, he realized that Alex Windmere was a surprisingly perceptive lad. He couldn't hear a damned word the boy was whispering furiously at the Captain who stood a foot taller than him. His mouth turned up when he realized that the boy was winning the argument. Again. Shaking his head, Felix accepted that the lad would grow up to be one formidable man. And it would work better in his favor not to make an enemy of Alex. Especially since his talk with his brother.

He didn't approve of Gareth's attitude towards their people. The lands entrusted to him by the very Queen he vowed to protect. Their upkeep should have been a part of his Knightly vows, but when Gareth said he hadn't returned because he knew his younger brother had everything under control, some of Felix's resentment ebbed.

Laughing under his breath, he watched Alex lift a finger and wag it at the Captain with a scathing hiss which made Gareth wince. And to Felix's astonishment, he dutifully turned and headed to where Sherry had disappeared with Arabella.

With a defeated sigh, he poured himself another glass of bourbon. There went his prospects.

The stool scrapped beside him and the glass was snatched out of his hand unceremoniously and downed.

For a moment his hand was held suspended even though the glass wasn't there. Deliberate crimson eyes finally turned to him with a silent warning.

Chest heaving, the lad slapped the heavy glass back on the table and leaned back in his seat, head resting against the back of the chair. "Oh thank god for alcohol."

Brow darkening he regarded him with growing fury. "Do you do anything that normal children do?"

The boy blinked at him as if he couldn't understand who he was talking about then sighed. "Please Felix," he rasped with more maturity than he was worth. "My brain is hurting."

Picking up the bottle, he slid it out of Alex's reach and took a swig from it directly. "You are not old enough to drink."

"You are not my father," he growled and Felix couldn't help but arch an amused eyebrow.

"That was a nasty trick by the way."

The caramel eyes that unsettled him flickered in confusion.

"At the lake," he clarified admonishingly.

As usual, the boy refused to be chastised. Instant mirth replaced the confusion and the mouth widened into a rather pretty smile.

Felix blinked and looked away with a frown. Pretty?

Alexa couldn't help but chuckle as the man's defenses came down like a visible shutter and stole the warmth from his eyes. These brothers were more alike than either of them liked to admit. "As opposed to claiming that I preferred ganders."

He had the decency to wince. "It was an honest mistake."

"That I would find you attractive?"

Felix's eyes snapped up in alarm and his blood simmered at the rather sensuous tilt of the boy's mouth, the caramel melting into rich honey. "I would appreciate it if we never speak of this again."

"It would be interesting, wouldn't it?" Alexa smirked. "If your gander theory was correct."

With a curse, Felix rose to his feet. "I do not have the measure for your teasing today boy."

Rancorous laughter shook his small frame and Alex held up his hands, mischievous eyes pleased with the reaction. Felix wanted to douse him with the rest of his bourbon. "I apologize. Please don't leave. We cannot lose you too. Looking for you would be hard enough."

He reconsidered it for a moment before dropping back in his chair with a spurt of annoyed breath from his nose.

"Especially with the number of brothels in this town."

He nearly climbed over the top of the table to strangle him, but Alex had darted away with laughter. "Peace!" He held up his hands in surrender. "Now. Sherry tells me you're the man to ask for the best places to hide."

Battling with the need to do bodily damage to a boy half his size, Felix wondered just what it was about Alex that brought out the worst in him. Disliking his lack of control over their sudden turn of events, the rakish Earl leaned his chair back on two legs and contemplated their options. It was true. He lived in Dhak. And he knew how to disappear in Dhak. But he wondered if he was happy with taking Gareth along. The self-righteous man would balk, he was sure of it.

Eyes drifting towards where the Captain had disappeared, he sighed. "I do know a place. But one most likely to offend my brother's sensibilities."

"What is with you and Gareth anyway?"

"We don't agree with each other's choice of professions."

Alexa couldn't help but raise her eyebrow. "I take offense to you implying he shouldn't be serving his Kingdom."

"Ah yes, you people from the capital think 'country' over 'kin'."

At the mocking bitterness, she leaned forward on the table and gauged the tightness of his shoulders even though he appeared outwardly relaxed. "What happened?"

"Nosey little thing, aren't you?"

She resisted the urge to demand an answer but rather settled to meet his gaze unflinchingly. It usually worked with Gareth. And she soon discovered it was as practical a course with his brother as well.

With a dejected grunt, Felix let his chair drop back on all four legs and put his elbows on the table, holding the boy's rapt attention. "My mother died because my brother wasn't here to look after her."

Alexa bit back the gasp. "Your mother...but...I don't understand."

"Gareth wasn't much of a son because he was more of a Knight." Shrugging he leaned back the chair, arms crossing in an age-old defensive gesture. "When he signed up for the Royal Guard he didn't look back."

"What was wrong with your mother?"

"She fell ill to the weather. Never recovered."

The sudden fist of guilt clenched around her heart. "I'm sorry to hear that. I'm sure Gareth wouldn't have gone if he knew."

"He knew. But he had received word that the king and queen had left the wayward princess alone and off he went to be a hero."

She flinched visibly, but Alexandra wasn't childish enough to think that it was her fault the woman was dead. Her own parents had died that night. Her own life had been torn apart and her Captain had made a decision. But one question still plagued her. Lifting her honey-colored gaze to the embittered man, she frowned. "And where were you?"

Vermillion eyes jumped to hers and held. They were cold but Alexa didn't miss the flash of guilt there. "Ah, I see." She nodded. "You weren't with her either."

"I returned!" He thundered, the sudden change in him taking Alexa by surprise. It was then she realized she really didn't know this man. Not really. Because suddenly he'd transformed from a cynical, womanizing scoundrel to a feral red-haired devil. She couldn't help but shrink back slightly. "But my ship arrived too late and Gareth buried her before I could even see her!"

"Where were you?"

"Away!" He snapped.

She let out a deep breath. "Look, I can understand that you would feel denied."

"Denied!?"

She winced. "Maybe that's not the right word."

"You think?"

Deciding to stay silent, she knew there was nothing else she could say. "I'm sorry about your mother. My own parents passed away when I was very young."

"You are still very young."

Her mouth twitched. "I keep forgetting."

Behind her, she heard the door slam and in walked Arabella, with her green eyes blazing. Alexa was contented in the fact that at least she was reacting. It must have been horrible to have Gareth collapse on her bleeding. She didn't know how she would have handled it. When she saw the two occupants of the saloon she stiffened.

Behind her emerged Gareth looking worse for the wear. Running a hand through his hair wearily he met Felix's gaze resolutely. "We cannot impose on Sherry any longer. We must leave. There are no boats leaving tonight. We might have to ride."

"That won't be necessary." Felix rose to his feet and took one last swig from his bottle. "I know of a place we can spend the night."

"But Felix…"

"Gareth," Alexa gently spoke to her bone-tired Captain. "Let Felix take care of it." Rising from her perch she walked to him and wrapped a hand around his waist, dragging one arm over her shoulder. "You can barely walk."

"I am fine," he grated out.

"Shut up Captain, that's an order."

Felix was already speaking with Sherry to borrow two lanterns.

*

Walking down the stretch of the beach Alexa took a deep breath of the sea air and smiled. Even though someone had tried to kill her and she wanted to collapse with exhaustion, she was exhilarated. Away from the confines of her castle, her troubles seemed far. When Alexa had tired, Felix had taken the weight of his brother who was already stumbling. Holding the lanterns up, Alexa and Arabella walked down the deserted beach, and the horses slowly pulled behind them.

"Where exactly are we going?" Arabella frowned into the darkness that stretched on for miles. The moonlight was hidden behind the tall cliffs as the night slowly progressed. She didn't like this lack of control over the events. More than that she was worried sick about the woman walking in disguise beside her. Someone had tried to kidnap their queen. Someone had meant to do her harm. Arabella hadn't had enough time to speak with Gareth and then she had been too worried about the bullet wound. Frightened for the man's life. Afraid she'd lose him even before she had him.

Felix hefted Gareth more firmly over his shoulder; the man's feet were already starting to drag. "I have a place here that will tide us until morning."

"Here?" Arabella wrinkled her nose, a touch of incredulous distaste in her voice. "In the middle of nowhere?"

Felix didn't appreciate the implication of her tone. "Yes, My Lady. Here in the middle of nowhere."

Gareth groaned with pain as his bandage jostled in the movement.

Over her shoulder, Alexa watched Felix struggle with the man. "Do you want to rest for a moment?"

"No, we're almost there." With a grunt, hoisted the listless Captain against a large boulder and held his jaw firmly. "But I don't like the color of him."

Arabella was by his side in an instant. "Let me see to him, you go and find the entrance."

"I'll help Felix," Alexa volunteered.

"No!" Arabella looked up sharply. "Stay with me, Alex."

The blunt concern in those dark green eyes was obvious. Alexa smiled at her teacher. "Relax Madam, I am sure I can handle Lord Felix Flamehart for a few more minutes."

The Earl bristled beside her and tromped off into the darkness. Alexa winked at Arabella's worried expression before trotting off after him.

Sighing, the older woman ran a hand over Gareth's sweat-covered forehead. "Damn you Gareth, you couldn't have picked a worse time to get shot."

Alexa had to run to keep up with Felix's long stride as they maneuvered around the beach. "So what exactly are we looking for?"

"Sometimes I wonder if you stick to me so that you can torment me, for some secret wrong that I've done to you."

"In a past life maybe."

"I don't believe in past lives."

"You should study the Mysticism of Tibetan Monks. Their fables are pretty interesting."

"I'm allergic to monks."

Alexa bit down on her lip to keep from giggling, as she held the lantern up so Felix could see whatever it was that he was looking for. "What else are you allergic to?"

"Nosey adolescent boys."

Her bark of laughter made him smile, but he was glad the boy couldn't see it. Felix could admit that, to at least himself. He liked the boy's sharp sense of humor. And he liked spending time with the lad. He was curious and perceptive. Good qualities in growing children. "Ah, here we are." Bending down he carefully riffled through the sand where it melted into tall looming cliffs.

Her head nearly tipped all the way back as she stared at the humbling height of the rocks. "My god, are we going to go over that?!"

"Not quite over it boy."

"Don't call me boy!"

Felix grinned wickedly. "I mean to go under it." And then to Alexa's growing astonishment, she saw him hook his fingers into a latch and lifted a hatch right out of the sand. A wide, low-stride staircase descended into the darkness, big enough to even allow the animals through. "Think I can trust you to go inside and light the lamps while I bring my deadweight brother?"

Alex gaped at him in horror. The mere thought of it made her knees quake.

The hand slapped her back, nearly sending her toppling inside headfirst. With a shriek, she hugged the lantern to her chest and snarled up at the man disdainfully.

Felix grinned at the light in the boy's eyes. "Be a man."

Alexa stared down into the depths of the tunnel and it seemed to gape like the open mouth of a beast. She swallowed thickly. How the hell could she be a man when all she wanted to do what run back and hide under his cloak?

The laughter was still ringing through the caverns well after they had settled down.

With the growl building in her chest, Alexa resisted the insane urge to do serious bodily harm to the snickering Earl.

The stairway had led inside to a musky old system of caves, she'd been shaking so hard when she reached the bottom that she'd nearly dropped the lantern. With trembling fingers, Alexa had managed to light the first torch. And as the light grew around her, so did her bravado. In fact, she'd managed to light the passage when Felix stepped back in.

But when she felt him come up behind her where she was leaning up to light a torch, his voice had startled her and she'd gone sprawling on the rocky ground.

The caves were inhabited. In fact, they were well lived in. Stocked with simple furniture, littered with beautiful white candles, and stacked high with books. And while they'd been helping Gareth to the daybed in the corner, she'd realized that the cream of the literary works was down here.

This was where Felix lived.

Felix came back from where he'd left Arabella with Gareth. One look at Alexa's face and he was back to guffawing like an idiot.

Rolling her eyes, she decided not to get incensed by how he was offending her royal sensibilities. But this man offended them so often, Alexa only turned and muttered about securing the horses.

Alexa was watching Stormy and Midnight whinny with their heads together where they were tied in a small alcove beside the stairs. The ease with which Midnight found his hay made her realize that the horse had been there before. She wondered why Felix had a place like this when he loved his Manor so much. She hadn't realized how long she'd been there when she hear Arabella's voice.

"Damn you Gareth! Leave me alone!"

Arabella stormed out towards the stairs, just as Alexa ducked behind the horses to stay hidden. What the hell was going on? Alexa frowned.

"Bella!"

Gareth burst out after her, but the woman had climbed half the stairs by then. Alexa was about to call out to them when Gareth grabbed Arabella by the arm and hauled her against him, his mouth coming down hard on the woman's.

Her breath caught in her chest, and Alexa watched Gareth claim her mentor with a fire that seemed to consume them both.

Going liquid in his arms, Arabella collapsed against him helplessly her hands sliding up into his hair for purchase.

The hunger was so potent, that the knot tightened in Alexa's gut before she realized she was envious. Stepping behind the horses, she only watched another moment to see a single tear slide out of Arabella's eye, glimmering happily in the moonlight before she finally turned away.

It never occurred to the Queen before. Her problems might have been solved had she had Gareth.

For the first time in her life, Alexandra Windmere wished she had had time for love.

Felix had been the unwelcome witness of watching Gareth carry the woman into the caves that housed his bedroom. The bourbon was starting to sing in his veins.

He picked up his dark cloak and walked out.

He found the boy sleeping in the hay the horses were munching on. In the soft scant light of the torch, Felix couldn't help but marvel at the radiant glow of his skin. He could grow up to be such a lady killer. Chuckling, he dropped down beside the lad and gently brushed aside Midnight's muzzle where he was almost gnawing on the boy's shirt.

And then his hand brushed against the distinct curves.

Every nerve in his hand on fire, Felix jerked away, nearly tumbling off the small pile of hay. Red eyes wide in the dark, he stared at the subtle changes that began to suddenly morph the small body and he shook his head violently to chase away the images. "Damnation, too much to drink. That is all," he repeated to himself, but his traitorous eyes were dragged back to the gentle rise and fall of the boy's chest. It had been his imagination, Felix assured himself. Just his loneliness that made him hallucinate.

Alex couldn't have breasts.

Could he?

Cursing himself to high heaven, he couldn't help himself from lifting his hand back towards the boy. Feeling like a lecher, he swallowed the bile in his throat but pushed on for the sake of his sanity.

When his palm flattened against the chest, his breath left him with a ragged gasp.

Concealed though they were, those were not masculine curves under the loose shirt and tightly bound cotton. And then the obvious began to take shape in his mind. The supple curve of that backside, the lithe length of the legs, the thin delicate fingers and the shapely waist. The smooth drip of the belly between the legs and Felix fell on his backside on the ground with enough force to jar him to his teeth.

Alex had more than breasts.

A man who could sketch a woman's body from memory had been duped.

And as the rage built in his skin, he decided he deserved to be sure. Crawling up the length of the slumbering cheat, he swallowed the mouth that drove him wild.

Alexa had been sitting there miserably one minute, watching the two horses nuzzle each other affectionately, and the next she went hurtling into the fires of hell.

It was when she gasped and felt the sinuous slip and slide of the tongue that she realized his hand had snaked under the shirt to fondle her breast through the tight wrap.

She was being molested in her sleep.

Stiffening instinctively, she dragged her hands up to shove him away when her eyes snapped open and were blinded by red.

It was then that comprehension dawned on her.

It was Felix and __ dear god!

His tongue was doing the most exquisite things to her mouth.

With a feeble moan that coaxed a shudder from the man above her, Alexa let the boy slip away and the woman wrapped her arms around him.

He snatched a breath through his nose when he felt her respond and then the kiss went wild.

His hands sliding up to hold her face, he slanted his mouth on hers and drank deeply. All the tension and insanity, that had plagued him for the past week because of this woman, exploded into an uncontainable passion. With her melting at his every touch, Felix came down on her with his entire being; without expertise, without his usual control. Like a starving man, his fingers mapped the bones in her face, feeling the depth of their kiss with his fingers, the novelty of it strangely erotic and coaxing a shudder out of him.

Alexa's sleep-addled mind forgot to reason that she hated this man. It forgot to remember she was the Queen and he had accosted her in her sleep. She forgot ethics and politics and right or wrong. She surrendered herself to the steady heat that built in her belly and began to spread. One hand speared into his hair and she held him to the kiss he'd initiated but she wouldn't let him break. Her free hand slid down the smooth hardness of his back.

When her palm passed over the base of his spine, his hips pitched forward and drove down between legs she didn't remember parting.

Her mouth wrenched away, her back arched with a jolt; her head thrown back, she cried out softly.

And everything stilled, but the crazed beating of her heart against his.

His face pressed against her throat, Felix took a few breaths to calm his screaming pulse until he realized just what he'd done.

With a startled hiss, he snatched his hands away from her and shoved himself away.

Staring up at the black rock, Alexa allowed the fire he'd laced through every part of her body to settle into a slow simmer before she dared to glide her eyes back to him.

His devil-red eyes glowed with betrayal.

"Felix..."

The firelight cast his face into a dangerous light. "Don't bother." With one last disgusted snarl, he left her there. Shaking and more miserably confused than when she'd fallen asleep.

And then her misery caught fire.

Jumping to her feet, she marched out after him. "Stop!"

"No!"

Eyes narrowing into scathing slits, she followed him up the wide staircase and into the night. "Oh for god's sake will you let me explain!"

"NO!"

If Arabella hadn't already given her the talk about men, Alexa would have thrown something at his head. Although she was sorely tempted to go through with it, she settled for grabbing his arm and spinning him around. "I realize that your pride is hurt."

"Madam, do you realize that I am inclined to throw you into the ocean?"

She quirked an eyebrow at the growl in his voice, his eyes flashing with barely restrained anger. "That would be a tad redundant don't you think?"

"Not from where I am standing." Shaking off his arm, he began walking again.

"Halt!"

She nearly walked into him as he spun around at her command. "I am at the end of my restraint Madam and for whatever its worth, I will not be held responsible for my actions."

"I believe it is a little late for that; you had your chance," she threw back at him nonchalantly, one hand planted on her hip as her eyes met his without humor.

He had the decency to wince. "I was just making sure."

"Under my shirt."

"Dammit woman, you kissed me back!"

An amused eyebrow shot up. "Only because you caught me by surprise first."

"You were pretending to be a man!"

"I can bet that you're perturbed because your gander theory is shot to hell."

"No Madam! I am perturbed that I found myself attracted to you, despite your gender!"

She couldn't help the twitch of her mouth. "You are attracted to me?"

"Madam, that was before I found you to be a lying, cheating___"

"Stop calling me Madam!"

"Oh that's right, you prefer 'boy.'"

Pressing her fingers into her temples, Alexa tried to will away the headache she knew was coming. "Look, I can understand that you would feel betrayed."

"Can you?"

She frowned up at him as he bore down at her menacingly. "There is a perfectly good explanation for the pretense."

"I'm sure. I would rather not hear it."

"It was for my safety!"

Pausing in his insane need to get away from this child woman, he finally turned to her and met those tantalizing caramels of her eyes that always bothered him. He wasn't entirely sure he liked having a name for all those confusing emotions he felt in her presence. "Your safety. And I suppose you're the Queen of everything," he spat sardonically.

Her shoulders slumping, she sighed. "Queen of Odyria actually."

He opened his mouth to snort when he saw the deep-rooted tenacity on her pretty face. And then the uneasiness that had always plagued him around this woman went up into smoke. "Queen Alexandra Windmere." For a moment he stood there staring at her in horror, unsure of how to address this new predicament he had found himself in. And then he realized he'd been groping the queen not five minutes ago.

Alexa wanted to relish the sudden flash of awkwardness in the aversion of his gaze and the nervous bob of his Adam's apple. Instead, she found herself saddened by the sudden wide chasm that had erupted between them. She tried a small smile. "But you may call me Alex."

His eyes made her wince. "I can see you're still angry with me."

"Am I allowed?"

She was startled at the new wave of animosity in his tone. "Well, I suppose…"

"Seeing as though I'm addressing the Queen."

Gaping at him in dismay, Alexa wanted to reach out and shake him and remind him that she hadn't guillotined him before. Why would she now? She hadn't changed. But then she realized that she had. In his eyes. "Oh Felix, I never meant to cause so much trouble."

He fell into an elaborate bow. "Anything for my queen."

Her eyes pricked with burning tears. "That was cruel."

"How about 'Your Majesty', would you like me to go down on one knee? I might not be Gareth's caliber, but I can certainly try."

The fist in her chest tightened until she flinched at the pain. "You're mocking me."

"I wouldn't dare Your Highness. Even if you're inclined to play your wicked games."

His cutdowns hadn't hurt as badly as they did now. He couldn't be the same man she'd joked around with. The man who'd laughed and played pranks on her. The man who had challenged her and made the troubles surrounding her, seem far away. "I played no games with you Felix."

"No?"

"No!" She snapped. "Will you stop acting like a wounded puppy?"

"If you command me."

God, he was frustrating. "Please Felix, this changes nothing."

"This changes everything!" He thundered.

Stilling under the weight of his words, Alexa wrapped her arms around herself, eyes flickering with unshed tears.

"Go back inside Your Highness, it isn't safe out here."

"You do not command me."

"Fine." He left her there on the beach.

Alexa stood there as the tide played with the sand at her feet and she realized she wanted to cry.

And if she'd felt alone before now, she was desolate.

Maybe Arabella had been right. The best stories were tragedies.

"Alone at last."

The voice froze the very marrow in her bones.

Lifting her chin, she stared up at the face.

Derek smiled widely, his face dark as the clouds blotted out the sun. "I was afraid he would never leave."

Alexa opened her mouth but the arms wrapped around her from behind, the handkerchief muffled her and her eyes began to water.

One solitary tear rolled down her cheek before her vision blurred and her eyes slid shut.

*

"Eloped!?"

"Why are you so concerned Gareth? It is what we had hoped for." The white-haired Councilman leaned back in his chair.

The wounded Captain slapped his hands against the thick table between them. "Alexa would never run and do anything! Much less marry!"

The older man raised an eyebrow. "Alexa?"

Snarling, the Captain jerked away, his hands itching to hit something.

Nothing could have prepared him for waking up in Arabella's arms and finding Alexa gone. He'd nearly broken Felix's nose and had a feeling, Arabella had caught the first boat back to her kingdom after all the things he'd said to her. He knew it hadn't been her fault. It hadn't been Felix's either.

It had been his own. He never should have left her side.

And then he'd received word from the Castle saying the Queen had returned. With her new husband.

"Gareth," the Councilman spoke softly, placing a hand on the Captain's shoulder. "We had both secretly hoped the child would marry for love rather than an obligation."

Gareth couldn't shake the burning red eyes that had stayed as silent as the man when he'd read out the parchment. "The Queen has never run in her life."

Sighing, the old man leaned back against the table. "She is still young. The young are given to reacting passionately."

"Not Queen Alexandra," Gareth lifted his dark gaze and grit his teeth to reign in his anger. "She would not have married that sniveling boy for all the silk in the world! That is why we had hoped to introduce her to Prince William."

"Maybe she had a change of heart."

"Is that, why I am not allowed to see her?"

"That is indeed troubling." The Councilman sighed. "But I'm sure that we will all get to see her at the reception. She's been away for a while. I can understand that she would need some time to herself."

Not from me, Gareth growled inwardly. He knew what had happened.

They had found her alone and bargained her Kingdom for her silence. And now she wouldn't dare see her Captain because she knew he'd see right through it. But what she didn't know was that her Captain knew her best. And he'd never let her down before. He wasn't about to let her down now, even if it meant he had to go through the Council itself.

But he knew he couldn't do it alone.

Gareth found him drowning at Sherry's bar.

He had stood behind him for at least a good minute before Felix had spun around and tried to take his head off with his fist. Through the cursing and the fists flying at him, Gareth had managed to drag him out with his arm wrapped around his neck.

Sherry sighed from where she was wrapped around her new client. "Here they go again."

"Who's that throttling Flamehart?"

"Gareth Van Buren."

"Is he going to kill him?"

"No. He's his brother."

"Let me go!"

"Damn you, Felix; will you listen to me?" Gareth ducked the empty barrel and watched it crash into the wall behind him. With a sigh, he held up his hands and faced his brother. Standing under the flickering light of the street lamp, Felix looked every bit like the pirate that he sometimes was. For the hundredth time, Gareth wished he had been there for him when he was young. "I know you're angry with me."

"Angry!? I'm furious! You trusted me for their safety and care but you couldn't trust me enough to tell me WHO she was? Damn you Gareth!" Felix nearly went spilling onto the dirt.

Gareth caught his arm and steadied him. "Calm down little brother."

"Do NOT call me brother!" The man thundered, his fiery eyes unsettling as he wrenched his arm loose. "I thought I had gone mad thinking the lad's smile was pretty!"

Gareth figured, smiling at the declaration wouldn't sit well with the perturbed man. "What are you angry at Felix? That she fooled you so well or that I lied to you?"

"You brought them to my house. I can forgive you for your cowardice, but not for jeopardizing the safety of my home and my people Gareth!"

"This coming from a man who spent most of his days playing pirate!"

"That was only until you decided to play the coward!"

"Dammit, Felix! I let you play the pirate because I never wanted you to be troubled by responsibilities." Gareth snapped. "I was tied down to my obligations; I wanted you to be free! And I still want you to be free! You're my brother! I've always wanted you to be happy!"

Scowling Felix strode to the wooden rail and looked down into the inky sea. He was drunk and he didn't want to hear it. "Go the hell away Gareth."

It was then that Gareth saw the faraway guilt in those fiery eyes. And he might not have been there for his brother growing up, but he did know the man well. "What happened that night?"

Suddenly the Earl was weary, head hanging down while his hands clasped there above the murky waters of the pier. "Is there a point to this?"

Gareth's anxiety sharpened and he came to stand beside his brother. "Tell me."

The flaming hair played with the wind and fluttered over the deadly glare. "Go to hell."

Under normal circumstances, Gareth would have replied with his fist, but the state his brother was in made him curious. "What is it that is really making you drink Felix?"

"I kissed her."

And then Gareth did hit him.

Nearly sprawling into the street, Felix caught himself with one hand around the thick metal lamppost. "Damn Gareth." He shook his head to clear it, to make the singing birds go away. "That hurt."

"You bastard!"

The Earl snorted. "Pot calling the kettle black Gareth. Is that really fair considering you failed to tell me who she was?"

"You kissed her!?"

Flexing the sore jaw, Felix shook his head. "It was a mistake. I assure you, I won't make a habit of being a fool."

"Hell, I could have told you that you are a fool!" Gareth snarled. This was an unexpected turn of events. When Arabella had expressed concerns that Alexa and Felix had gotten close during the forced 'vacation', he had told her he knew his brother. Even if Felix found out that Alex was really a woman, the Queen wasn't his brother's usual flavor. He'd seen enough of Felix's women. He preferred lithe, curvaceous girls with experience. He never had much patience with stubborn little women.

Then something occurred to Gareth. He frowned at the troubled man. "What did she do?"

Felix blinked at his brother as if he was deranged. "Who?"

"Alexa. When you kissed her."

"Why?"

Because anyone who had ever tried to lay a hand on the woman walked away with lasting scars. His Queen might have been a small woman, but she knew how to use a sword. And especially handy with the dagger, that was always strapped to her thigh under all the layers of her skirt. Even as Alex, she had carried the weapon in her boot. And Gareth had taught her enough so she could defend herself if needed.

"Must we relive my mistakes Gareth?"

"Humor me."

The Earl's brow darkened. He had no idea where his brother was going with this. With a defeated sigh, as if it pained him to admit it, Felix finally spoke. "She kissed me back. But I believe she said I took her by surprise."

"No one takes My Queen by surprise."

Now thoroughly confused, Felix didn't bother hiding it as he met his brother's cautious gaze. "What?"

Gareth's mind was churning. Grabbing his brother's elbow he steadied him. "This will require some rethinking, but it is a long way off to the Capital." The Captain's mouth stretched into a wide wicked grin much like his pirate brother's. "Although, I do not believe a – what was it you called me? Ah yes, righteous, uptight, arse can pull this off."

Felix didn't like the look in his brother's eye. "No."

"I will need a pirate."

"NO!"

*

"Are you quite mad!?"

Gareth handed him the rope. "Wait until you see my light."

"Gareth!?"

"Remember that her window is the fourth from the left."

82

"You cannot expect me to go along with this!"

The Captain pulled the sac's string tight and sealed it. "Strap this to your back."

Batting away his brother's busy hands, Felix took a step away from him and pointed to him purposefully. "Cease now. I am not going to be a party to this!"

Gareth sighed wearily. "Are you uncomfortable wearing the pirate patch?"

"Damn you Gareth, I am NOT kidnapping the Queen!"

"Why not?" The Captain seemed confused.

Felix stared at his brother as if he'd gone mad. "Because they'll hang me!"

"Bah! The only one who can hang you is the Queen. Who in this case will happen to be with you."

"And what about the new King? I am sure he wouldn't take kindly, to having his wife carted off in the middle of the night."

"You leave the king to me."

"Somehow brother," Felix shouldered the sack, "I am not reassured."

"Don't you trust me?"

"No?"

Laughing, Gareth slapped a good-natured hand on his back. "Think of it as your debts repaid to the Kingdom."

Interest sparking in those vermillion eyes, Felix narrowed his eyes. "Don't riddle me."

"You do this and I will remove the bounty on your head."

Felix felt his jaw go slack. "You always said it was a lesson I had to learn."

Gareth shrugged. "I would consider it learned."

"Selfish bastard."

With a wink, the Captain turned to leave. "And remember; do not underestimate her because she's a woman."

Felix didn't understand what Gareth had meant. He contemplated the intelligence of his brother's plan and his own stupidity as he scaled the wall. But he was infinitely glad, that his career as a pirate and his forced retirement hadn't left him ill-equipped to handle his brother's harebrained assignment.

He'd managed to creep into her room without incident. He'd even excused himself those few moments he'd spent staring at her sleeping form. He'd expected her to be lying straight on her back, hands folded on her stomach, like a royal corpse, but what he found was astonishing.

She lay on her stomach, one arm wrapped around a pillow, the nightgown having hiked up to her waist, the sheet twisted around her torso. Having rolled in her sleep, the petite woman lay diagonally on the bed in the very center, one tantalizing creamy leg peeking out of the rich royal blue sheets. He turned his head sideways and let his mouth twist up into a smirk at the amount of skin she seemed to be showing. Then he shook his head, angry at himself. She was a married woman. And she was his queen. He had no right to entertain any thoughts of the sort about the woman.

But try as he might, he had never been able to shake the image of her vibrant caramel eyes flashing with mirth. They haunted him at the bottom of his rum bottle and the setting sun, even the blaze of the morning through his window.

When he placed one hand on the bed beside her shoulders so he could reach with the other and wrap it around her mouth to muffle her scream, he realized what Gareth's parting words had meant.

With a gasp she came awake, her hand fishing under the pillow and before Felix could grab her, she rolled and the blade was placed at his throat. "Damnation!"

Sleep-addled, Alexa had reacted instinctively. And then she was blinded by the red.

"Oh, Lord!" She rasped, honey eyes beguilingly wide. "Felix!?"

Felix had to physically restrain himself from kissing the soft, parted lips under him.

Alexa's heart had started thumping when she'd felt someone lean on her bed, but staring up into the swirling depths of the scarlet gaze, her heart hammered against her ribs like a mad thing. She couldn't understand what he was doing here. Of all the people in the world to be stealing into her room, this man was the last she'd expected. His hair was the color of blood, his eyes glinting like rubies, his goatee a tad unkempt. He really was nice this close.

Then she realized Felix was staring at her open mouth like a hungry lion.

Heat flooding her cheeks, she pressed the knife harder against his Adam's apple, but not enough to cut. "What the hell are you doing here?"

White teeth gleamed in the light of the single candle that burned by her bedside. "Are you sure you would like me to answer you while you hold a knife at my throat?

Lips curling away from her teeth, she growled. "The same knife is about to cut into your jugular if you don't."

"I missed you, sweetheart," he purred, leaning closer and delighting as the blade moved with him rather than against him.

He had expected her eyes to widen in panic, instead, they narrowed and then he realized what else was in jeopardy besides his neck. He cleared his throat, her knee flicking gently against his groin for emphasis. Caught on the precipice of lust and hesitation, his mouth twisted knowingly. He chuckled. "Alright, I'll tell you the truth – If you put the weapon down."

"Which one?"

His smile widened at her quick quip. Ah, he had missed her, he realized. He hadn't felt as alive as when dealing with this royal elf. "How about I let you choose?"

Alexa was beginning to tingle as he leaned there over her, his body slowly but surely pressing down on hers. The sudden flashes of his kisses and caresses rushed back to her before she could rein control. Noticing, that if she didn't find the upper hand, he would disarm her, she lowered her knee but tightened her hold on the knife. "How about you stop playing games and tell me what the hell you're planning." Then she frowned up at him. "And why are you wearing a pirate patch?"

"You should ask your good Captain."

That floored her. "Gareth sent you?" And she had thought that maybe he had missed her.

Felix would have caught the flash of disappointment followed by the flare of anger, but before he could answer her, her leg had hooked around his torso and was tossed off her. With a laughing groan, he lay there on the floor, as she fluidly rose out of the sheets and glared down at him. "I'm glad you're amused Flamehart. But do you realize that stealing into my royal chambers could have you beheaded!"

Lying there with his elbows propped under him, he gave her a lascivious grin. "And I wonder My Queen, what you will tell them."

The blood boiled in her veins. "Damn you, Felix, what the hell are you doing here? Tell me now or I WILL call the guards and have you clapped in irons!"

He really should have just thrown her over his shoulder and climbed back out, but he couldn't help but rile her up a bit. She looked smashing in a temper. And there was no reason why he couldn't enjoy this just a bit. After all, he was out on a limb, so to speak.

Damn, but he looked good laying there on her bedroom floor. If only she wasn't the Queen.

And then she realized just who she was. She was a married woman.

Felix could see the exact moment the woman he knew disappeared and in its place was the Queen.

"Get up off my floor immediately." This time there was only authority in her voice and ice in her eyes.

With an exaggeratedly dismal sigh, Felix rolled to his feet. "Sometimes I swear you rile me up just so you can shoot me down."

Arms crossed, she glowered up at him and demanded, "Now tell me why you stole up into my chambers."

"To kidnap you."

For a moment she thought she heard him wrong. The shock of his words made the ice-queen mask crumble around her and she blinked up at him in bewilderment. "I apologize; sleep seems to be clouding my senses. I thought you said you were here to kidnap me."

"You heard correct, Your Majesty."

Her mouth dropped open in almost comical shock, but Felix had reached forward and tied the gag around her mouth. For the second time in her life, Alexa was dragged away like a sack of flour.

The body was lowered into the waiting arms.

"Easy boys," Felix smiled at his men. "That's precious cargo there."

The eyes shot daggers at him accusingly.

Jumping down the rest of the way he gazed up at the window and chuckled. She had nearly made him drop her twice. He'd never met a woman like her. She opposed him at every step of the way. Her wit was entertaining as hell and he itched to get his hands on her. He hoped to hell Gareth completed what little political maneuvering he had to complete, or the Queen would need rescuing from him.

"Your Grace?"

"Let's go." Walking to Midnight, he swung up onto the saddle and held his arms out until the bound woman was placed in his lap. Her shoulder dug into his chest and his breath blew out in a whoosh. Felix realized their ride to the port would be penance for his sins, an absolution for his will to resist grinding against her pert little behind conveniently resting in his lap. A feat worthy of Goliath. Arms wrapping securely around her waist, he pressed his mouth against her ear and hissed. "Hold still or else."

Freezing in his arms, Alexa decided she didn't really want to break her neck before she had a chance to break his, as Midnight carried them away from the castle like the wind.

She wanted to feel bad about leaving her new husband and her kingdom behind, but for the first time in the past two weeks, Alexa let herself relax. Tomorrow, she decided. Tomorrow she'd deal with tomorrow.

*

The Curling Wind was a beautiful vessel. She had tried to protest when he'd thrown her over his shoulder, but their brief stop had made one thing clear. She would go with him, whether she liked it, or not. And even though, she had no option but to accompany him on whatever crazy adventure he'd embarked on, she refused to speak with him. Not after their argument in the cabin.

"Get dressed."

Alexa stood there, arms crossed stubbornly as he blocked the only exit out of the little cabin.

Felix sighed when she continued to glare at him silently. "Come now Elf. I miss the boy who used to battle wits with me."

"It is customary to have an opponent who HAS wits to battle with."

The thin lips tilted. "Get dressed. Please."

Her eyes narrowed at the memory he was referring to. "And if I don't?"

The grin was vile. "I am a man of questionable morals; do you really want me to answer that?"

She wasn't completely innocent that she didn't catch his implication. "You wouldn't dare."

He took one step towards her and she didn't waver. He took another and she lifted her chin to glare at him. His last, had her craning her neck back to continue holding his gaze. She didn't dare look away or bat an eyelash.

Felix reveled in the woman's bravado. He wanted nothing but to make good on his threat. For a second he felt a stab of regret when he realized that she now belonged to someone else. And the last time he'd been this close to her she'd been his. Almost. "Your Majesty, I plan to take you away on my ship. Most of my crew members, save for the ones who belonged to Gareth, are indeed men of questionable character. Do you really want to go dressed as the only woman on board?"

His proximity was jarring enough, but the potent concern in those red eyes was what floored her. Not the threat. And with it came the stark realization that she couldn't be attracted to him. Not now. "I will dress. If you answer my question, then we will not speak again."

A scarlet eyebrow arched. "Then I'd rather not answer your question." He turned and headed to the door.

"Why did you do this Felix Flamehart?"

Turning on the threshold, his unreadable face suddenly morphed into the sweetest smile he'd ever given her. "It is my last service to My Queen."

And with that enigmatic declaration, he was gone.

That was then.

Now as he stood at the helm with his first mate he couldn't stand her silence. She stood there in her little boy clothes, her hair still cropped short, body bound in its confines. Back in her bedroom, he'd finally been able to see her as a woman and he had marveled how he'd never noticed.

"Your cabin boy's rather forlorn."

Felix sighed. "Is that way of your saying you'd rather take his place, Jack?"

The short balding man snorted. "As if you'd trust anyone else on your back Felix."

That was true. The world he lived in was indeed wrought with betrayal. It made, what Alexa had done, seem like a slap on the wrist.

"Something bothering you, Boss?"

Shaking his head, he handed the wheel back to the man. "Nothing that can't be remedied. Keep an eye on things."

"Will do."

Walking down the narrow stairs, he stepped onto the deck and nodded at the men who he passed before coming to stand beside Alexa. "Come inside."

Her spine stiffened. And she'd finally relaxed. Relaxed enough to marvel at the ocean. She'd never realized how much she loved the colors of it. The way it rippled as if alive. Busy with state affairs, she'd never had the chance to truly travel because it was fun. She had used boats, stayed in royal cabins and come out on the plank when they docked. Now standing on the port side of the beautiful vessel surrounded by pirates, the Queen was envious. She was envious of the beauty that eluded her even though she owned half these waters they were traveling.

"Come on elf, you cannot give me the silent treatment forever."

Watch me; she threw back silently with a flick of her chin.

The man sighed. "Come inside or I'll drag you there."

If looks could kill, Felix would have keeled over. With a slow deliberate pivot, she led the way to his cabin.

The door closed and she stood there in front of him, her hands on her hips.

Felix smiled softly at her. "Are you hungry?"

She wondered if she could tell him to go to hell someway without speaking a word.

He raised an eyebrow at the indecision on her face. "Your Highness, don't speak. But please eat." He held out a plate of sumptuous pheasant. He sighed when she looked away. "Gareth will kill me if you don't eat."

Her eyes told him, *good*.

Unable to comprehend how to appease this woman, he broke off a leg of the pheasant and flopped back on his bed. "Fine. Don't eat. Don't talk. Even my men have started to wonder what is wrong with you. If you don't fit in, you might be exposed."

She didn't like his implication.

"So I've decided, tomorrow you will help them scrub the deck."

"What!?"

Eyes twinkling, he munched on the leg and grinned. "Ah, how I have longed to hear your dulcet tones."

"I will not scrub floors!"

"You are my cabin boy. What else do you plan to do; draw my bath maybe?"

"I don't want to be your damned cabin boy!"

"Then what would you like to be?"

He chewed on the bone and her eyes instantly riveted to the mouth working the rounded end. When his mouth tilted at the corners, she realized he had caught her staring. "I'm hungry."

"I would be delighted to help you out, Your Majesty."

The cocky eyebrow warranted a black look. "Not for you."

"Can I help you change your mind?" The eyebrow didn't go down.

Scowling, she looked away and let out a sigh. "Why do you insist on making this difficult? I'm married!"

"I know."

"Then stop dangling yourself hopefully under my nose!"

Rolling off the bed, he placed the clean bone on the plate and nibbled on his thumb. This time she purposefully held his gaze. She would not look at the offending digit. She would not!

"My Queen; was our argument at the beach that troubling, that you had to marry a halfwit moron like the Duke of Dungberg?"

"Dunberg!"

He rolled his eyes. "Whatever."

"And he is the King now."

"So I hear."

She frowned at him. "What is wrong with you? A week ago you couldn't wait to be rid of me! Especially when you realized I'd made a fool of you."

"Don't flatter yourself, Your Highness. If anyone made a fool of me, I believe it is I. Sometimes I take too many things at face value. Trust me; that is not a mistake I plan to make repeatedly."

Crossing her arms haughtily, she lifted her nose in the air. "Are you the sort of man who thinks kisses move mountains?"

"A romantic?"

"An idiot!"

The sharp bark of laughter made her want to smile back at him. Laughing had completely changed the man. Now in this exciting setting of a pirate ship and his pirate patch, she realized, it gave him a rough attractive edge she hadn't noticed in the civilized world. Even though it was her royal responsibility to rid her Kingdom of this filth on the high seas, she realized that she envied their freedom. "We kiss once – once! And suddenly you think you have some claim on me."

"I have no claim on anyone. Least of all you, Your Highness."

"Stop calling me that!" She snapped at him, the troubles of the night returning. His words stabbed new pain into her chest. But he had been right. Everything had changed.

"What would you have me call you?"

Her vision blurred and she balled her fists, trying to restrain the tears that threatened to fall. She hadn't cried.

She hadn't cried when she'd woken up in Derek's bed. She hadn't cried when he had shown her the marriage certificate. She hadn't cried when he'd forbid her to meet Gareth. How she'd stood in her window watching him storm into the castle. She had had to physically restrain herself to keep from running to him. But here, without the weight of the crown on her head and the support of her Queenly vows, the word was out of her mouth before she could stop it; "broken."

The arms came around her like a vice.

She screamed, muffled against his shoulder and struggled. Her fists beat against him until everything burst inside her and she went down in flames. Her wails of pain were drowned into his shirt as he held her tightly. "Go on Elf. Cry it out. I'm here. I won't let you go."

His words only made her cry harder, clutching him close. She let her knees give out under her as he lowered them gently onto the ground, her sobs tearing into his soul. "Dammit Alex, what did they do to you?"

She shook her head, unable to speak. Everything inside her was raw. Everything seemed to bleed.

His questions cut into his heart, but he held her as she cried herself to sleep. He wondered if he should have pushed so hard. He wondered if it had been better to let her be the Ice Queen. The woman who was queen. Not the queen who had been a woman.

Later when she awoke, she sat in the middle of his bed and ate.

He reclined in the chair; watched the child-woman slowly and steadily find solid footing. "Why didn't you tell Gareth?"

Her eyes snapped up sharply. "I didn't tell YOU anything."

His gaze burned. "You told me enough. They found you on the beach after I left, didn't they? What did they tell you? What did they bargain with? Everything? The people? Your kingdom?"

The darkness clouding her brow told him he was right.

Shaking his head, he pulled off the Pirate patch. "It was foolish to keep this from Gareth." Standing, he pulled off his deep red velvet coat.

Alexa although feeling lighter was still weighed down by the future. So she was a tad slow to react to Felix's resolute feet leading him to the door, but she caught up to him before he could leave completely. "Where are you going?"

A muscle worked in his jaw. "To turn this damn ship around."

Her mouth dropped open. "You're taking me back?" Why did the dread suddenly pool in her belly at the thought? She wasn't one to shirk her responsibilities. She wasn't one to abandon anything she was responsible for.

Felix wanted to break something. He wanted someone to be punished for that one singular emotion that had been introduced to this beautiful woman. Because the woman who had flown headlong into bushes full of thorns, the woman who had been level-headed when they had been attacked. The woman, who had laughed in the wind as they rode at breakneck speed towards Dhak, was now looking up at him in fear.

Unable to help himself, he slid one hand up and held her fragile jaw tenderly, thumb stroking along her chin. "Sweetheart, I will never take you back. If you ask it of me."

Dear god, he couldn't say it like that and expect her to be rational.

He dropped his hand and dragged his gaze away from her.

All his life, Felix had prided himself on his ability to have any woman. Now that same ability unsettled him. "I meant to go back and break his legs."

The irrational laugh bubbled out of her before she could stop it. "God, I would pay to see that."

"How much?"

She lifted her tear-brightened eyes to smile sadly at the grin. "Don't make it seem so attractive Felix, or you'll find a Queen at your door, who has freshly run out of excuses."

"Maybe that's what I want."

Her smile vanished. "Don't."

His brow darkened. "Why? You're certainly not happy with him."

The notion suddenly stole the breath from her. She shook her head, stepping away from him. "And what, I'd be happy with you?"

"You were never this bitter."

"You were always good at avoiding answers!" She snapped, eyes flashing with misplaced fire.

His hands lifted in surrender. "I apologize if I pushed when I shouldn't have, Your Highness."

And she still flinched. Why did it stab when he said it?

Because she realized, it widened the chasm that had opened between them that day on the beach. Oh, how had things gotten so complicated? She had thought of him as a friend. "Will you answer a question for me? Honestly?"

"I've never lied to you."

She didn't like this new intensity about him. It implied things that were beyond her reach now. "Why did you bring me here?"

Because I missed you. Because I wanted to save you.

But he didn't say any of those things. "Because Gareth asked me to."

She was startled at his answer. "That's all?"

"That is all."

"And you followed his order blindly?"

"Didn't I follow his order blindly when he said two random women would be staying at my house?"

Rubbing her temples, Alexa wondered if her migraine would ever go away. She hadn't been able to breathe right since she'd awoken that fateful morning. No. She mentally shook herself. She would not think of that. She had to move forward. She wasn't one to rehash her past and ruin what little future she was going to have. Gareth might have meant well when he asked Felix to kidnap her. Felix was just doing his part, she realized with a sad little hiccup in her heart. She had entertained the notion that he might have come to her for his own reasons, but she was partially glad that it was only an obligation to him. It would certainly complicate matters less.

"Running away was the stupidest mistake I ever made. I should have just agreed to their terms. It would have been easier to bargain from that position, rather than a wayward queen everyone thinks ran from her responsibilities."

"Is that what they told your people?"

She sighed and sat down on the edge of the bed. "It doesn't matter what they say to my people. It matters what I say, but with my new leash, I'm afraid, even my words, are limited. My allegiance is what is holding the council from undoing all that I have accomplished in the past years. Trade, farming. They could deem it all unfit and this time, I wouldn't have the clout to overrule the new sovereign."

Felix watched the slump of her shoulders. "I know what Gareth is secretly hoping for."

"What?" Her question was tired.

"Love."

She looked up sharply. "Excuse me?"

There was no humor in his gaze or the straight line of the way he held himself. "He's hoping I can convince you."

The color in her face turned as white as sheets. "No."

The pirate shrugged and leaned there against the wall, arms crossed. "It could work."

"No!" She was on her feet in an instant, her heart hammering against her ribs. He couldn't have agreed to the mad scheme, he couldn't! Her mind in a frenzy of insane possibilities, she turned away from him, the panic welling in her gut. Gareth couldn't have planned for this. "No, that is impossible!"

"Impossible that we might love?"

She spun on him. Rage and confusion mixed with fear in her caramel eyes. "We cannot!"

A cocky eyebrow drifted up at her expletive. "Cannot or will not?"

"Cannot!" She bit out at him. "I cannot possibly choose another! The scandal would destroy everything!"

"Even when they find out how you were already betrothed to me?"

Her fear exploded into horror. "Gareth cannot prove that!"

Felix wished there was an easier way to break this to her, but he knew his brother. And he'd understood the light in the man's eyes. It didn't take a genius for Felix to guess what his brother was planning. "Gareth can prove anything once he sets his mind to it. He means to denounce your current marriage and call out the King for blackmail and treason."

Knees turning weak, the woman shook her head, eyes trained on the Earl, her thoughts spinning out of control. "They'll kill him. They will kill him rather than let him get away with this, Felix!" She was on her feet in an instant, across the room and grabbing his shirt in her fists. "We have to go back. You have to take me back!"

He wished he could make this easier on her. Gently clasping the whitened fists, he kept his voice gentle. "I can't do that."

"I command you!"

His smile was crooked. "You realize that pirates have their own code?"

"Damn, you Felix!" She tried to shake him, the fear beginning to broth in her stomach. "The councilmen will not give him time enough to accuse anyone! They will be rid of him! They bit me and spit me out without a whimper! Gareth will not stand a chance!"

He was afraid to touch. Afraid she was not the woman right now, but the queen. Even though the wild concern in her eyes was for her Captain, Felix wouldn't allow himself to hold her. "The Duke cannot be allowed to escape judgment."

"The councilmen will protect him!"

"You are queen Alexa!" He snarled, his hands catching her shoulders despite his apprehensions. He held her there against him, his glare melting through the stormy disquiet in her beautiful face. "He cannot be allowed to walk free!"

"And he is the king!"

"He is a man!" Felix softened his tone, but the venom, he couldn't remove. "A manipulative nasty little man! He's been king one day! You've been queen since the day you were born! The people won't listen to him."

"But the council..."

"Hang the council!" He finally gave in and wrapped his arms around the petite woman, gathering her against him, his mouth resting against her forehead. "The council is nothing! You're the queen. Neither Gareth nor I will allow them to hurt you."

Caught between the uneasy safety she felt in his embrace and the need to hold him forever, Alexa couldn't let go of her fears. "You cannot protect me forever."

"We can."

She shook her head. "Please Felix, this is madness..."

"Probably, but for the first time in your life my queen; let the men find a solution. "He felt her stiffen in his arms and smile against her fragrant hair. "You are entirely too efficient, but you need to sit back and let us do our jobs for a change."

Unable to resist the obvious comfort he was offering, she let her body relax against him and laid her cheek against his chest, his heart soothing her frayed nerves. "You're just a pirate."

"Damn right I am." The chuckle rumbled in his chest and echoed in her bones. "Give me all their names, and I'll find you every last bit of dirt on them. Enough to even make your head spin." Tilting her head back she gazed up at him, disbelief melding with amusement. He smirked down at her, reveling in the relinquishment of power in his favor. "Dungburg is going to hell already at my hands, the others will too." Her shoulders shook with silent laughter, eyes dancing with mirth he had missed so much. "I will give you so much dirt on them, they'll snivel at your feet. And if they still defy you, then we can try them before your people."

"Felix the council is an important check and balance on the monarchy."

"And the monarchy is not a check on them?"

At his quick retort, she wavered, her lip caught between her teeth. "I..."

"Gareth might have taught you how to fight. But he only taught you to fight fair. Let his crooked brother teach you how to fight dirty Your Highness."

Her smile was beautiful. Alive like the sun. The way it had been in the stables.

"If you still want to be the queen."

He'd expected her to think over it a moment, but she didn't. "More than anything," her wish was blunt in the passion behind her words.

"Then say, you trust me, sweetheart."

Her eyes flickered with mischief. "You trust me, sweetheart."

Safe to say Alexa was spared from scrubbing the decks, but she was not spared from the suspicious glances that everyone kept throwing her way. What was worse, although Felix kept an eye on her, he let her roam the ship alone and explore to her heart's content. Maybe it was his way of apologizing, but Alexa could have used his company.

"Ye cheated!"

She winced as the old man threw his hand of cards on the barrel top. She really should have tried to lose. And that was what she had intended until the old pirate kept smirking at her smugly. "I certainly did not!"

"I tell ye Morgan, this uppity lad needs pistol whipping!"

With a muted snarl, she lifted her scathing honey eyes to the big ugly crew member that towered behind the old man. If Alex had been of lesser will, she might have flinched at his face. It was mangled and twisted as if by a crazed animal, but the sheer size of him bothered her. So she realized she should have played it safe, but the old reference to being pistol-whipped prickled her. "You stay out of this Hogsbreath."

The crooked teeth flashed at her in less of a smile and more of a threat. "I saw you slip the Ace out of your sleeve boy."

There was no arguing with this bunch, that much she knew of. From what the scrawny pirate had told her, they were a day's sail away from land. Felix hadn't been around much to answer questions. He was always running around, tending to one problem or the other. The storm that had hit them the night before had left a lot of them drained and tired. So, Alexa had taken out the old deck of cards she'd found and decided to cheer them up. This 'cheered up', she hadn't intended.

Leaning back in the rickety old chair, she rocked it back on its hind legs as she'd seen Felix do, and fixed the other men with a cheeky grin. "Two out of three?"

The old man slapped more gold coins on the barrel and snorted. "You're on!"

When the Ace landed on their makeshift table, Morgan screamed like a raging bull, knocking everything away with one swipe of his hand.

It was then that Alexa pondered the intelligence of her decision. These were not village people she could tell old stories and tech lessons to. These were bloodthirsty pirates who demanded retribution for childhood trauma and had a code, which included the dismemberment of various body parts. Alexa had to grit her teeth to resist the urge to run screaming like a little girl. "Ah, Morgan. You're a sore loser," she lamented with a shake of her head.

"On yer feet lad!"

This had gotten decidedly worse. She was reasonably equipped to handle herself. Gareth had sparred with her enough, but she didn't know how this old man fought. Felix had already demonstrated that he fought dirty. She was strictly classroom trained. She'd never actually had to fend someone off if the need arose. It never did.

Until today.

Felix was walking out after a short nap and a shave.

He hadn't been able to rest as much as his body demanded so he caught slumber when he could. After the storm had hit them, Felix was unhappy that he'd been set back another day. They'd veered off course and he'd lost two men. Tired and taxed, the Earl wished for the simple comforts of his home in Caerleon. He missed the manor. He missed the sunlight and he sure as hell missed the food that hadn't been preserved for weeks.

He'd lived the life of a pirate in his younger days. He now craved the silence of Flamehart manor so he could spend his plunder and write his adventures.

But there would be no respite from the life of a pirate for now.

Especially when he saw the thick burly pirate lunge for his queen. "Hoth!"

His angry bark went ignored.

Alexa had sidestepped out of the way, effectively avoiding the attack, but she was unprepared for the flying tackle that came from her side. It took everything in her not to screech with surprise as Felix's arms wrapped around her and he rolled her away from the weight that hit the deck a few inches away. Gaping up at the scarlet-haired devil, she lay there as he growled low under his breath and sprang at the two pirates that had been fighting her.

"Oh no," she whined.

She winced as the fist connected with flesh.

She flinched when she heard the snap of bone.

But heinously she watched her vermillion demon take down the goliath of a pirate and the sturdy old man who was more technique than power.

The thick body smacked into the side of the ship and slid down with a groan until the stocky man sailed into him and everything became silent.

And then those devil eyes turned to her.

This time she neither flinched nor winced. With an awkward mutter, Alexa stepped over the legs of the unconscious men and walked into the Captain's quarters with her head held high.

"Are you deliberately trying to get yourself killed?"

She evaded the hands that tried to push her away, but doggedly she weaved around them and slid the cloth and disinfectant over the cut on his lip. Hissing at the sharp stab of pain his accusing eyes narrowed in distaste.

With a sigh, she relented. "I am not suicidal. It was just a card game."

"You were gambling with Pirates!"

"YOU happen to be a pirate!"

His anger was slightly mollified at her snapping retort, but he stubbornly held his ground. "I am trying to protect you while they will not think twice before taking your hide and you are bent upon getting me killed!"

"Your death was never on my agenda," she muttered dolefully and dabbed at another cut on his brow before moving to the angry bruises appearing all over his jaw and ribs. Shirtless and shading purple, Alexa still couldn't help but admire the sharp slants of his frame. He really was a beautiful man. A devil tempting the saint. She snickered at the silent metaphor. She recalled the way he'd tried to charm Arabella and outwit an adolescent boy. Those moments seemed years past although they had only been a week before. So much had changed.

"Maybe you should supply me with a copy of this agenda. I'm having a hard time keeping an eye on you as it is."

"He implied I cheated!"

His mouth twitched with a smile at the imperious tilt of her head. For a woman with the weight of their world on her shoulders, she was surprisingly innocent. Unlike the women he usually preferred, he wanted to caress this one. He wanted to whisper in her ear that all would be well like a besotted fool. Displeased with his own train of thought, he reminded himself that he would have to return her once Gareth had everything prepared. "Never cheated in your life?"

She looked back at him without blinking and Felix chuckled. "This coming from a woman who pretended to drown. Who thwarted me in my own home. Who sniped at me every moment she could. Your tongue Alex could cut glass."

Alexa found that on his tongue, the acronym of her name actually sounded lovely. "I suppose I have brought you nothing but trouble."

"How can I argue with her highness?"

Her hand connected with the side of his head and the man burst out laughing, his bruises and cuts forgotten, he reached down and pulled the woman into his arms, holding her tightly. "Oh, I've missed you, Alex."

Shaken by the sudden tenderness in his voice, Alexa was about to tell him she had missed him as well when a great tremor shook the boat and sent them both sprawling onto the floor.

Clutching her closer to his body, Felix looked up just as his cabin door slapped open. "Captain!" Jack panted, eyes wide with panic. "We're under attack!"

Felix rolled off her and reached for his shirt. "Who the hell would be mad enough to attack us?"

Jack hesitated, eyes skittering to the cabin boy sprawled on the floor like a sacrifice. "Pirates."

"What!?" Alexa gasped, her caramel eyes impossibly wide as she sat up. Felix gritted his teeth. "Hell's teeth."

Eyes slowly glided to the Earl as he dressed hastily. "Pirates my Lord?" Her voice couldn't have been sweeter if she tried, but her eyes spat fire.

Felix met her gaze only briefly, his face etched with worry as another tremor rocked the ship.

She sat there on the floor, legs stretched out in front of her arms, crossed. "I suppose wearing the pirate patch won't save us will it?"

He had the decency to look sheepish before he ran out to defend them.

*

Alexa winced as the Captain of their vessel was held at the point of a rather sharp cutlass.

Once they had been boarded their resistance had been small. Most of them had been overly concerned with making their cabin boy inconspicuous.

Bundled in a thick coat, she didn't appear too much of a threat and now that she was surrounded by every crew member shielding, she realized the farce she'd stepped into.

She wanted to scream for bloody murder. Felix and his deception deserved nothing less.

The skinny Captain Crowe hadn't wasted time in finding the man in charge.

Felix had graciously accepted.

"I can assure you we have nothing on board that you might need. We're just a traveling vessel of vaudeville actors." Felix spoke calmly to the thin man who sported a disturbingly cold black gaze which implied where he'd gotten his name from. Nothing seemed to miss his eye.

"Impoverished actors posin' as pirates? Crowe thinks yer lyin'."

Alexa tensed, but the thick rough hand wrapped around her arm and held her steady. Looking startled she saw Hoth cautiously standing behind her like a towering giant. Mouth gaping she wondered just how much of a stage these actors had set. She really was a blind fool. Glaring crossly at the man who now was the only barrier between the pirates and getting everyone killed, she wondered how he was going to get away with this. And she couldn't believe Gareth of all people had conspired against her.

"Damn it, man, you don't rob fellow pirates."

"No? Who said?" Crowe gave him a partially toothless smile before skimming his gaze over their gathered crew members. "They don't much look like actors to Crowe."

"We're very good?"

With a snort, Red Beard slid the tip of his sword deeper into Felix's throat. "Oh, Ah can see that mate. Aren't you the one they call Red Devil?"

Alexa's head snapped up at the name.

The scarlet-haired man's eyes hardened. "You must be mistaken."

His sword never wavering, the man grabbed Felix's arm with surprising strength and lifted the sleeve to see the crescent of faded old scars on the inside of his elbow. "Ahh, yer tongue might lie Red, but yer scars sure as hell don't. Ain't it be here that the wolf sank his teeth on the Isle of Myrrh when ye were searchin' for that Goblet of Fire? Crowe knows his business well mate."

Snatching his arm away, Felix scowled. "How nice for you."

"Gettin' the drop on the Red Devil. Wowie! Who'd have thought it?"

"I've retired."

"Oh, Ah don't doubt it, mate." Crowe's smile suddenly turned disturbing. "And ya got Old Crowe to believe there be nothin' of value on this vessel. Now tell me. What's o`value here?"

"Nothing Crowe, I'm just an actor now!"

The thin pirate leered at the famous pirate then turned to one of his men. "Find anything?"

"Just some important lookin' papers and barrels o`rum."

"Ah, Red yer disappointin'."

A muscle worked in his jaw, but Felix stood perfectly still. His eyes were on everything but his own men. They'd been given strict orders to offer no resistance. It was damned unfortunate Crowe had such luck to find royal bounty and a legendary pirate all on the same vessel. Only Felix wasn't about to give his other secret up. "Your raid is futile Crowe. We have nothing of value."

The black eyes narrowed, searching the red for answers. "Buck," he called back one of his crewmen. "Have we ever gone back empty-handed?"

"Nope!"

His lips spread into a helpless smile. "Now that Crowe's here, he'll have to have somethin'." Shifting his eyes to one of Felix's silent crewmen he grinned. "How's about his head eh?"

The man stiffened, and a sharp breath dragged through his nose in alarm.

Alexa's lips parted in growing dread.

"Pointless bloodshed Crowe, we have nothing!"

"I wonder if ye'll still be singin' the same tune when I lineup them heads pretty as a picture on this here deck." Chuckling, he pulled his sword away and grinned at his men. "Make sure he watches."

"STOP!"

Felix's heart plummeted into his gut. He watched his men discreetly try to keep the owner of the voice between them. Hidden, but to Felix's dismay, the boy squeezed out between them and stood in front of his crew, caramel eyes troubled. "What the hell are you doing boy!"

Crowe's eyebrow cocked at the sudden surge of blackness in Red's face, his body tensing to break free from his men's hold at the boy's coming forth. Interest piqued he turned to the blonde lad and scrapped his thumbnail with his sword tip as if bored. "Volunteerin' lad?"

Alexa's heart was pounding.

Behind her, Felix's men had broken into a frenzy as the pirates drew their swords and held them in place.

She was sure now. Felix's men were not pirates. She could bet her life on it that they were Gareth's men meant to protect her, and she knew that all of them would go down without so much as a flinch for their Queen, and even though Alexa understood her importance she couldn't. In the end, she might lead an army, and she might take someone's life but she was also responsible for the safety of her people. She didn't grow up thinking of the greater good and then selfishly sitting back. Her father had never done that.

Neither would she. Her people's blood would not spill on this ship. Not while she was around. "He's lying."

"Damn you Alex; go back!"

Squaring her shoulders she lifted her chin and met Crowe's gaze without flinching. "There is something of value onboard."

"Ye don't say." Crowe stepped closer to the imperious little boy and smirked.

"Don't you dare Alex! Don't you dare!"

"I am what they are protecting!"

Both eyebrows hiking up Crowe looked him up and down before snorting. "You?"

"He's lying!" Felix spat, struggling so violently that two more men had to hold him down.

"I'm not." Alexa bit back the shudder as the scrawny pirate started to circle her like a vulture. "If I'm lying, would they be reacting so strongly for the life of a lowly cabin boy?" She met those disturbing black eyes as he stopped before her, his sword in one hand, the other stroking his chin thoughtfully. "I am Queen Alexandra Windmere of Odyria." Her eyes hooded she allowed the thin man a second to blink in confusion as she slid her hands daintily behind her and tilted her head in a winsome smile that screamed everything woman. Around her, she could hear Felix's cries, but her attention was on the stunned pirate in front of her. "And you're lynching on my turf."

Crowe only had a moment to hiccup as the tiny woman stepped forward and the small dagger sank into his heart.

Everything around them stilled, as Crowe stared down at the ornate hilt of the knife, the seal of the Royal House of Windmere embellished in gold before he fell like a stone. Alexa palmed the cutlass as it slid out of the dead pirate's hand before turning deliberately toward the men that held Felix immobile. "Now that Captain Crowe has forfeited his position," she began with a half-smile before lifting the heavy blade effortlessly, "I believe his slayer now holds his rank." She slid her smirking honey eyes to Felix. "Would that make me a Pirate Queen?"

"You are the most infuriating woman I have ever had the displeasure of knowing!"

Alexa was having too much fun to feel chastised. "Come now Red, you of all people should commend my brilliant stroke of genius."

"Genius!? Dammit, Alex! A Pirate Queen? Are you mad?"

"A little insanity is healthy I've heard." Smirking from her place on the high-backed chair in Crowe's surprisingly neat cabin, Alexa watched the Ex-Pirate wearing a hole in her floor.

"You could have been killed!" He thundered.

Her mirth fading, she sighed and sat up straighter in the chair. "You give me very little credit Flamehart."

"This isn't a game Alex!" Stalking up to her, he grabbed her by her shoulders and shook her. "Death would have been easier! Do you have any idea what they could have done to you? You with your books and castles, you don't know the kind of…"

Shrugging off his hands, she rose angrily to her feet, her nose nearly touching his. "Don't you dare lecture me! I'm not a blushing virgin nor am I a hapless woman that you need to protect! I am Queen and do you really think I would be where I was if I wasn't able to at least wield a blade? What kind of monarch do you think I'd be when people have to die left and right just to save me?! How dare you question my ability to stand up for my people! Did you think I would sit back and watch that odious man slaughter those men just so I could live on? Do you really think that low of me Felix?

"If it had been a King standing there before Crowe my duty would come before my safety and I would be remembered as a brave and noble king! He would be revered and I am an infuriating WOMAN? I am NOT a woman! I am queen!"

Staring down into those flashing eyes Felix felt his heart slowly but steadily fall back into its usual pattern. It hadn't calmed since he'd seen her facing Crowe. He'd been crazed with concern for her and now there was no doubt in his mind why.

Queen Alexandra Windmere demanded love and loyalty.

How could he refuse?

It was physically painful to hold himself back from holding her. From kissing her until she was gasping in his arms. His blood roared in his veins and he couldn't smother the shudder that skirted down his spine. His gut tightened when he recognized the emotion settling in his belly like a satisfied, but coiled rattlesnake.

She was right. If she was a King, he wouldn't be contemplating ravishing her, putting aside his gander theory, and declaring his undying devotion like a besotted fool. Because not only had she made it painfully clear to her own self that she was untouchable but to him.

Ex-Pirates didn't fall in love with Queens.

He just wished his brother had warned him, because, for the first time in his life, Felix realized why Gareth had never come back.

*

When Gareth saw the two people step off the plank, he raised an eyebrow in surprise.

Alexa stood beside an equally mute Felix, their eyes weighed down by unsaid things.

The short ride to the Inn was just as silent. It was only when they had seated around a table of food and drink in the room, did Gareth ask them and the story left him astounded.

"You killed a Pirate?"

Running a hand through her short hair Alexa nodded. "Yes."

"Dammit Felix, where were you?"

"At a knife's point," Alexa snapped before the Earl could open his mouth. "Are you questioning me as well Gareth?"

The Captain sighed and shook his head, bracing one hand on the back of the chair as he stood over the table where Alex and Felix reclined. "No, My Queen. I am not. Still, it was risky."

"My life's like that Gareth; let it go. But I was wrong to stay silent," Alexa admitted. "And I was wrong to run. I should have stayed and faced them then. Now, I've ruined everything."

"It was not you, My Queen. You have Derek the Bastard to blame for that. But I do wish you had come to me. You came to me when Stormy tossed you and broke your wrist. You came to me when the stable boy tried to kiss you. You came to me when you couldn't find your kitten. I had thought I was your friend."

Chin trembling, Alexa didn't care for decorum as she rose from her chair and threw her arms around the reassuring strength of the man who had always been there for her. And she held onto him tightly. "I'm sorry," she whispered. "I have let you down Gareth."

"Never, Your Highness." Gareth smiled against her soft golden hair. "Not even if you tried. Now." Pulling away he wiped her cheek tenderly. "Tell me. Tell me exactly what you remember; don't leave anything out."

The story spilled from her.

And for the second time that night, Felix felt like a fool. The way she spoke of the beach confirmed his fears. He had been overly harsh in his drunken rage and rampant desire. Blinded by his words. He watched her recount her experiences. The Duke's plot and his guilt caught flames of vengeance. This woman was sacred and he wouldn't rest until the bastard paid for his crimes against her. He didn't care if she could take care of herself, he would protect her and her honor beside Gareth, for as long as he was alive.

Gareth was pacing like a caged lion. The retelling of his fears only managed to increase his fury. "Where did he take you? Which church?"

"I don't know." She nibbled on the bit of bread, not really hungry, but feeling weak. Weak after weeks of turmoil. All she wanted to do was curl up on the little bed and sleep, but Gareth and Felix wouldn't let her. They went over her story again and again.

"What town?"

"I don't know."

"Alexa! You must remember something."

"I don't," she moaned and leaned her head back, fingers pressing into her eyes to lessen the burning of tears. "I don't remember anything until the morning."

"Then how the hell did you find out you were married to the bastard?"

Hating what she was about to reveal, she dare not meet their eyes. "I woke up in his bed. He had papers I had signed with him. A marriage contract. I must have still been drugged."

Gareth was struck speechless.

Eyes blazing, Felix confirmed his fears. "You mean you never actually consented..."

"No."

"I'm going to kill the bastard!"

Felix was out of his chair and holding the furious captain from stalking out of the room as if he meant to ride over there and kill the man himself. Although he admitted the idea was appealing, he held his brother steady. "Gareth! Calm down!"

"No Felix," snarling and spitting with anger, the raven-haired man jerked away. "I will not calm down."

"You think I don't want to tear him to pieces?" He didn't bother hiding the blinding rage from his brother and the matching fire there seemed to calm Gareth to a few degrees. Felix held his gaze without question. A silent agreement that there would be hell to pay, but they needed to think clearly for now.

Turning to the silent woman, Felix evened his voice. "Did he hurt you?"

"I don't remember, but in the morning he said we consummated the marriage so I couldn't leave him."

"Bastard! This constitutes rape."

"Yes, Felix." She snapped at him. "I believe I know that!"

It was Gareth, who finally interrupted the silence that prevailed softly. "How sure are you?"

Alexa blinked at him. "What?"

"How sure are you that you did consummate the marriage?"

"I was in his bed!"

"That doesn't necessarily mean..."

"Without my clothes!"

The two men fidgeted uncomfortably. Gareth couldn't believe how much he wished Arabella was here to aid them, but he had to be sure. "Alexa, you were a virgin."

Her cheek tinting with embarrassed color, she glared at him. "Oh stop hedging and be done with it!"

"It should have hurt." Gareth met her eyes painfully. "I don't know what Arabella told you..."

She couldn't help but roll her eyes. Men. "I'm not an idiot Gareth. I've extensively studied farming and delivered cows with my bare hands, I think I know the mechanics."

"Dammit Alexa, you're not listening to me. For your first time, it should have left bruising, if not blood!"

It was then that the implication sank in and her mind only provided a blank. "I...I don't know. No." She looked up at the two waiting men in growing wonder. "No there was no blood and I didn't hurt, but I don't know for sure."

Gareth met the red eyes briefly. "Send for the woman."

"Gareth what are you doing?"

"I have a hunch. Trust me."

The midwife walked out of the room and glared at the two men who had dragged her out of bed in the middle of the night. "She's cleaner than the day she was born. And the poor thing's scared to death! What did you say to her?!"

Gareth was through the door in an instant.

The relief seemed to soak every corner of Felix's body. Unable to contain his grin he wrapped his arms around the tall woman and hugged her tightly.

"Oy! Hands off me!"

Planting a romping kiss on her cheek Felix grinned down at the woman wildly. "Thank you. Thank you!"

Oh, but he was a handsome devil. Muttering and blushing under the gorgeous man's attention, the woman mumbled under her breath, looking pleased. "Aye Lad, you're welcome. Now, what's this about anyway? Why bring the poor lass here again?"

Felix blinked down at her in confusion. "Again?"

"Aye. Those rough and tumble boys brought the lass here on a ship. Sickly she was then; I remember. Told them I'd bring soup in the morn, but when I returned, they'd gone. Without a word."

Grabbing the woman by her shoulders, Felix tried to reign in the hope that threatened to burst through his chest. "You saw her. You saw that woman in there."

"Yeah. That husband of hers carried her like a sack of flour. No way to treat a woman," she clucked her tongue disapprovingly. "But ye can't expect much from his kind of man."

"What kind is that?"

"The cheatin' kind." She glared. "Went right off with one of me girls! Fat good it did him."

Nearly gasping with it, Felix swallowed thickly. "Millie! Millie, tell me exactly what you mean?"

Gareth was holding the shaking, but relieved woman in his arms when Felix stormed into the room, devil eyes blazing with wicked triumph. "The bastard couldn't consummate anything because he's unable!"

For a moment Gareth and Alexa stared at the smirking man in stunned silence.

"You're not married Alexa." Felix held the Queen by her shoulders and shook her until her eyes focused on his, the beautiful peach returning to her cheeks. "You're not married to him!"

Gareth snorted. "I was kind of looking forward to making her a widow."

Then the Queen's eyes blazed and the Red Devil's grin was feral. "I believe it is time to return our wayward Queen to her throne."

She stood there without her boyish clothes. They provided a certain protection she realized. They reminded her of happier times. A time and when politics and conspiracies didn't taint everything. They were of simpler times. When her country and her throne didn't hang in the balance. When she wasn't about to pull off the biggest sham of the century.

The story had been concocted.

The papers had been prepared.

The Queen had married Felix Van Buren, Earl of Flamehart at the climax of a whirlwind romance.

She sighed.

Arabella was sorely missed right now. She wished her tutor was around. If only to remind her that the best love stories ended in tragedies.

It would make letting him go easier. Because somewhere along the way the woman had fallen in love with the pirate. But the Queen and the Earl could never be anything beyond a staged and practiced play.

"You should be asleep."

Shivering in the night despite the warm, moist wind of sea around her, Alexa didn't dare turn around. "I don't want to do anything today that I should."

Felix should have read the signs screaming 'danger'. But in her simple borrowed brown dress, she was poignantly approachable. Ignoring the warning in her words he crossed the deck and came to stand beside her. "Today is only a few hours from tomorrow."

Her heart clenched painfully at the double meaning to his words. "Here to mock me?"

Felix was silent for a long moment. "I will walk you inside."

"Because you should?" Lifting the glittering eyes, she watched his impassive face. How could this man stand so still when everything around her was in such a frenzy? But then she saw a bone clench in his jaw and sighed. "I am sorry. That was deliberately evocative."

"Aren't you always My Queen?"

Her eyes slammed shut. "Must you always remind me what I am?"

Feeling slapped, the man didn't lift his eyes away from the gentle waves that lapped against the hull. "I think it is more to remind me, Your Majesty."

Shuddering beyond her control, she shook her head, the heat building behind her eyes. "Don't. Please don't call me that." Felix dreaded the flickering promise in her eyes and he meant to turn and leave her there, because he knew like he knew the seas that no good would come from this. But the woman had shifted closer, her hand lifting up to touch his jaw. "It hurts to hear you say it."

Skin singing where she was touching him, Felix let his eyes close to the softness of her fingers, his own fingers gripping the railing as if to physically restrain himself. "Go to bed. I will not play this game with you."

"Cannot or will not?"

"I should say cannot." Lifting one hand he clasped her wrist firmly, but tenderly. "But I will not." Finally unable to help himself, he met her gaze and drowned without even touching the water. "It is grossly unfair to expect a pirate to play gentleman."

"Why won't you call me Alex?" She pleaded, her wrist still warm in his grasp as she gazed up into his fathomless eyes, his face deliberately trying to stay stoic, but his eyes – they pitched and swelled like the ocean waves.

"You're not Alex anymore."

"Then call me Alexa."

"I don't think so." He lifted a foot to step away, but her hands caught his sleeve and she glared up at him in defiance.

"I am married to you Felix. You can at least use my name."

Why the hell was she doing this right now, he lamented. The mere flash of her brilliant eyes had heat rushing straight from his heart to his groin. He didn't need this right now. The legalities were tantalizing. "Those damn papers are a sham!"

"Did we both not sign them?"

Eyes shuttering he took a deep breath. "Do not do this tonight."

"Tonight is all I have." The tear slid down her cheek, unbidden. "Why did you agree with Gareth's scheme?"

He looked at her sharply. "What?"

"When he told you to kidnap me, why did you agree?"

His eyes glinted a deep maroon in the darkness, skittering over her face like a deer's and Alexa knew she'd cornered him. "I considered it a debt repaid."

"You owe me nothing!"

"I owe you an apology."

She staggered back at the reply. "For the kiss."

Keeping his eyes on the dark horizon, he nodded. "For the kiss."

She wanted to slap him. She wanted to grab him and shake and kiss him. She wanted to demand why he was choosing now to be noble, when he'd been nothing but a vagabond with the boy.

Then her eyes hardened. "Penance for kissing the Queen." His head jerked as if she had struck him. She had meant to. "Back in my chamber when you lay over me with a knife to your throat you desired me. Was I not your queen then? Or in that little cabin when I refused to dress and you imagined stripping me down yourself. Was I not your queen then?"

The ruby gaze darkened. "What would you have me say?"

"The truth!" She snapped angrily. "I want the goddamn truth Felix!"

"You've a filthy mouth sometimes."

"I kissed you with this mouth, you didn't complain overly much!"

Throwing up his hands Felix turned his back to her. Trying to rally his courage and skating thoughts he wondered what the hell she was trying to get out of him. "I made a mistake alright?"

"Which time?"

"For the love of God Alex, what the hell do you want me to say?"

Grabbing his arm, she spun him around and snarled up at him. "Tell me the truth! I want to hear it from your mouth!"

"No!" He roared. "No I didn't think you were my Queen. Not when I kissed you the first time and never wanted to stop. Not when you stood on that beach asking me to be your friend. Not when I wanted to kiss you in your bed. Not when you sat on that damned horse and I wanted to take you there. Not when you were dressing my wounds or dressing yourself! Damn you woman that was then!" She stared up at him in confusion. "You were not the Queen. You were a beautiful, stubborn infuriating woman!" His voice softened when he saw the glistening happiness in her eyes. He hated himself more as he continued. "But today the woman who saved my life and her own, the woman who is travelling to reclaim her throne and the woman who will prove that a Queen does not need a King to sanction her rule, IS a Queen."

For the first time in her life, Alexandra didn't want to be Queen. And the realization was staggering. Clutching the railing she had to open her mouth to drag in much needed air. "Maybe I didn't need to hear all that."

"Maybe you did."

Her breath caught as he spun her back around to press against him, his arms wrapped around her tightly. His rough hand palmed her cheek and the woman who could face off armies and political takeovers felt her knees buckle. "I've never met a woman like you Alexandra." Her gasp was mingled with a painful sob and his arms tightened around her, his forehead resting against her. "You give yourself so little credit for how exceptionally strong you really are. You're determined. You're intelligent. You're patient. You're fiercely loyal, forthright and fair-minded. But that's not why I respect you now. I respect you because you've a light about you that is blindingly courageous. You make people want to believe in you. Just the way you promise to keep a roof over their heads. The way you say nothing will harm them so as long as you're alive. You demand loyalty! How can anyone know you and not love you?"

"Felix..."

"You asked me for the truth Alexa and you will hear it." Jaw hardening he met her gaze unflinchingly. "I love you."

The world seemed to spin out of her grasp, her vision blurring at the admission. She had expected her heart to sing, but it was physical pain to finally have him say those words to her.

Be careful what you wish for.

"Did you hear me Alex? I love you more than I've ever loved anyone. More than my damned life. For whatever it's been worth, running away from my responsibilities, from my family obligations for my brother – utterly aimless wandering and mindless until I met you." His fingers tightened on her arms, shaking her slightly as if it would sift his words better. "I thought I was free!" The scarlet gaze followed the tear that slid down her pale cheek. "I thought I was free, until I nearly fell off my library ladder, until I nearly drowned in my lake, until I laughed and screamed and met the boy who just wouldn't stay out."

Alexa just watched the stoic face melt into the fiery intensity of the Red Devil, her own heart screaming with every emotion his words brought forth.

"I want you. I need you," he whispered raggedly. "It hurts to look at you and know that I cannot have you, but I will never lie to you. Even if it means putting my damned heart at a knife's point," he hissed as if the pain was as palpable as her own. "I love you Alexandra. Enough to believe in destiny, to believe in blind faith and soul mates and love at first sight because whatever brought you to me, saved me from the worthless life of a lonely aging pirate! And I know that makes me a scoundrel."

She shuddered, her hands trembling where they hung uselessly beside her, but her eyes never left him. They stared up at him wonder. "You idiot," she whispered achingly. "That was the worst thing to say."

Startling at the paradox of berating tenderness and the soft smile that touched her mouth, he blinked. "What?"

"I love scoundrels."

With a rough tender bark of laughter, he grabbed her against him, his arms wrapping around her tightly, cheek pressed down against her head. "No good will come of this." He murmured into her hair for propriety's sake, but savored the feel of her body pressed against the length of his and thanked whoever was listening that he'd found her again.

Arms twining around his waist Alexa held onto him and let the tears soak into his shirt. "How much longer do you think today will last?"

Felix's gaze slid from the tantalizing darkness of the horizon to the woman in his arms. Desire flared low and dangerous. He was out of his mind to even be here. They both were. One of them had to be rational. One of them needed to remember. He swallowed thickly. "A few hours."

Alexa lifted her head from his chest and tiled it back to look up into his crimson gaze. "Then give me today."

His breath leaving him almost explosively, he wanted to kiss her and shake her back to her senses all in the same breath. She was mad. He was crazed. No good would come from this.

Gareth would skin him from his bones.

"No."

Her usually soft, tiny hands clawed into his back and she coiled for attack. "You selfish, teasing, heartless bastard!"

He knew she'd leave him. She'd be angry and heartbroken, but it was necessary. He would do this for her. Even if it tore him into shreds.

But the woman never conformed and neither did the Queen.

Hands wrapping around his throat, she lifted herself against him. "I love you too." Then she swallowed his shocked gasp, her lips covering his and stealing the last of his protests from him.

Felix's senses swam in surprise, and then something seemed to snap and uncoil inside him, as if he'd been waiting forever for this stolen moment with her.

Her nimble little fingers twisted into the crimson hair, pulling it free from the string that confined it neatly. With electricity roaring down his spine, Felix slid his palms deftly over the small woman's supple curves and pulled her closer. Alexa's mouth opened over his with a soft demand and she coaxed his tongue to tangle with hers.

As it had before – the kiss caught fire.

Tears mingling with helpless giggles, Alexa heard more than felt his surrender. With a growl that sent her heart careening in her knees, he nipped her chin. Soft feathery kisses walked down the gentle slope of her jaw and the heat flared across her ears long before he found the earlobe.

Before she'd been half asleep and more surprised, but this time when his hand slipped into the neckline of her dress she couldn't help arch into him with a muffled gasp. The husky chuckle against her demanded she slap him, but then his mouth ducked down without warning and his mouth and tongue on her flesh stole all reason. Senses exploding with new sensations, she gripped his shoulders and hung on for dear life.

Her spine unlocked until her head fell back, the sweetness of her surrender nearly drove Felix wild. Tasting. Caressing, Felix paid homage to her, savoring the reality of the woman in his arms. But it wasn't enough. Dropping down on his knees and cursing the flare of her skirt, he tilted his head and buried his face between the apex of her thighs.

Hands braced on his shoulders, Alexa squeaked in surprise holding onto the trembling man as he pressed into the most intimate part of her. "Felix!?"

With a laughing groan, he lifted his head and dancing vermillion eyes gaze up at her, the moonlight making them inky. "If you say 'no' now, Alex, I will die." Smiling, he seduced her with his blunt desire enjoying the childlike wonder her honey gaze. "Without tasting you, without touching you, without__"

Trembling and on the verge of collapsing, Alexa slid her hands into his thick hair and tugged gently. "Come up and kiss me. Now."

His mouth widened into a nefariously teasing grin. "Yes, Your Majesty." Rising from his perch, he brought her feet with him and Alexa's world tipped off its axis, as he swept her into his arms.

This time the title didn't cut into her soul and the realization alone had her wrapping her arms around him and burying her mouth against his neck. Kissing every part of him she could reach as he carried her towards the cabins.

Alexa was a few short seconds away from spontaneously combusting. She'd shared a few kisses of ardent nobles trying to win her favor. She'd taken walks around the gardens with eager to please monarchs. But nothing had prepared her for the unashamed and blunt hunger this man had for her. It left her reeling and trying to recall everything she knew about an act she'd never actually experienced, but nothing could prepare her for when he laid her down on the silken sheets and his hard, heavy and all male weight settled down on her.

And he was hers.

Felix tugged at the edge of her simple gown. "This has to go."

"I could help if you move."

"Not on your life," he smirked. "Do you doubt my expertise Madam?"

Rolling her eyes at his blunt display of ego, she lifted on leg along with the caress of his hand up its length. "I hope you don't mean to tear it off me My Lord?"

His grin widened, and Felix discovered he rather liked the way she called him that. "The thought did cross my mind."

"Don't you dare," she glared at him as he slowly unbuttoned the bodice. "It's the only womanly article of clothing I own at the moment__oh dear god!" Eyes rolling back into her head, her head fell back against the pillow as his mouth suckled its way down her throat. With a moan, she wriggled under him. "Get it off."

Crimson eyes slid over every exposed contour of her body sending red heat flaring underneath her skin. Twitching nervously, she tried to free her hands from where he'd pinned them beside her head, but his fingers tightened on hers and he breathed out his words reverently. "Beautiful."

Blushing to the roots of her hair, feeling nothing like her royal self, Alexa tried to angle away from his probing gaze but was suddenly lost in the intensity of those magnificent eyes. How had she ever thought them to be frightening? "Felix?" She whispered his name as if speaking any louder would break the spell.

"Do you trust me?"

Swallowing tensely, she bit her bottom lip and his gaze instantly caught the movement hungrily. "No."

An eyebrow arched, his eyes fixed on her mouth.

"Not when you're like this?"

Amused red eyes lifted up to hers. "Like what?"

"Like you want to eat me."

"Smart girl," he purred and pulled away to sit back on his knees. His hands loosened from hers, trailing down the bones in her shoulders over the soft roundness of her breasts and down the flat belly. Her breath hitched in her throat as his fingers brushed down the length of her body before lifting up to pull his own shirt off his head.

Alexa had seen men train without their shirts, but she'd never seen a man she was in love with. The combination of her own spiraling emotions and the satin skin stretched over hard muscle, set off a curious tingle through her. He was a beautiful man. So busy was she marveling at the expanse of the hard lines of his chest, that she didn't notice him unbuckle and push down his pants until he was free of their confines finally.

The shirt and pants flew over his shoulder and his mouth twitched in amusement at the suddenly silent Queen under him.

Like the Greek statues of old, he knelt there over her, only the rich color of him paled any artists' creation she had ever seen. The red strands she loved so much framed those demon red eyes that still sent shivers skating down her spine. His mouth twisted into an amused grin and Alexa's heart skipped a beat, leaving her lightheaded. She drank in the sight of him unabashedly naked, inviting and wicked. And completely hers. Any shyness she'd been feeling went up into a tuft of smoke as she reached out to touch him.

With a smile of acceptance, which only came with a deep sated love, he came to her.

Shuddering at the exquisite feel of his bare skin against hers, Alexa let out a soft breath against his ear. "Felix…"

His name left her lips with a whispering desire. Soft but intense. It sent raw, carnal awareness rushing through the man at alarming speed. "Hold on to me sweetheart."

Her arms and legs came up around him in an instant, fingers rushing over his back, exploring every rise and fall of his body ravenously. His desire spiraling out of control, Felix bit back a chuckle against her mouth before he kissed her hard. "Mmmm, Alex?"

Flaring red eyes met hers reverently. Even though desire was exploding in every nerve of her body, Alex held his gaze. "Yes?"

"I believe now would be a good time to remind yourself that the gander is always on top of the goose."

Laughter mingling with longing, Alexa took his face between her palms and kissed the smug man into silence. Felix had never enjoyed union more with a woman in his life. The laughter, the tears, the prayer, it was exhilarating.

When the haze of desire faded, Alexa was happy to see that it still left behind the tenderness, the friendship and so much love. She stroked him gently where she lay with him, speaking soothingly against his ear as he had. Nonsensical, silly promises she never thought she'd make. But the night was almost over. Her heart keened in her chest to know she might not have this forever. Every day. Oh god, it hurt.

But when she tried to shift underneath him to untangle herself, Felix pulled her tightly against him and his mouth pressed a poignant kiss against her forehead. "No."

"Felix?"

"I've changed my mind," he growled possessively. "I'm keeping you."

Alexa nuzzling against his jaw, stilled. Pulling back to look up into his face. "What?"

"Queen or no Queen Alex. You're mine," he stated and his tone left no room for argument. "No one gets to have you like this but me."

Heart hammering in her chest, she swallowed. "Do you know what you're saying?"

"Explicitly."

Slack jawed she gawked at the resolute firmness of his mouth. "King!?"

"If you'd have me."

"If I'd..." At a loss for words, she couldn't believe what he was telling her. "But...how...I mean...what about..."

A gentle finger was placed on her mouth and he smiled. "Do you trust me?"

Gazing up into those eyes, she sighed.

He really was a scoundrel. That's the worst thing to say to a girl when she doesn't know where her clothes are!

*

"This is outrageous!" The thick man named Verdin sputtered. "This is high treason!"

Felix stood in the center of the room the six council members sitting in a semi-circle around him. Behind him sat the Queen on her throne, Gareth dutifully by her side. "I believe it was high treason when my wife was stolen from me."

"This is the Queen you're talking about!"

"Precisely," Felix agreed calmly, "this is the Queen who is legally bound to me in marriage."

"You kidnapped her!"

"It is all about perspective," the scarlet-haired man crossed his arms nonchalantly and shrugged. "Wife, Queen. Kidnap, rescue. Depends on where you're standing councilman. All I know is that my wife was stolen from me in the middle of the night and I know it was the righteous and noble Duke."

"King!"

"We're still debating that I believe."

Marlin, the oldest of the six Councilmen narrowed his gaze calculatingly at the Earl. "You cannot have us believe, that a witness has now, conveniently, come forth."

"Are you implying it's all a scam and our marriage papers are forged?" Felix met the gaze head-on. "Maybe we should call an expert and have her signatures verified, but then I demand you examine both marriage contracts."

"Preposterous!" Verdin snorted. "There is no need."

It was finally the white-haired man who had been silent previously. "And what does the Queen have to say?"

Marlin shook his head. "The child is obviously confused and exhausted Rogan."

Alexa opened her mouth to protest, but Gareth's hand on her arm stilled her.

Felix kept his devil-red eyes on Verdin and walked up to him, his hands splaying flat on the console that separated them. The man leaned back with a touch of fear to him. "I wonder councilman if we call in the witnesses whose establishment he used to sleep in that night, what he will say about the Duke's royal cargo."

Verdin's face turned red with anger. "Lies! How dare you threaten the King?"

"Where is he then?"

"He does not need to concern himself with paltry matters as his wife's infidelity."

"Infidelity!" Alexa snapped instantly to her feet. This time Gareth couldn't hold her in place as she marched forward and stood behind Felix, her warm caramel gaze a rich amber with anger. "I wonder how YOU are speaking of infidelity Verdin when you were the one who left that poor wife of yours in Helax to marry that lovely Duchess with her fat purses!"

The man instantly paled. "I...slander!"

"Slander, Verdin?" Leaning forward Alexa growled low under her breath as she bared down at the man. "Do you think I don't know what goes around in my own Kingdom? Do you think I don't know that you have her holed up in that little town of Helax in that run-down little cabin in the mountains? Do you think I don't know the pittance you send her so that she can care for your daughter?"

Gareth stared wide-eyed in shock before he caught the self-satisfied glint in his brother's eyes. Mouth twisting up at the corner, Gareth sat back and decided to enjoy the show. With Felix, he watched in satisfaction as their Queen fought back.

"Is this true Verdin?" Rogan questioned his fellow councilman with ice in his voice.

Verdin struggled with his words, jumping to his feet. "I will not sit here and be maligned!

"It is indeed interesting that you speak of maligning your honor Verdin when your son not only abducted me against my will but fabricated our marriage vows, and my signatures and lied to consummating our marriage."

The gasp was instantaneous.

Verdin turned as white as snow.

"And do you know why I find that interesting Verdin? Because your son is unfit to consummate anything!"

There was a murmur of shock around the room, and Alexa pulled away with a scowl of distaste.

"My son is already pronounced king! He will have a say in this!"

"I doubt he has a say in anything anymore," Felix's voice rang clear. All eyes turned to him as he sprawled on the throne, one leg dangling off the arm smugly. "You realize that providing witnesses and proof were a formality of this council. Because I believe, since I AM legally married to Alex AND perfectly fit in every way, which would make me...King?"

Verdin stared at the couple in shocked silence.

"Would you like to do the honors, My Queen?"

With heinous pleasure, Alexa lifted her steely gaze to the councilman. "You conspired against me in hopes of putting your pitiful son on the throne and you undermined the purpose of this council." Straightening her back, she held his horrified gaze with her resolute one. "I hereby relieve you and your son of your positions and assets. Gareth? Arrest them for high treason."

Teeth flashing in blunt satisfaction, The Captain of the Guard withdrew his sword and stepped towards the cowering Verdin. "With pleasure."

Alexa stood there grinning, hands on her waist as the Councilman was carted off. "Felix?"

"Yes, my Queen?"

"You are in my seat."

"Allow me to rectify that immediately." The King grinned maniacally and dragged her down into his lap.

As King Felix Flamehart continued to show Alexa just how willing he was to adhere to her wishes, Queen Alexandra Windmere learned that sharing was a lot more fun.

EPILOGUE

Alexa watched him strap his belonging onto the saddle. "You will hurry back?"

Looking over his shoulder, Gareth grinned at her. "Unless she decides to resist. Then this could take a while."

Biting her lip, Alexa looked around at the two knights that stood, mounted and waiting for their Captain. "Ah, hell with it." Leaping forward she wrapped her arms around the man's neck and embraced him tightly. "I will miss you."

Laughing, he held her against him and swung her around once before placing her back on her feet. "I will miss you too Your Highness." Delighting in the pink in her cheeks, she slid the back of his knuckles against the happiness that colored her. "You wear him well."

The pink darkening, Alexa smiled cheekily, pushing the golden strand of her growing hair behind her ear.

"Are you flirting with my wife again brother?"

Turning around, Alexa's mouth widened into a grin and Gareth frowned at his brother as he swept his wife into his arms possessively. "She is not just your wife, you pompous arrogant boy!"

Felix smirked at his older brother, his arm wrapped around the Queen. "That's King pompous arrogant boy to you Gareth."

"Hmph." Waving an indifferent hand at the besotted couple, Gareth turned to his mount and lifted himself into the saddle. "Sometimes I think Felix, you married her for the attention."

Alexa kissed her King's ear teasingly. "He did Captain." She winked at the raven-haired man. "For my attention."

"I do like the best in life."

Gareth rolled his eyes and picked up his reigns. "Well, I'm off. I need to travel fast. Can't have Arabella alerted to my arrival. No telling what will greet me at her door."

"Rattlesnakes."

The Captain shuddered. "God I hope not." He took a moment to see his titan-haired brother draped over the little girl, who had wailed for him when she scraped her knee. He felt a rush of pride for them. "Take care of her Felix."

"You know I will." The King nodded without blinking.

With one last glance at their smiling faces, Gareth turned his horse and rode off for Arabella's home.

Alexa snuggled against Felix's arm. "I hope Arabella finds her happy ending."

Kissing her temple, the King watched the fading figure of his brother. "She will."

"I certainly hope so." Pinching a hefty pick of his backside she grinned up at him. "So how does the gander feel about being on the bottom tonight?"

Wrapping his arms around her, Felix nuzzled her nose with his. "I knew there was a reason I married you."

"There is." Alexa smiled winsomely. "I blackmailed you with your gander theory."

The castle rang with shrieks of laughter as the King threw the Queen over his shoulder and carried her inside.

THE END

THE

MEMOIRS

"Sure you want to do this?"

The question was redundant considering I was riding up the elevator to the penthouse for my latest assignment. It was also a little insulting considering my boss has said either I could do this or be fired. Unemployment was worse than death for me considering my loans and credit card bills. He knew just how badly I was drowning. Truthfully I had a feeling he was waiting for me to fail so he could fire me.

This assignment was a do-or-die situation. There was no point in the question.

Besides, I was utterly curious now. The beautiful man who opened the door and led me into the building was a tawny creature with the most astounding green eyes in history. If I could have afforded indulgence, I would have said 'once around the park my good man'.

"Miss Emily?"

The files nearly spilled out of my arms. Catching them quickly, I braced them against my chest and smiled apologetically through my black-rimmed glasses. "I'm sure."

His brown darkened as if he wasn't pleased with my decision. Almost, as if he was disappointed. "Right."

PING.

The elevator doors opened and he didn't bother with chivalry. Merely walked out imperiously.

Gorgeous and rude. With a deep sigh, I stepped through the elevator and yelped.

The head turned slowly as I gaped at him with a wide-eyed stare. The eyebrow lifted in silent inquiry and I bit my lip. "The elevators almost… never mind."

"This way," he spoke as if I was five years old. Opening two ebony doors, he positioned us in an 'L' shaped hallway. "Wait here," he instructed with one hand raised in warning before disappearing ahead and through a door.

Finally letting out a breath, I sighed. Harry had sent me here to get me fired. I was sure now. The apartment that I'd been led to was in one of the most opulent and luxurious parts of our city. The building was everything ancient wood and red brick. Expensive lighting, beautiful tapestries and furniture, priceless artifacts and impeccable taste. For a woman who lived in her jeans, wrote articles for a tyrannical newspaper man and spent her nights with a beat-up old laptop, this was a nightmare from a horror movie.

"Adam?"

Startling, my things nearly went flying out of my arms again. Heart panting, I stared down the corridor to my right and swallowed thickly. *Geez Emily, get a grip!* I scolded myself. Despite the setting, this was not an Alfred Hitchcock movie.

There was a slightly ajar door on the other end. The hallway I stood in was poorly lit, to begin with, but there was nothing but darkness on the other side of the door.

"Adam!" The man's voice demanded with growing irritation.

Gaping like a fish, I looked towards the door the tawny Adam had disappeared through and wondered what the hell to do now. There was no sign of his return. Now what?

"Grrrr…"

Head whipping back towards the dark door I took a moment to decide if that had been a growl or my imagination. But the rational part of my mind naturally assumed that whoever was calling for Adam had probably lost his patience. So swallowing down my panic I cleared my throat. "Um…Adam went to get something."

There was absolute silence for a heart-stopping moment before the gruff voice spoke again. "Come inside."

Eyes widening abnormally I debated whether I should just turn and run. Then I remembered how he'd reacted when Adam hadn't spoken up. Swallowing thickly, I hurriedly placed my armload of books and papers on the mantle and straightened my coat and hair. If that was my assignment, I didn't want him to think I was a bag lady. Although it was of no consequence what I looked like, being in the beautiful colonial building demanded some semblance of dignity.

My hand flattened against the door, and I took a deep breath to calm my nerves. After all, I was here to jot down a few notes for the old man's memoirs. I had to face him eventually. He couldn't very well shout through the thick door.

"Are you coming or going?"

Startled at the amusement in his voice, I glared at the door and pushed it open. "Coming," I assured him with a voice that was steadier than I felt.

Beyond the hallway was a large room completely shrouded in darkness. But the huge windows streamed moonlight and touched everything it could reach. And there was no one inside. I frowned, taking into account the ornate paintings, the countless rows of bookshelves, the grand mahogany desk and the gilded lamps. Was I hearing voices?

"Miss Brown?"

I jumped, nearly toppling back into the hallway until I saw a wine glass appear from the side of a high-backed chair facing away from me. So someone was there. Letting out a relieved breath, I took a step forward. "Mr. Jackson Black I presume?"

The hand beckoned me forward.

Maybe the well-known dialogue was too decrepit and old even for him. With deliberate footsteps echoing across the wooden floor, I finally stopped beside the chair before finally taking a step forward to look at him.

"Jesus!"

The wine glass lifted back up to his lips and the black eyes glistened up at me like onyx.

He quirked up one end of his mouth in a way that was neither a smile nor a grimace. "Miss Brown, they'll say you're blasphemous." Then his teeth flashed at me in what couldn't be anything but a smile. "A black Jesus?"

Gaping in shock, I missed the humor in his situation, even though I'll probably come back to laugh at myself later. But the rotting old man I'd expected to greet me was not the man who was smirking up at me now.

In the black chair, nearly invisible against the thread was a dark man with fine dark chocolate skin stretched over only what could be called chiseled bones. Like something out of a painting, he sat there, one ankle resting on his knee, one hand cupped over the top of the wine glass, his free hand curled around his ankle. But it wasn't the sheer beauty of the man that took my breath away, now. It was the lack of wrinkles on every inch of revealed skin, from his shiny bald head, and neat hands to his face and the slight peak of the collarbone from the pitch-black shirt.

"You're staring Brown."

Snapping out of my daze I felt heat rush up to my cheeks before shaking my head. Looking at anything else but him. "I'm...sorry. I thought... I mean I assumed you were…I didn't mean to…that is…"

"Relax. If this is Sean Mackenzie's idea of a joke, you can tell him I am not amused."

Neither was I. It was painfully obvious Jackson Black was no decrepit old man who wanted to write his memoirs before he died.

Because sitting in front of me was the most physically fit man in his early thirties, I'd ever seen. And did I say gorgeous?

"You know Mac?"

"Unfortunately," he wrinkled his nose for a fraction of a second before narrowing those glittering eyes at me. "You can tell him that any favor I owed him is void." He waved a hand over his shoulder. "You may leave now."

Mouth dropping open I stared at him. Oh dear god, I was being fired. Even before I'd started, I was being fired.

When I didn't move from my spot, he lifted his eyes back to me with a question clearly etched across his perfect face. "Yes?"

"I…"

"Speak up Brown; I don't have all night, contrary to what he told you."

Gritting my teeth, I clenched my fists and decided to hold my ground. If I was going to be fired, then I would at least have my say. "Contrary to what *you* may believe, he told me nothing. From what I was informed, that too through an email, was that I was to meet a Mr. Jackson Black here for an introduction for memoirs he needed to chronicle or be fired. Now if you're not Jackson Black or in need of a writer to assist you, I would appreciate that either you point me to the right man or that you tell me why I am being dismissed."

For a movement he watched me. And in those few seconds, I felt him take inventory of my whole life. To say his gaze was penetrating would be an understatement. He gave me the shivers. And they were not the pleasant kind. They were an uneasy reminder my body was sending my brain. Don't prolong it, as it's advised to leave now.

"I believe there has been a misunderstanding."

"You don't need to document your life?"

"I do."

"Then you're not Jackson Black."

A muscle ticked in his temple. "I am."

"Then I guess you're going to have to tell me why I'm about to be fired."

"I will, Brown, if you stop interrupting."

I didn't like him. Whoever the hell he was, I hoped to hell that his answer was good or I'd have to kick him in the shins which I had a feeling would only hurt me. I nodded at him as if to tell him that I was conceding for his turn to speak.

Tilting his head indulgently, he placed the wine glass on a nearby table and leaned back to get a better look at me. Those eyes drank in every detail of the simple black pumps, up the length of my calf to the knee-length straight black skirt, the white cotton collared shirt and the black jacket. Then his gaze lingered on the length of my throat, the curve of my hardening jaw, the flare of my nose up to my blazing eyes before his mouth quirked in the corner again. "I am Jackson Black and I do need a writer to help document some facts for me. Memoirs are too much of a commitment to what I'm planning. Sean happened to be a man to whom I owed a favor, a mistake that I intend to remedy immediately. And you're being sent back because I believe your boss has played a rather nasty trick on you. You weren't what I asked for."

Hackles rightly risen, I narrowed my eyes deliberately. "Is that a reference to the fact that I'm a woman?"

"Among other things or I misjudged just how much Sean owed me." If he thought smirking at me was helping he was sadly mistaken.

He was a frustrating man. But before I could tell him what I thought of his connotation the door slid open and Adam stepped in. "Master Black, I apologize. Miss Brown, you should have waited."

The black eyes were still trained on mine, and he lifted one hand to acknowledge his employee. "It's quite alright Adam. I invited her inside. But you may walk her out."

Teeth grinding together, I couldn't help the grunt of distaste. "Sexist pig."

"Miss Brown!" Adam stepped forward angrily.

The black eyebrow hiked, the smirk morphing into a rather sexy grin. "I assure you Brown; it's not your expertise I doubt."

I was still unsure of what he was referring to, my ability as a writer or as a woman. But I had a feeling he was enjoying my confusion as well as the lecherous innuendos. "And I assure you Mr. Black; it is not your gender I doubt."

When Adam stepped forward to bodily drag me away, the hand lifted up to hold him back, the black eyes now interested. "Tell me Brown; are all female writers natural feminists?"

"Tell me Mr. Black, are all former slaves as naturally eloquent as you?"

That remark would have had me thrown out. I was sure the moment it left my lips, but it was too late, Adam was gaping at me like a beached whale and Jackson Black had lost the humor on his beautiful face. Shouldering my bag more firmly, I held my head high despite my low blow. "For the record Mr. Jackson Black, I am the best damn writer in Chicago today and my being a woman or a feminist has nothing to do with it. Good night."

Weaving past the tall form of the stunned assistant, I marched straight for the door.

"Wait."

I should have kept walking.

His voice caught me with my hand on the doorknob. I paused because the panic that I was going to drown in debt froze me in my tracks. It was not his voice. It was the sheer terror that my life would swallow me whole if I lost that halted my feet. So when the resounding footsteps of expensive shoes sounded behind me, I turned with trembling limbs.

He was tall. Abnormally. Almost Six four. With his hands shoved into his dark pants, he gazed down at me curiously. There was open interest in those onyx eyes as he tried to get answers to the questions on his face. For a few moments, I stood under his scrutiny. This time it wasn't superficial to take a tally of my feminine assets or lack thereof, it was deeper as if he was trying to figure out my hopes and dreams. And that unsettled me even more than when he'd been trying to imagine me naked.

"Shorthand?"

I blinked at him. "I beg your pardon?"

"Can you take shorthand?"

I was a journalist; it was second nature. "Of course."

He seemed to like the finality of my answer because he nodded with a slight smile. "Adam, give her stationary."

My breath of relief was nearly explosive. I wished to god he hadn't heard it, because it painfully spoke of just how much I wanted to keep this job. Trying to muster some dignity I cleared my throat. "That won't be necessary." I looked up at him when I knew that it wouldn't hurt my eyes. Although I doubted looking at him wouldn't ever hurt my eyes. "I have my own."

He nodded rather imperiously. "We start tonight."

Like a blithering idiot, I watched him stroll back toward his chair.

"Tonight?"

"Adam will pick up your things and move them into the guestroom."

"Move my stuff?" I squeaked.

Over his shoulder, he quirked an eyebrow at me. "That was the initial request."

What the hell was I getting myself into? Swallowing noisily, I closed my eyes and prayed for my soul before walking forward. "Anything else in your request I should know about?"

Picking up his wineglass he met Adam's eyes, which instantly resulted in our being left alone and the door closing soundlessly. My unease instantly became panic.

Drowning his wine glass, Mr. Black smiled reassuringly at me. "How about we move this to my desk?"

I gaped at him. "Move what?"

His eyes twinkled with mirth. "The story you're going to be writing."

Get a grip, I muttered to myself. Just because he'd turned out to be a rather virile and beautiful black man, there was no reason to think that I was a banquet and he was a starving castaway. Trying to get over how I didn't like the situation, I reminded myself to think of the pile of bills that would be sitting on my doorstep. Walking to the mahogany desk, I bit my lip as I weighed my options.

"You can sit behind the desk. I like to move around."

I hated how everything he now said sounded like a damned innuendo. It was his fault for reminding me I was a woman. Moving around the table, I sat in the chair gingerly and stared at the moonlit study around me.

"There's a pen and pad on the table, you can start with that for now."

This was insane.

"What now Brown?"

I huffed and looked up at him crossly. "First of all, with the way you keep calling me 'Brown', I feel like you're speaking to my father. I have my own name. Secondly, I'm only human."

Standing framed against the illuminated window, he frowned at me. "I don't know your name and I know you're human."

"It's Emily and I don't see in the dark."

There was a flash of confusion on his face before he walked over to the desk and leaned almost all the way over it.

Oh dear god, he was going to attack me!

Eyes widening slightly, I drew back into the plush leather of his desk chair until I saw him reach for the lamp and warm golden light blinded me.

The sharp smell of Kenneth Cole hit me unannounced.

Blinking away the stars blinding me, I heard him drop into the chair on the other side of the desk, mirroring his previous stance. Finally, when my vision cleared I got a good look at him.

In the moonlight, he'd appeared ethereal, untouchable and something out of an old fairytale.

Now in the pragmatic light of the lamp, he was dazzling. Carved from dark marble he sat there looking back at me without so much as a flicker of emotion on his face. If I hadn't seen him walking and talking for the past few minutes, I would have thought I'd imagined him. I don't feel bad for the time I took to catch my bearing and gather my wayward thoughts. "I think it's time for you to tell me exactly what I'm going to be doing here Mr. Black."

He rested an elbow on the edge of the desk and wrapped his hand around his jaw while he contemplated me. This time I didn't fall prey to his intimidation. When he seemed to notice that, the corner of his mouth twitched and his hand fell away. "You are to remain in my household until I see the need or until the book is completed. Your schedule will be a tad odd considering I have no time for anything during the day. We will meet in the evenings. Your days are yours to do with as you please, Adam will leave a car at your disposal, and you're welcome to go where you please as long as you're here at seven. Although I will warn you that our sessions might make you somewhat nocturnal like myself. I sleep very little. Also, you will have Sundays off. Until you are working as my employee I will provide a stipend for your stay here which you will be paid every Sunday morning."

Throughout his tirade I stared at him silently, my mouth slightly parted.

Entirely too pleased with the effect he had on me, he leaned back in his chair with a victorious grin.

"Do I get a chauffeur?"

He blinked in surprise before chuckling huskily under his breath. "You want a chauffeur to drive my Bentley GT?"

My mouth dropped open. "You have a Bentley GT?"

His grin was teasing. "It stands next to my Jag."

1.   Rolling my eyes, I relaxed into the chair and met his black eyes deliberately. "Should I take specs in case you need this logged into your memoirs?"

"It's just a story, Brown."

"Emily."

"Regardless, it is my story. And the cars are insignificant."

With a sigh, I picked up my pen and paper and propped one shoeless heel on the edge of the chair and propped the yellow legal pad on my thigh. "You can begin when you're ready."

He was eerily silent so I lifted my eyes from the paper to the man gazing at me with profound interest. "What?"

"That's genuine cowhide leather you have your feet on."

The foot in question thumped back onto the ground and I felt the color rush up my cheeks. "I apologize." Again his silence made me raise my eyes. "Now what?"

"Are you sure you want to do this Brown?"

"Emily!" I said firmly. "Mr. Black, must you insist on being obstinate?"

"You may call me Jack."

"You may call me unimpressed." I narrowed my eyes at him.

His hand returned to his jaw, his lips partially hidden behind his palm. His eyes glistened with silent regard. "Would it impress you if I said I'm not human?"

This time it was my eyebrows that hiked up. "Is this where you expound on how infinite money sucks out one's soul because I'd love to trade places with you."

I could feel him smile behind his hand. "No, you wouldn't. And no," he mumbled around the hand, "it is not the money, as infinite as it is not, that has taken my soul."

The weight of his voice melted away all other emotions. This time he sighed at my silence and pulled his hand away from his mouth and my eyes were drawn to it like a moth to a flame. Cursing under my breath I dragged my eyes away only to glare back at him when he chuckled knowingly. "I'm sorry that Sean didn't tell you."

"Tell me what?"

"How old did he say I was?"

"He didn't."

The wince wasn't heartening. My brow darkened. "What's going on?"

"I suppose there's no other way to say this." Shifting lower in the seat he met my eyes matter-of-factly. "I'm a vampire."

If I'd been confused before, my mind spun off its axis and left me swimming in bewilderment.

Now I realized why Sean had done this to me. This man was insane and I was going to be degraded to playing housemate with minimum wages. "Okay."

This time his shoulder shook with deliberate laughter. "You don't believe me."

"It is a little hard to…er…swallow."

His eyes flickered with mirth before he held his hand out to me. At my warning glance, his lips stretched away from his teeth in a grin. "I don't bite."

More to humor him, I reached across and slid my hand into his.

"Jeez!" Wrenching my hand away I stared at him in astonishment. "You're freezing! Adam should turn on the heat, you'll fall sick."

Rolling his eyes, he sat back and shook his head with utter disappointment. "Would you like to see the fangs?"

"No, I'd love to see the coffin you sleep in. Honestly, Mr. Black, if you just want me to leave, I'd prefer you to not play around and say it plainly."

"How plain would you like for me to make this Brown? I am a vampire."

"You're insane is what you are." Smacking the writing pad on the desk, I stood and re-shouldered my bag.

"Please sit down."

Walking around the desk, I yelped when he was suddenly standing before me. Staring up at him, I realized that my head barely grazed his clean-shaven jaw. "You cannot write my story Brown if you don't believe me."

There was a strange magnetic pull to those onyx eyes. Beautiful and captivating. For a few seconds, I couldn't remember what he'd said to me, and then I saw a flash of gold in those black depths. I gasped as his lips parted and I saw the twin-pointed teeth. Mouth opening in shock, I could see him physically brace for the screaming fit. But with the blood pounding in my ears, all I did was stare unblinking at the canines flashing at me with a grotesque appeal. I didn't care that the monsters under my bed had been real. I didn't care that horror movies had a base. I didn't care that death was staring me in the face. All I could think was that I'd never seen anything so beguilingly macabre. There was no other way to describe them.

And the creature hissed out a breath when one of my hands reached up as if to touch them.

Jerking away, he put at least a foot of space between us as he glared at me. "Not the response I was expecting. The screaming, the stumbling, the horror I'm used to."

Gulping down the panic attack that threatened to do exactly what he was expecting, I fisted my hands at my sides. "I'm sorry Mr. Black."

"I'd prefer Jack."

"Yeah well I'd prefer Emily but you're not exactly complying," I muttered dryly.

This was an entirely new ballgame. I should have been reassessing my commitment, but strangely enough, all I could think was that this would be one hell of a story.

With a deep breath, I strode around the desk and dropped back down into my previous chair. "I only have one question really. Well two now that I think about it before I agree to this."

His black eyes were fathomless. "What?"

"Are you going to eat me? And is this significant enough to be part of the book?"

At first, I realized he couldn't believe what I'd asked, then his mouth widened into a breath-stealing grin. "No, and yes."

With a nod, I picked up the writing pad and paper. "Great. Now you expound your troubles while I get the violins going." I motioned the strumming of the instrument with one hand over my arm.

The vampire dropped back into what would be his usual chair and laughed heartily. "You know Brown, I think this is the beginning of a beautiful friendship."

"If I get to drive the Bentley."

"Done."

I grinned widely at him.

"So maybe you should start from the beginning."

Reclined in his favorite chair while I leaned against the desk, I waited for him to throw something at me. "Why?"

Not what I was expecting. "Well, it helps to know what happened in the past to speak of the significance of the present or future."

"And who decided that?"

I had no answer for him. It would be the first time I learned that

126

nothing was predictable about this man. Not his disposition. Not his nature. Not his appetite.

"It would help me to understand."

"What do you define as the beginning Brown?"

It was irritating how he wouldn't use my first name. "How about a date of birth?"

"Which one?"

"Are you being intentionally irritating Mr. Black?"

An eyebrow arched; amused. "The date depends on whether you're asking me when I was born as a human or a vampire. Which can also be my death day if you believe in resurrection and all that."

He delighted in throwing me for a loop and watching me flounder. I smiled tightly. "The date you were born as a human."

"Why?"

Throwing up my hands, I let out a frustrated breath. "Oh come on."

"No, I'm honestly curious Brown. What does it matter when the human was born?"

I stared at him incredulously. "Are you saying that your human life is insignificant?"

He shrugged before taking a sip from his wine glass, which I suspected was carrying nothing alcoholic. "Thirty-two years of an earthbound farmer isn't much of a comparison to five hundred years of history in the making."

I suddenly felt like a child. He had the effect on most people, I gathered, but that didn't faze me. "But don't you think that man you were, shaped the vampire you became?"

He seemed confused by my question. "Why would it?"

"Well," I wondered how to approach it without offending him, "let's put it this way. Physically, did you look like you do now when you were a farmer?"

"Yes, but why does that matter besides the fact that I was a dark-skinned vampire?"

"What about your genetics? Your family tree? Your parents?"

"What about them?"

"They made you who you are."

"Which parents?"

"Mr. Black," I glared at him. "Now you're going to distinguish between your birth parents and those that turned you into a vampire."

His grin was satisfied. "You're catching on."

With a huff, I dropped into the visitor's chair beside the desk. "Work with me on this, will you? We need some sort of background to ground this thing or it's going to make no sense."

"To who?"

"Anyone!"

Rolling his eyes as if it was a waste of his time, he slumped lower in his seat, which was, as I learned with experience, a sign of his boredom. "I was born in 1556 in the once prominent capital city Gao of the Songhai Empire in pre-colonial West Africa."

My mouth has appropriately fallen open because his eyes are shown with triumph. If he had thought to shock me, he had succeeded. Nonchalantly he nodded to the forgotten writing pad I held in my fingers and instantly I jerked my eyes down to start jotting down the details as he spoke. But the color in my cheeks stayed for a while.

"It was a time when Timbuktu was a blossoming Centre of learning and a thriving cultural and commercial center. Arab, Italian, and Jewish merchants all gathered for trade. A revival of Islamic scholarship also took place at the university in Timbuktu. Neither of which matters to my story."

"You were Muslim?"

"When I was human."

"And now?"

"Now I think a bloodsucker is in no position to conform to any religion, don't you agree?"

It was troubling to note the lack of consequence he placed on things we held dear, like religion and time. "What was your life like?"

"Simple. I was a farmer. I plowed land, cleaned dung, plowed more land, cleaned more__"

"I get it," I grumbled and shook my head at his stubbornness to put any worth to his time with a beating heart. Maybe it was my own prejudice. "How about a name?"

"When?"

I had to bite back a smile. "Did you have many?"

He shrugged as if it was extremely normal to have several names. "I forget."

"The one you were born with."

For a moment his eyes were humorless, but then he must have realized how I wasn't going to budge. "Han. My name was Han Yama Danku."

"Han." I rolled the name in my mouth and smiled. It seemed to suit him. "So why Jackson?"

"The name changes as I change location. Can you imagine a man called Han Yama Danku popping up in random places over the last five centuries? The social security agency alone would have a field day." His grin was wicked. "Not to mention the questions and taxes and let's not forget the IRS."

I decided I would let it rest. For now.

"Is there anything that you remember about being human? Something significant that would help make a distinction between your vampire years?"

"My culinary preferences?"

God, he was being difficult. But taking a calming breath I smiled encouragingly. "Besides the obvious."

"What's obvious?" He threw back promptly.

There was no way to avoid his questions. I could already see a pattern. "The blood-sucking, un-dead, creature of the night references."

"Bloodsucking, yes. Creature of the night – more of a preference. Un-dead…mostly philosophical stereotyping."

I frowned at him in confusion. "I'm sorry I don't follow. Aren't you a nightwalker?"

"Only because it's easier that way."

"Aversion to sunlight?"

"Myth. "His chuckles were teasing. "Have you ever exposed dead skin to UV rays? It shrivels and wrinkles. It's more of a cosmetic disposition rather than a spiritual deterrent."

"So you can walk in the sun?"

"When it's not too bright and I wear adequate sunblock, yes."

It was disconcerting that there was a possibility they walked among us under the shroud of sunblock. Eerily unsettling.

"You seem disappointed."

"I was thinking disconcerting."

"Understandable."

I swallowed nervously. "And the blood-drinking?"

"Wouldn't that be more than disconcerting?" The arched eyebrow was mocking. There was no way else to categorize it. "Yes, to answer your unasked question. I killed people. I sucked them dry. I was a murderer and an animal of baser instincts for many decades. But I assure you it got old after a while."

I had to clamp down on the need to scowl at him. "How sad for you."

His teeth glistened in the lamplight. "All children go awry sometimes."

"You weren't a child," the antagonism was hard to smother.

"Wasn't I? I'd been thrown into a life of almost limitless power and control. It's like picking up an orphan off the street and giving him a hundred million dollars in cash to do with as he pleases for as long as he likes. No questions asked."

"You don't need to justify the monster status to me, Mr. Black."

"Don't I Brown?" Standing out of his chair he strolled to a crystal decanter and poured himself another glass of the crimson liquid. The bile rose in my throat as I realized that it could be a person.

He threw a smile at me over his shoulder. "Relax. You're assuming again."

"I'm not."

"You humans have telltale hearts."

He was right, my breath was harsher than when he was just a man. Now he was a monster I was supposed to write about and understand. "Is it blood?"

"Yes."

"Human?"

"Yes."

"Fresh?"

"Unfortunately, no." The crystal stopper musically clinked back into the mouth of the decanter before he sauntered back to me and stood there. "Compliments of the Chicago Central Blood Bank." I wrinkled my nose when he took a whiff and grinned. "Adam makes sure it's 98.6. Almost fresh."

"When was the last time you killed someone?"

"For blood?"

"For anything," I grated out mechanically which only seemed to please him more.

"Let's see," he pretended to contemplate his past while I wondered if his answer to make a difference to my decision to stay, "what are we now? 2008? I'd say about a hundred and fifty-four years."

The number wrenched a gasp from deep in my chest and I realized I'd been holding my breath.

At my stunned expression, his patented smirk melted away to leave his face impassive. "Bleeding Kansas. I was in America then. Around the passage of the Kansas-Nebraska Act of 1854. Border wars broke out in the Kansas territory, where the question of whether it would be admitted to the Union as a slave or Free State was left to the inhabitants."

A sickening knot tightened in my chest. "John Brown."

His face was deadpan, but his eyes burned. "He thought 'Slave Power' was seizing full control of the national government."

John Brown had been a well-known Abolitionist during the Civil War. He'd killed many people. Many slaves.

I flinched despite my greatest efforts. "I…"

"Probably a coincidence. But you see now that sometimes our family tree and our parents don't shape us into who we become."

But there was no coincidence. My ancestors had probably been responsible for Bleeding Kansas and I had a feeling he'd known it long before he mentioned it today. But his words rocked me to my bones.

Suddenly calling him a 'monster' was relative.

I was unpacking my traveling bags, marveling at how Adam had managed to pick everything I needed, including adequate underwear, toothbrush, toiletries, shoes, socks, makeup, moisturizer and other necessities. I tried not to imagine him going through my underwear drawer or rifling through my tampons, but he hadn't missed anything. It was all there.

My cell phone trilled happily.

Flipping the silver phone open I sighed. "Emily."

"I was wondering what to do with the things you left in the office Em."

I couldn't help the un-lady-like grunt. "Hello, Mac."

"And I will need an official resignation from you Em. You can't just, not show up for work one day. There are procedures."

My blood frothing in my veins, and I grit my teeth. "What makes you think I quit?"

There was absolute silence on the other end for a few precious seconds. "You never called me."

"Are you sure *you* didn't call me to find out if he's eaten me or not?"

"Wha.... uh...so you...are you with him?"

"Isn't that what my job was?"

This time the silence extended longer. "And you're staying?"

"Didn't I say I would?"

"No you said you were taking the job, I just figured you wouldn't stay with it."

"You figured wrong Mac. I'm staying. Which means you leave my stuff alone and make preps to pay my paycheck for this month."

I could practically see him glaring at the phone.

With a victorious smile that I hoped would reflect in my voice I spoke. "Oh and Jack says that any favor he owed you after this is completely void, but he's still got a few favors he holds over you." It didn't matter that I didn't call him 'Jack'. Mac didn't need to know that.

"Oh."

I jumped up on the bed and did a little victory dance complete with hip swivels. "If you can't get me on my cell Mac, you're welcome to call at his house. Adam will put you through. I'll email you a progress report at the end of the week. Ciao." Flipping the phone closed, I tossed it on my bed and whistled 'Brand New Day' under my breath while hanging my clothes in the closet.

Since it appeared that I was the only human in the apartment, he decided to introduce me to his own brand of cooking.

Sitting in the kitchen, with four bowls of odd sauces in front of me, I started when he spoke the name of the country.

Head snapping up I stared at him in alarm, the spoon stopping in midair. "China?"

"There was a lot of fun to be had with the kind of insanity the Allied troops were sporting." Jack was stirring the pasta, his booted feet echoing on the fine marble floor, an oddly soothing rhythm as he cooked and spoke of his life. I'd been in the Black household for six days and already I was exceedingly embroiled in the stories he spun with the least amount of drama. Today he was telling the tale of the Boxer Rebellion of 1898 in China. As I'd already learned, his perspective was completely different from what the history books said. It was fortunate that I had been good at world history in college or I would have been lost.

"Wait, wait!" I frowned at him from where I was perched on a stool beside the huge island table. The kitchen was well-lit, but the shadows still followed him. "The Allied troops were sent in because the Boxers with their Yihetuan, the Boxers United in Righteousness, were crippling communication, torching schools and churches and murdering anyone foreign or related to foreigners."

His eyes were, as usual, mocking my lack of knowledge. I was sure now that he enjoyed throwing my carefully explained social history out of whack. "The Eight-Nation Alliance was a 20,000 men campaign of indiscriminate slaughter, rape, and pillaging." Pointing to the sauces, he added the silent question.

Tasting the last one I wrinkled my nose before handing him the one I liked best. He didn't bristle at my snort of disbelief. "The Boxers were responsible for the death of 48 Catholic missionaries and nearly 18,000 Chinese Catholics. Not to mention over 200 Chinese Eastern Orthodox Christians were also put to death, along with 200 more Protestant missionaries and 500 Chinese Protestants! Dammit Jack, just because you were a reformed pillager taking financial advantage of the chaos, doesn't mean those decorated officers of the 9th Infantry Regiment of the United States Army were a bunch of rapists and anarchists."

His grin was hedonistic, almost as if he enjoyed my patriotic ruffled feathers while he cooked my dinner. "Are you saying that the Opium Wars of the 1900s had no contribution from the foreigners?"

I glared at his back, wishing I had some darts handy. "I'm not. But it's wrong to blame them entirely. And why the hell are you taking the boxer rebels' side anyway; they were nothing but a bunch of violent xenophobes!"

Walking to me, he leaned against the counter beside the stool I occupied and leaned into my face, his nose nearly brushing mine as he grinned victoriously. "All I'm asking Brown is that you see this from another perspective."

There was a time when his mere proximity would throw me off, and send my heart racing with genuine fear, but after spending more than a week in confined quarters with this creature, I had firsthand knowledge that his hunger was well-reigned. So I met that unshakable gaze and held my own. "I could say the same to you, Mr. Black. It was one of the very well-known Chinese Professors of Philosophy, Yuan Weishi who said these criminal actions brought unspeakable suffering to the nation and its people! He knew these were the facts, and admitted that it was a national shame that the Chinese people cannot forget. If the Eight-Nation Alliance hadn't lent their aid, the imperial government would have never been defeated and the Republic of China would never have been established a decade later."

His eyes sparked with genuine interest as they usually did when we argued. "You can't deny that it conveniently lead to Japan's rise to power and Germany's attainment of the nickname 'Hun'. You do remember who the Huns were, right? Don't you understand anything sweetheart," he purred and I knew the punch line was coming, "history is told through the eyes of the victor."

There was no denying that. So with a wince I snatched my eyes from his hypnotically convincing gaze and grunted. "Fine. It's your book anyway. Authors can afford to be biased."

Spooning out a serving for me on a plate, he placed it in front of me. "China was a lot rawer than it is now. I miss it sometimes." With a chuckle, he handed me a fork and winked.

"I can totally imagine you as a boxer."

He took an elaborate bow as if I'd complimented him.

And that's how it was. While I took notes and argued, he tried to break and unhinge everything I believed in. I should have been afraid of what all I was losing for a few wads of hundred-dollar bills.

It didn't help that he cooked like a gourmet chef.

There was a knock on my slightly ajar door. I'd just returned from a jog.

My notes kept growing. It was almost that I spent my days compiling and deciphering the quick scrawls I'd jotted down on my papers while he talked. And he talked pretty fast. I'd taken today to air myself out. I barely had a life outside the Beast's castle. I remember mentioning the reference to him once.

He'd been amused.

Blinking over my shoulder at him, I took in the sleek black suit over a black silk shirt open at the throat.

Damn, but the man could dress.

Hiding a smile, I straightened from where I was rifling through my clothes. "Mr. Black."

"Hey Brown," he purposefully scanned the contents of my room before frowning. "This place is entirely too small for you."

I chuckled at the distaste in his voice. "It's bigger than my own room back at my place."

"Adam should have known better than to put you in one of the service rooms. I'll have him make the guest bedroom." I opened my mouth to protest but he held up a hand. "It wasn't a request." Turning away I rolled my eyes and unconsciously started to tidy my room. Arrogant as always. But something about him was different lately. He seemed lighter than when I'd first seen him in that dark study. More human than a demon.

When I finally met his eyes he frowned at me. "Where were you?"

"Jogging?" I chuckled before dropping onto the bed and unlacing my sneakers. "Not of all us have un-dead metabolism and naturally perfect physique."

"Perfect?"

Heat rushed to my skin and I avoided looking at him where he was probably smirking. Could this be any more mortifying? My mouth did tend to run away with me. Hoping to change the subject I decided to speak of our next topic of discussion. "Was there something you needed? Our session isn't due for another two hours."

He watched as I wiggled my toes free, black eyes darkening for a moment I wondered if he disapproved of me being barefoot in his house. Then I wondered if my feet smelled. Self-consciously I stood up and walked around the bed to hide them from view. He'd already said his sense of smell was as acute as his hearing. "We're speaking about the Mughal Empire of Asia today and something about the biggest diamond in history, right?" I finished with an indulgent grin.

"Spoken like a true woman." Laughing, Jack walked in peering at my old notebook, fingers sliding over the notes I'd taken about Asian empires in the last 17th Century. There was very little I knew about the region and the great expanse of information was already crowding my brain. Then I frowned, as he seemed engrossed in my notes. This was unlike him. First, to come to my room, and then to proceed to go through my things without my asking.

When he moved to rifle through my closet, I dove over the bed and snapped it shut. "Hey! Does the word privacy mean anything to you?"

His grin was lascivious. "What could you possibly be hiding in there that I've not already seen?"

Cheeks pinking much to my chagrin, I stayed between him and my poor collection of clothes. "Well, you've not seen mine."

"I could."

I glared hard up at him. "Was there something you needed?"

His eyes slid over my shoulder as if trying to look through the wooden lapels of my closet before sighing. "I need assistance," he winced at the word as if it gave him physical pain to admit it.

I held back a smile at his reluctant request. "I'm sorry to hear that, but I'll do what I can to help."

Realizing that I wasn't about to let him poke through my belongings she walked to the little window and frowned out into the orange sky. "I am invited to a Fund Raiser for the Chicago Hospital Children's Ward."

I blinked startled. "Huh?"

Turning to me, he gave me an admonishing glower. "I do have a human life for pretense sake. Did you think I spent my days in a coffin?" Then he smirked. "Better yet, did you think I got the Bentley by eating Walter Owen Bentley?"

"Smartass. Hmph." Grumbling at his superior tone I stomped to my bed and picked up the clothes I was going to wear after my shower. "So go to the Benefit."

"I had forgotten that it was tonight and I was meant to bring a date."

Foot catching in the charging cable for my cell phone, I tripped and landed on my bed in a heap. Eyes wide as Ping-Pong balls I gawked at him. "Are you suggesting…"

Crossing his arms, he looked down his imperious nose at me, the muscles in his arms flexing under the exquisitely tailored suit jacket. It looked like Boss Tweed. "If you can bring yourself to accept."

"ME!?"

Exasperated by my alarm, he leveled his patented scowl at me. The kind that made grown men cowers. I merely went deathly still under its weight.

Clearing my throat, properly chastised, I sat up slowly; afraid the head rush might make my brain explode. "I see."

"Do you suppose you could prepare yourself in twenty minutes?"

"Sure if I had a magic wand."

My humor didn't seem to amuse him. He merely narrowed his gaze, fine-tuning that glare and causing gooseflesh to erupt all over my body. "Forty?"

I swallowed and quit while I was ahead. "I think I can manage," I squeaked.

With a satisfied nod, he turned to leave. "I'll meet you at the Bentley."

Panic slowly and steadily welling inside me I wrung my poor little t-shirt into an anxious ball. A social event on the arm of the most gorgeous man on this side of the world. Like the proverbial Cinderella. Where was a fairy godmother when you needed her?

"And Brown?"

I looked up with dread seeping into my bones.

"If you make it in thirty, I'll let you drive."

I dove for the bathroom as my bedroom door closed before the explosion of rancorous male laughter.

"Remind me never to let you behind one of my wheels again."

Rolling my eyes, I let him lead me up the steps to the convention center as the valet drove his precious car to the parking. "I can't believe I'm getting the speed and safety speech from a vampire."

"Unlike a vampire Brown, you have human reflexes."

"The fire hydrant was like ten feet away!"

"Have you ever heard of the concept of breaking distance?"

"I'm guessing it's the years speaking now." The adrenaline was so busy singing rhapsodies in my blood that I hadn't realized we'd strolled through the entrance and through the crowd of stunned people without breaking stride.

Then I noticed it.

The charity was themed in black and white.

If Jack had thought to tell me, I'm sure my break-neck speed had forced him to forget. In a roomful of men and women only dressed and black and white, I was red. Heart screeching to a stop, I wobbled in my three-inch heels. "Oh, my god."

If Jack hadn't been a vampire, my nails would have torn flesh through his jacket and into his arm.

Wrapping one hand firmly around my viselike grip he smiled pleasantly at a fat balding man that approached. "Fix your face Brown; they'll think I stepped on your toes."

With the world spinning around me, I pasted on my best 'I'm just the date' smile while my eyes darted around in absolute horror.

"Hello, Mayor," he greeted warmly as the man shook his hand, the portly man now flanked by a group of aging businessmen and their young giggling wives.

"Ah, Jackson! A pleasure to see you, my boy. I'm glad you could make it. It wouldn't have been the same seeing as how one of our most generous benefactors was missing." The man smacked Jack heartily on the back before his eyes drifted to me and widened. "And who is this, may I ask?"

The geek in the red dress?

Pulling me forward, he presented me like the arm ornament I was with a gallant smile. "Mayor Becket this is Emily Brown. A talented journalist for the Chicago Times and presently helping me write my memoirs."

My hand nearly shook out of its socket, I was awed by the fact that not only did he know my name, but his praise also sounded genuine. I gave a wobbly smile to the Mayor who suddenly decided I had to be introduced to at least ten more men because his life depended on it. And Jack carefully maneuvered me through the group of men who were startled when they got their first look at me. I'd been running on pure adrenaline since my drive, but soon I could feel it effervescing and leaving only terror in its wake.

When the final politician had been introduced, Jack thankfully led me to the refreshments table before leaning down to whisper in my ear. "Would you kindly explain to me why your heart is screaming in fright?"

Gasping for breath previously denied, I tilted my head back and let him see the horror in my brown eyes. "I'm red!"

He blinked in confusion. "You're nearly as white as a sheet; although, I do prefer you with your natural color when you don't appear as if you're being led to the guillotine."

"No!" I hissed under my breath as the waiter handed each of us our drink. "Everyone else is in black and white! I'm red! Did you see the look on those men's faces?"

Black eyes danced with amusement. "It was a tad hard to miss."

"And the women!" I moaned softly under my breath, the Champaign glass trembling in my fingers. "My god they looked like they'd seen a cockroach!"

Both his eyebrows hiked up and he regarded me silently for a moment while I glanced around in abject mortification.

"Brown?"

"Oh, dear god!" I wheezed. "They're ALL looking at me!"

"Brown!"

Wide, horrified gaze snapping back to him, I found him smiling down at me with the oddest little smile. Like I was a delusional little child and he found that endearing. But that was probably my hysteria talking.

"The reason those men were staring at you is that they're lecherous old bastards who've never seen a beautiful woman in their life." My jaw dropped at the simplicity of his lie. "And the women are glaring at you because they'll never be as beautiful as you." Patting my hand on his arm gently as if I was being silly he smiled wider. "Now, can you please remove that catatonic look from your face or people will think I held you at gunpoint to accompany me."

Swallowing down the sudden lump in my throat, I let him lead me through the people, stunned at the rather elaborate lie he'd concocted for my benefit. But did he have to sound too sincere? It did funny things to my stomach. "Jack?"

"What?"

"That was very sweet of you."

"Hmmmm."

"I mean it. I've never had anyone make something up with such sincerity just to save my__"

The rest of my words died in a gasp of breath as I went sprawling into his arms, the Champaign glass nearly spilling all the bubbly on his jacket. I don't know where I got the self-mastery to hold onto both the glass and his arm as he gathered me with enough force to bring every inch of me to press against him. "You are the most infuriating, exasperating..." My eyes went abnormally wide as I saw a flash of fangs, eyes opaque with anger before he let out a frustrated breath and handed our drinks to a short balding guy with enough authority to shock even him. "Dance with me," he commanded although he shouldn't have bothered because already he'd nearly carried me to the dance floor.

With suave, imposing expertise perfected over five centuries, he led me around the floor forcing me into the easy rhythm of his body. I was doubtful my feet ever touched the ground. This was simply another one of our arguments, another relentless battle of wits. Mind you, a coordinated one, but a struggle, nonetheless. He was holding my hand a bit tighter than was necessary, and that fact alone threw me off balance. With a quiet force, he turned and twirled me between the beautiful couples like some distant exotic prince. A distant exotic extremely pissed-off prince.

With a wince, I braved the fury I could see simmering beneath his chocolate skin; the fine bones of his face undulating as he gritted his teeth. "So about this colossal diamond…"

A muscle worked in his jaw, but his eyes flickered back down to mine and they slashed through me like a knife.

I smiled a wobbly smile up at him apologetically even though I didn't know what I'd done besides pick the wrong dress. "How colossal are we talking?"

As if he hadn't already been holding me like a second skin, I felt his arm tighten around my waist and I braced for the verbal reprimand that was coming. But bizarrely enough, his mouth twisted up into a pleased smile. "About a hundred and five carats."

My knees turned to jelly. "Holy mother of…"

His shoulders shaking with amused laughter, his black eyes finally sparked with humor. Slowly, his arms relaxed and my feet finally touched the ground. "I was traveling to Delhi, India with a French Jeweler named Tavernier in 1665. We saw it and the throne it was placed in. They called it the Kohinoor Diamond. Literally means 'Mountain of Light'. It originated at Golconda in the state of Andhra Pradesh in India, belonged to various Mughal and Persian rulers who fought bitterly over it at various points in history, and was seized as a spoil of war for Queen Victoria of Great Britain in 1877."

Embroiled in the story, I blinked up at him curiously. "Is it in London now?"

"Part of the crown Jewels and like all significant jewels, the Kohinoor had its share of legends. It is reputed to bring misfortune or death to any male who wears or owns it."

I muffled my snicker. "I take it; it deterred you from stealing it."

"It was definitely de-motivating, especially since Tavernier was set against it. They say conversely, it is reputed to bring good luck to female owners. According to another legend, whoever owns the Kohinoor rules the world," he finished with a wink.

I gazed over his shoulder into history wondering what it would have been like to see it all. The grandeur of the Mughal Emperors who sat on thrones of precious stones and wore gilded armor. To have lived in the time of diamonds as big as a man's fist.

"Come back to me, Brown."

With a sheepish smile, I met his teasing gaze. "Sorry. So tell me about Delhi."

"I was there the year they built the Taj Mahal."

"Didn't the king cut off the hands of all the craftsmen who made it?"

Chuckling low under his breath, he rested his chin against my temple and I couldn't suppress the shiver. He was warmer tonight, but the contrast was still chilling. "Not so my sweet. Shah Jahan planned to build a similar Mahal next to it for himself as the Taj was for his beloved wife, but he fell ill."

Resting against him, finally relaxed in the circle of his arms, I let my eyes drift shut as we swayed gently to the orchestra. "If he cut off their hands, he would have had to find more artisans."

"And he already had the best."

"What was Delhi like?"

"Dusty."

Choking my laugh, I lifted my head and smiled up at him. "The man trapezes across the globe and finds the land of the Taj Mahal dusty."

"Not so my dear," his eyes twinkled with mirth. "Venice was wet."

By the time we walked through the door to give our coats to Adam, Jack had completely forgotten his near-homicidal anger.

"You SAW Napoleon?"

"From a distance. He conquered Venice in 1797 and brought to an end the most fascinating century of its history. Venice had been one of the most elegant and refined cities in Europe, greatly influencing art, architecture and literature."

"Didn't he liberate the Jews?"

"The Jews certainly tell it that way."

"Oh, right the victor tells the tale."

"Although Napoleon was seen as something of a liberator for the city's Jewish population; it can be argued they had lived with fewer restrictions in Venice. He removed the gates of the Ghetto and ended the restrictions on when and where Jews could live and travel in the city."

"Whose side were you on?"

"Napoleon's."

"Whoa!"

He chuckled at my childlike awe then blinked at the gaping Adam. "Yes, Adam?"

Shaken out of his surprise, the tawny man blinked between us in confusion before clearing his throat. "Would you like me to get you something to drink Master Black?"

Jack waved him off with a hand and a grin. "I'm not invalid Adam. It is late. Go to bed. I'll fetch it for myself."

The assistant stared at me kicking off my high heels and then at his Master as if he'd just sprouted horns before lifting his nose in the air and leaving us.

I blinked at the imperious attendance and grunted. "What is his problem?"

"I've never given him a day off?" Jack seemed to ponder that.

"You've NEVER given him a day off!?"

He winced at the aghast look on my face. "I've never refused his request."

"Has he ever made a request?" I narrowed my eyes at him, hands braced on my waist.

For a second his eyes slid over me and then to my absolute shock, he lifted one hand and slid it gently across my jaw. "Never." Then he chuckled at my glazed expression. "Thank you for coming with me tonight. I really appreciated your assistance."

Smiling crookedly at him, I wrinkled my nose. "Even if I looked like a big red sore thumb?"

He let out a long breath. "Go to bed Brown. You're giving me a headache."

And then without another thought, he turned on his damned imperious heel and disappeared. I reached for an ashtray to throw at him, but I doubted it'd even dent him. Throwing my hands up in the air, I marched into my room.

I'd never understand that vampire.

It was a Sunday I finally took to go home, grab some more essentials, pay pending bills and clean my apartment. I was in the middle of dusting the tiny living room when I realized I was happily cleaning and humming under my breath. Screeching to a painful little halt I stood amidst the place that had been my own for the past four years since I moved to the big city. My home. My sanctuary.

My cozy little pigsty. It had always been cozily cluttered. Now in the two hours, I'd cleaned enough to see the rugs and the upholstery and even straightened the hanging pictures on the wall. No longer did they hang characteristically askew!

And there in the middle of my home, I was suddenly lost.

The walls were too white, the furniture too stark and the rugs too barren.

In the three weeks I'd been with the arrogantly affluent vampire, I'd lost my home.

The staggering realization hit me hard enough to sway me on my feet so that I had to grab the edge of a nearby chair and drop into it gasping.

It would be insanity to get attached to the warm browns of his home, the sumptuous breakfasts, the scintillating lunches and the long talks over mouthwatering dinners. Already I dreaded the coffee that would come out of my coffeemaker. My head dropped into my hands with abject remorse.

In those few hazy days, I'd been corrupted. I missed the warmth of his central heating. I longed for the plush softness of the four-poster bed he'd moved me into. The tall skyscrapers that greeted me every morning.

Oh dear god, I moaned.

I'd gone over to the dark side.

"Brown?"

The shriek exploded out of my chest, my legs tangling as I went sprawling into the weathered old rug.

Under the weight of his shoulder, my flimsy door gave way and I watched in humiliated fascination as he barreled into my little apartment with concern flashing across his face. "Brown!"

Wincing from my spot on the floor, I rose up on my elbows. "Down here."

Startled black eyes snapped down before crinkling at the corners. "And what an interesting place to be."

Glaring from the awkward sprawl, I held up one hand. "Don't be a jerk, be a gentleman. Give me a hand."

"Who said I'm a gentleman?" Raising an eyebrow, he held out the cold hand and lifted me up to my feet as if I weighed like the wind.

"The tabloids say you're quite the ladies man."

"Ah, so that is what you do in your free time. Research your boss."

Dusting my backside, I belatedly realized that he was standing in the middle of my living room in his refined threads and taking in each and every nook and cranny with childlike curiosity. "Why are you here anyway?" I had hoped to distract him from the fine scrutiny that swam in his eyes.

Momentarily distracted, he met my gaze and his mouth widened into a heart-stopping smirk. "There was something I needed to ask you," he clarified before darting around me in the blink of an eye. "What's this?"

Huffing and resisting the need to stamp my foot, I pulled the old soccer trophy out of his hands and placed it back on the mantle. "Honestly Jack, what are you doing here?"

"Honestly?" He turned halfway to look into my face. For a moment I saw the veils lift, and something dark stared down at me. Something I'd never seen on him before, his eyes inscrutable. "I don't know."

My little apartment was suddenly too small for this vampire's presence. I wondered how he'd managed to come inside without being invited. But he'd decimated every notion I had about the undead, so why not another. Deciding on changing the topic, I cleared my throat and stepped away from him. For someone dead and decrepit, he sure as hell smelled nice. "I thought vampires needed to be invited inside."

"Yes and salt is supposed to trap spirits," he twisted his mouth mockingly. He lifted one hand towards me. Going deathly still, I held my breath as a cold finger wiped a smudge from the bridge of my nose. "Been playing housewife?"

Flushing at the idiotic tremble in my bones, I frowned at the tip of his finger and took a deft step away from him. "I don't have an Adam to wait on me." Pointing to my simple two-seater couch, I hoped I looked as firm as I sounded. "Sit."

Black eyes twinkling with mirth, he obediently walked to the couch as I made a beeline for my bedroom.

But he made sure I heard the 'woof' before slapping my bedroom door close behind me.

To have Jackson Black as my pet was the absolute last thought I needed in my head. Morbidly fascinating.

Rummaging through my closet I settled on my favorite lived-in old blue jeans and tugged on a soft gray sweatshirt before gathering my hair into a high ponytail.

Ever since the benefit, something had been brewing in his black eyes as if he was trying to humanize himself for me. It unsettled me when he'd spent every day before that proving just how fantastic and inhuman he had been. From his retelling of history to the way he spoke of global politics and philosophy, everything besides him became insignificant.

So why was his presence in my apartment troubling?

Shaking myself out of my thoughts, I pulled open my bedroom door, determined to get to the bottom of his visit.

This time I had the good sense to stifle my shriek.

He stood there leaning one shoulder against the doorway, eyes dancing with mischief. Like he delighted in my jittery nerves. That was familiar.

Everything else was out of place, but then it had been unlikely for him to take me dancing.

Arms crossed, he arched a knowing eyebrow at my unflattering choice of clothes. Suddenly I felt silly for making it a point to be as imperceptible as possible. "Stop that."

His only answer was a leisurely sweep over my frame. Slowly taking in the unruly ponytail, the hunched shoulders, the invisible waist and the straight long denim-clad legs. Seething under the deliberate scrutiny that I knew was surely meant to unsettle me, I growled low under my breath. "Are you quite done?"

That only warranted another, more penetrating trek back up my body before meeting my eyes. "I assume it was deliberate."

I hated how he nailed everything on the head about how I felt. Crossing my arms defensively, I frowned irritably. "What is with you today?" Ducking past him I made a beeline for my tiny kitchen and opened the fridge to find something that would distract me. Grabbing the bottle of beer, I turned around and nearly dropped it in panic with a convulsive gulp.

The low chuckle was anything but human and if he was domineering in my apartment, in the kitchen he suddenly made me claustrophobic. The sound was not human and what was worse it didn't frighten me. Just unsettled me. Like something was going wrong. As if in response to the hitch in my heartbeat, he stepped further into the kitchen. "I should be asking you Brown; what is with you today? I've never seen you so jumpy."

"I've never seen you this pushy!"

He shrugged, but the smirk didn't waver. "I'm a vampire sweetheart. The fear feds the beast," he purred and my eyes widened abnormally, it was only the flash of triumph in his eyes that made me realize he was teasing. Testing my boundaries.

"I thought you despised that Disney analogy."

"Only because they got it wrong."

"Let me guess, the Beast was a vampire."

"No," his voice dipped lower and my bones chilled, "the Beast killed Beauty in her sleep."

I couldn't help the sharp stab of fear, but the sudden mental images were of him holding me down in the bed and drinking me dry. Christ, how did this creature go from man to monster in a matter of seconds? And why the hell didn't I stay?

"I'm not afraid of you," I offered feebly. Flattening my back against the closed refrigerator, I tipped the beer bottle back and took a hefty gulp.

My panic was palpable when he called my bluff and stepped closer. "You should be little girl."

And suddenly his intimidation game was sickening. My fear caught fire and turned to fury. "Newsflash Mr. Black," I bit out, eyes narrowed at his game. "I'm not a little girl."

But that's exactly what I felt like under the sudden expanse of the dark man as he leaned forward to play with the magnets that held my odd little lists and reminders. "Mmmmm," he murmured, "sometimes I wonder Brown. Sometimes I wonder if you're even real."

And then almost like he'd never been there, he was back in the living room inspecting my things.

Swallowing down the nervous lump in my chest, I frowned after him. What the hell was his purpose today? I glanced at the slightly open door of my apartment where the wood splintered when he'd come in. Not once had he apologized for the misunderstanding. "You broke into my house."

"I thought someone was with you."

My brow darkened at the loaded implication. "How?"

"Your heart."

Damn my heart. No damn his sensitive hearing. I couldn't say that I didn't like him anymore, but hated how he could read me without a single word spoken across my face. It was a kind of intrusion that went beyond his burst into my apartment uninvited.

Tipping my head back, I downed half of the beer. He was exhausting.

Even though I knew Jackson Black, I didn't know the man now exploring my apartment as if it was more captivating than history. He opened every drawer. Some of them he only glanced at, others he chose to touch the contents of with the tips of gloved fingers. I watched, mutely fascinated by the way he went over everything, his eyes not missing a thing.

It was disconcerting. More so than his diet.

His fingers trailed over the back of my couch, and it made me uneasy. As if he was touching more than just my couch. I'd fallen asleep there. I wondered if he knew. I'd cried there when I was watching 'Casablanca'. I'd made out with the first man I brought home.

He slid his hand over the back of the armchair, and I bit my lip. The memories there were just as palpable.

He examined every DVD, every CD beside the stereo. He ran one finger over the spine of every book on bookshelves that dominated one wall of the room.

He studied the photos hanging on the wall with the intensity of an art student. He stroked the soft throw I'd tossed over the arm of the couch.

Suddenly it was getting really hot in the kitchen. The heat flared under my skin uncomfortably.

Leaving him to his inspection, I stalked into my bathroom. Glaring at my flushed reflection, the unusual anger slowly bubbled in my belly. I wasn't territorial. Not usually anyway. So why the hell was it bothering me?

"For a moment, she let her lips hover over his until she heard him growl softly, then she brushed her lips against his once, twice, three times, more intimately each time."

My eyes snapped open in alarm as the sultry voice drifted out of my bedroom, and my heart thudded once in my chest.

He heard it.

Chuckling on the other side of the door he finished the paragraph. "His gloved hand slid around to fist in her hair, and she molded herself against his lean hard body, and slid her tongue into his mouth."

His chuckle morphed into a barking laugh as I burst out of the bathroom, snatching the paperback out of his hand. "Do you have to touch everything!?"

"Does it bother you?" He grinned; leaving no doubt that he already knew how much it bothered me.

"Of course it does!" I threw back disdainfully before stuffing the book back into my nightstand. "Snoop," I grumbled under my breath. But he heard me as usual.

"But don't you see Brown?"

Everything went deathly still as I felt his voice right behind me. It took every ounce of my strength to hold the nervous quakes. I didn't like him. I didn't like him at all. Not then. "See what?"

"There are many ways to look at things."

Turning around I meant to put him in his place, but my breath froze in my chest.

Crowding me against the nightstand, his voice dropped to a husky murmur, his grin maddening as ever. "You should know better that things aren't always what they seem." I should have panicked then, but I didn't. His eyes held mine, hypnotizing in their intensity. This was a side of the man I'd never seen. Or maybe this was the vampire. "Sometimes," he said as if following my train of thought, "one must touch things to truly understand them." He brushed his thumb over my cheekbone and I felt the blood rush back to my face.

Whatever spell he'd been weaving seemed to come to a crashing close when he touched me.

The asshole was pulling my leg. Because there was no way in hell he'd look down at me with the hunger that shined in his eyes. Like he wanted me. "You're a scoundrel, Jackson."

Snickering, he took a step back, thoroughly pleased with my accurate deduction. "I'm a vampire Brown."

Flattening one palm against the hard steel of his chest, I pushed him away and he let me pass. "Very good. You nearly had me forgetting."

"It's always good to have things in perspective." I didn't like what he was implying. Honestly, I didn't want to understand the reason he was here.

"I'll remember that." Furious at how easily I'd played into his intimidation games, I turned and glared hard at him. "Are you ready to tell me now why you're here? It is still my day off last I checked."

In his expensive suit, he dropped onto my bed, the shiny shoes up on my mattress. He stretched out as if he owned the place, hands braced behind his head. "I realized that there was an important human aspect of my life that I should have told you about."

I quirked an eyebrow. "Something that isn't insignificant?" I threw his words back at him.

His mouth twitched, but this time, he didn't grin. He could tell, it wouldn't go well. Far from it. A moment I stole to be the man I wanted to be."

"And it couldn't wait?"

He curled his lower lip in a makeshift shrug. "I might forget."

Scheming, manipulative leech! Tilting my head I decided to humor him. "Tell me."

"After I became your proverbial Beast." He grinned and I wanted to spit at him that he wasn't 'my' anything, but it might have been childishly defensive. "And before I went to Europe," he paused dramatically for effect, "I went to Algiers to meet Barbarossa."

"Whoa, whoa!" I held up my hand, effectively thrown for a loop. It was a norm when dealing with this man. "Barbarossa? As in Pirates of the Caribbean Barbarossa?"

"That was Hector Barbarossa, and for the record, must you Disney-fy everything I remember?" He reached out and picked up my alarm clock, twisting the hour hand to his whims.

Snatching it back from him, I placed it back on the table. "Let me get this straight," I sighed and pulled my desk chair to sit in. I took in his languid profile on the bed, "after being turned into a vampire, you became a pirate?"

Turning to me lazily his twinkling black eyes smiled. "Doesn't every little boy dream of being a pirate?"

It took me a moment to answer and I blame the rather debonair mental image I was battling of him in black pirate garb, complete with cutlass and eye patch. And some scrumptious leather pants. His mouth twisted into a knowing smile and I diverted my gaze in embarrassment. Conceited ass. I couldn't help the morbid curiosity that this man nurtured in me. So I used my secret weapon. When in doubt – hedge. "Did you have a pirate patch?"

"Funny you should ask," his fangs flashed with arrogance. "The eye patch was first worn by an Arab pirate Ramah ibn Jabir al-Jalahimah, who wore it after losing an eye in battle in the 18th century."

"The eye patch is..."

"Arabic origin," he smirked. "Bet Disney didn't tell you that."

I shook my head at his glee. "Sometimes I think you take heinous pleasure in destroying all my preconceived notions."

"A vegetarian vampire needs some way to get his thrills."

"Vegetarian my..."

The husky chuckle demanded that my heart fluttered with it as he fluffed the pillows and sat up slightly. "Now. How would you like to begin this history lesson?"

And he effectively reduced me to an inexperienced child. But it was a familiar sense of demotion that I was used to in his presence. "So you were in Algeria during that early 17th century when the Barbary Pirates were terrorizing the Black sea."

"Terrorizing?" He snorted. "That's a bit harsh."

I glared at his trivial tone. "You are not serious! The Barbary Pirates had more than 20,000 captives imprisoned in Algiers alone. The rich were allowed to redeem themselves, but the poor were condemned to slavery. Their masters would on occasion allow them to secure freedom by professing Islam. They were Crusading Taliban terrorists on water!"

146

"Can you be any less judgmental?" Jackson rolled his eyes. "The Taliban didn't even exist in Algeria until the 20th century which by the way is also a cause of western pressure."

"I am not battling religious politics with you Jack."

"You brought the Taliban into it."

He was infuriating. "Argh! Fine. Forget the Taliban, how can my calling them terrorists be harsh when they were responsible for a dozen American ships being captured, their goods being stripped and everyone enslaved? Considering how much you were against slavery in the confederation, I would think you'd realize they gave rise to slavery, to begin with."

"The Barbary pirates, or the Ottoman corsairs, were originally Muslim pirates and privateers that operated from North Africa, but not all of them. When I was there, there were Dutch, and there were Spanish. There were even Portuguese. Algiers was a safe haven for a lot of scum Brown, no one's denying that, but I will reiterate all my previous arguments that the times demanded their presence."

"That's how you justify their tyranny and debauchery!"

"Debauchery? That was only on all hallows eve." His smirk was depraved. "It was a night started with feasts and excellent spells of drunken revelry followed by a dance around the bonfire."

I didn't want to smile, so I held my lips in a thin line. "Of course it did." It unsettled me that the first thing his human instincts compelled him to do was maul and pillage. Maybe that's what his true purpose was tonight, as he'd hinted. To remind me of what he had been rather than who he was now.

"Naked," he added with extra relish.

It took every ounce of my willpower to not imagine the gorgeous vampire in his birthday suit dancing sinuously around a crackling fire. At the knowing smile on his face, I glowered and refused to be sidetracked. The mental image could be filed for future reference. "That's your universal excuse, isn't it?"

Rolling his eyes, he threw up his hands in defeat before rolling off the bed in one little move. Instantly I could see the man I argued politics with. The man, who cooked dinner for me. The man, who took me dancing. It was uncanny the way he shifted moods. "I don't know what your history books say Brown, but the continued piracy was due to competition among European powers. France encouraged the pirates against Spain, and later Britain and Holland supported them against France. In the 18th century, British public men were not ashamed to say that Barbary piracy was a useful check on the competition of the weaker Mediterranean nations in the carrying trade. I bet it'd surprise you to know that payments in ransom and tribute to the Barbary States amounted to 20% of United States government annual revenues in 1800."

147

Mouth dropping open, I considered denying his claim, but one thing I knew of Jackson Black. None of his facts were made up. And if I pushed, it would only mean endless hours digging in the library and then having to suffer under his smug satisfaction for weeks.

Biting down my naturally patriotic American sentiments I grit my teeth. "What does this have to do with Barbarossa anyway?"

"You asked me how I became a businessman." He absently toyed with the cosmetics on my bureau.

"I thought you ate a duke or something."

Infinitely amused and pleased with my retort, he wiggled an eyebrow at me. "That would have satisfied your morbid appetite, wouldn't it Brown?"

"You're one to talk."

Relishing my unease, he moved back to tower over me while I sat in my chair, like a warring goliath. "At about the time Spain was establishing its presidios in the Maghreb, the Muslim privateer brothers Aruj and Khair ad Din -- the latter known to Europeans as Barbarossa, or Red Beard--were operating successfully off Tunisia. I joined him before acquiring a fleet of my own."

"By acquiring you mean you stole."

His cackle was dark and sexy, clearly enjoying my tilting moral ruler. Jack patted my head in a degradingly reassuring way. "Rest assured my sweet." I swatted his hand away and the masochistic bastard only seemed pleased. "The dozen sunken American ships that you speak of eventually lead to the formation of the United States Navy in March 1794. So you see, everything is about cause and effect. It's political maneuvering. When you live as long as I do, you begin to see a pattern. The world doesn't change Brown." He smiled that devastating smile that was meant to weaken women and disarm grown men. I'm dignified enough to admit the world under my feet suddenly trembled. "It's just the weapons that change."

Already teetering on the edge of my wisdom and his ability to throw me off-balance I let him wrap one hand around mine and draw me to stand. "Now," he spoke confidently as his hands gently rubbed my knuckles. "You can type up those notes on the plane while I take care of a few business matters. I hope you don't get airsick, the cook makes a mean lobster."

Pulling out of the haze his eyes were starting in my brain, I frowned up at him. "Where are we going?"

The gorgeous mouth widened into a fiendish smirk as he triumphantly held the passport I had kept in my dressing table drawer. "Algeria."

To say I had barely ever made it out of the country was one thing, but the truth was I'd never been farther away from Chicago. Coming from a simple town outside of the most bustling cities in the country, I figured I'd seen everything. But then I stepped off the plane and instantly fell in love with Algiers. There's something about the city that would stay with me forever. Like the black and white streets of Casablanca, Algiers has its own sights and smells. Its own lure.

The airport brought us at least 20 kilometers inland. In the heart of the city.

From what little he'd told me on our ride to the port city, I knew that Algiers was built on the ground level by the seashore. White skiffs and yachts anchored in the crystal blue waters. On route N5 direct to Bab Ezzouar, the nondescript black car gently rolled towards the ports from the heart of the city.

"You seem lost."

"I'm soaking it in," I reassured him. The tall aging buildings seemed to speak secrets.

"I thought you might like it."

Glancing at his knowing smile, I frowned at the man. Today he was serene and patient. Like a damned parent hovering over me, pointing out sights, offering answers while I explored. I didn't understand half the reasons for his actions and it floored me that he would bring me along with him for a business trip. "Are you going to tell me why we're here?"

Sprawled in the backseat beside me, Jackson offered me a cursory glance. "There's a friend I need to see."

I can admit it. He was a formidable man in his element. It was the first time I got to see this side of the vampire that paraded as a man by morning. It humanized him more and worried me. Was it just wrong that while he was issuing orders with fatalistic finality, my eyes were glued to him? The folklore said that vampires had their lure, but I had a feeling any lure that Jackson Black possessed was because of the man he was and had become. The fangs and cold flesh only added to the enigma. But that didn't make him who he was. And the harder he pushed to remind me of the demon the most certain I was that he was afraid to let me see the man he was.

I was curious to know who he was because the 'mild-mannered farmer' claim didn't fit the sharp business mogul seated across in the opulent white leather of his private jet.

"That's great," I muttered. "Great time for a reunion."

My breath choked in my chest when his hand caught mine, fingers wrapping it, hard. Eyes darting up, I wondered if I should flinch, but his mouth was twisted into a confused, almost painful line, eyes narrowed on me as if he couldn't grasp something that was at the edge of his mind. "What do you want from me?"

The question wasn't as simple as it sounded.

I took care in choosing my words. "I want nothing from you Jackson. I never did."

The snort was mocking, but his hand loosened on my fingers and my breath evened. "I don't believe you, Brown! Everyone wants something."

I took a chance. "I do want something." The returning tension in his muscles was palpable. "But not from you Jack."

I'd meant to reassure him; instead, I met the scalding golden pools of his eyes. "Why not?"

Quirking an eyebrow, my mouth hitched up in a half smile. "Do you realize that your mood swings faster than a menopausal woman's?"

The laughter shimmered in those black eyes, but he didn't reach his mouth. "You're hedging."

"It's the best I do next to baiting."

His smile was sheepish. "I suppose I've been rather troublesome lately."

"You have." My eyes narrowed. "Are you ready to give me some answers?"

His hand gave mine one last squeeze before pulling away. "Not yet." Looking out of the window, he spoke again after a moment. "Do you know the reason I don't like the Beauty and the Beast analogy?"

"Too sweet?"

"You're not my prisoner Brown."

I couldn't help the chuckle. "I would have thought you'd say, 'you're not much of a beauty Brown.'"

He glared at me with an odd fire. "I can understand now why beauty comes with no brains."

I wasn't sure what he meant. Was Ismart or that I was ugly? I felt it prudent not to ask. His new thing seemed to be talking in riddles.

"For the record, you've already given me what I want."

His shoulders tensed. "What's that?"

"You've proven that the bogeyman exists."

Turning his head he frowned. "That shouldn't be a comforting thought."

"At least now I know what I'm up against." I chuckled at the anomalous affection in his voice. "I'm better prepared for what goes bump in the night."

"As if you weren't already a poster child for monster attacks."

I smirked. "Because I'm pretty?"

"Because you're suicidal," he retorted.

"How do you figure that?"

The eyebrow lifted archly. "You're traveling with a bloodsucker Brown. You pour me blood without flinching. You sleep under my roof without fear and I've yet you see you disgusted when I touch you." I had the sense to keep from reacting too much to that. "What you should be is afraid of me."

"I am afraid of you." I relaxed back in my seat. "But I know you won't hurt me."

"I can."

"Yes. You can, but you won't." I pulled my window down and let in the salty air pull my eyes shut. I didn't want to discuss this further. I didn't want him to convince me that he was the monster and I was a helpless victim. I was here of my own free will.

Right?

I'd thought we'd be staying in a quaint little hotel, but instead, I stood staring up at the buttresses as the man of the house gave me a tour.

Murat Haarlem was nothing like anything I'd ever seen before. Like something out of an old storybook, he kept an old browning manor in The Kasbah, a citadel some four hundred feet above sea level. Overlooking the newer parts of Algiers, the Kasbah formed a triangle with the two quays. Historically marked, Haarlem told me; the Kasbah sat right on top of the ruins of old Icosium, an ancient city said, to be founded by Hercules' companions.

It was like finding the cesspool of history and all I wanted to do was wade in.

So when I appeared enthralled Haarlem happily insisted on a tour.

Jackson had sourly refused.

"You seem distracted!"

I blinked at the soft smile in his words and turned to Haarlem's crystal blue eyes. "I do?" I'd already established, that he shared Jackson's culinary tastes; only that he wasn't a vegetarian. I had thought it would bother me, but the fact that Jackson trusted him to lead me through the winding passages of the old home with him, I wasn't overly stressed. Also, Haarlem had yet to appear anything but accommodating and sweetly thrilled to have my attention.

It helped that the man was beautiful. Not as finely chiseled as Jackson, but since he led the 'merry' life according to him, Haarlem was softer around the edges. He dressed in simple clothes, jeans and a collared shirt. Not as tall as Jackson, he was golden whereas my vampire was all chocolate and coffee. But it saddened me that Haarlem was happier. Maybe Jackson's dark disposition was a fair price to pay for his self-imposed restrictions.

Haarlem's eyes crinkled at the corners. "Worried about your friend?"

I couldn't help but frown at his accurate deduction. I didn't care what Jackson said about my heart. I felt like I was damned transparent. "We're hardly friends," I corrected him before turning back to the beautiful hand-painted panels. "You have a beautiful house."

"It was once a palace that belonged to a pirate named Simon the Dancer."

Hitching an eyebrow, I stopped beside a low chair, fingers grazing the soft velvet that covered the arms. "A dancing pirate?"

"Hardly," his chuckle was sardonic. "They say he moved quickly upon his feet. Almost like...a boxer would."

My breath stilled, my eyes cautious as his smile widened. "Are you toying with me Haarlem?"

His chuckle was positively gleeful. "I see now what he meant."

"About what?"

But he was already shaking his head. "Never you mind Emily Brown. How would you like to see the library?"

I was torn. Torn about staying right where I was to demand answers and my insane need to see what sort of treasures he had hidden away. "You're a cruel vampire Murat Haarlem."

Laughing uproariously, he wrapped one affable arm around my shoulders. "I wouldn't eat you sweetheart even if you came to me on a silver platter."

"Who said you would!?" I gawked at him.

"Jackson knows I have a weakness for pretty belles."

"Jackson's a wicked tease," I muttered sourly.

Everything about me seemed to amuse him. Just not in the same way as Jackson. Haarlem seemed to genuinely enjoy my company. It was a relief from the exhaustive pace I'd fallen into with Jackson. It was a welcome change. It made me smile more. "So this is his house?"

"It used to be my dear; until he wagered it on a pretty little bird with blonde curls."

My teeth ground together. "Good for you."

Snickering happily at how he'd found a partner against the dark surly vampire, he pushed open the doors to the library and took my breath away.

The lobster on the plane had been sumptuous, but it was nothing compared to the banquet Haarlem laid out for me the night we were supposed to leave. I found it sweet that the two men went through the motions of the dinner for my company when I could have been the main course. I learned not to take offense at the teasing hunger in Haarlem's eyes. He never apologized for it and the constant compliments that fell from his lips soon began to make me smile rather than blush.

He was easy to like and he had an astonishing way with women. I didn't need him to polish his skills on me to know how easily he must have won the house. Jackson's people skills left a lot to be desired, I didn't even want to think about how he must have been with his women. Demanding, mocking, arrogant, I wagered.

All through my meal, Haarlem spoke of his runs with Jackson on the Barbary Coast. His tales kept me sleeplessly entranced well into the night until the second round of coffee was served on the balcony that overlooked

Old Algiers, the new city beyond and the ocean that went on forever.

Staring out at the black horizon it wasn't hard to see the pirate ships moored in the harbors.

"Come back to me, Brown."

Like whiplash, my attention was snapped back to the dark man leaning on the stone paling beside me. Once before he'd spoken those words to me, but here in the timeless cracks of his life they took on a new disconcerting meaning.

I must have stared at him in startled awe because I felt Haarlem cut the tension deliberately as he came to stand beside me, a hand on my elbow turning me back to the horizon. "You're right to be fascinated, Emily." Dragging my eyes away from the disturbing heat in Jackson's gaze I let Haarlem point out the various sights of importance in Algiers. "It is a small city built on this very hill you stand on. It goes down towards the sea and divides in two there." He pointed to where the modern building built an illusionary wall. "The High city and the Low city. One can find masonries and mosques of the 17th century there. If you would like, I can take you to the Notre Dame d'Afrique tomorrow."

"No." Jackson's voice cut through the confusion that seemed to surround me between the two vampires. "Our flight leaves tomorrow morning."

"Come now Zymen, the flight is your own. You may leave when you please."

"It's Jackson now."

"Bah!" The golden vampire waved a casual hand. "I cannot keep track of all your names."

Gathering what was left of my bearing, I wrapped my hands around the warm mug of coffee. "Maybe next time Haarlem." I smiled reassuringly at him. Trying to soften the sudden steel in Jackson's voice. "I doubt even I can soak in all of Algiers in one visit."

His grin was pleased. "You are welcome anytime Emily."

"Thank you." I sipped the finely brewed coffee before interrupting whatever the dark vampire was about to growl. "Tell me about Simon the Dancer."

Jackson went deathly still.

The chuckle was knowing as Haarlem came to lean beside me on the paling. "He appeared on the Barbary Coast around 1580. After terminating his employment with Barbarossa, Zymen de Danseker became a Dutch privateer and freelance pirate on the Barbary coast."

"Freelance?" I turned towards him, forgetting that the very same man stood not two feet away from me, but I had a feeling this wasn't a story I was going to get from Jackson. He liked to speak about the world as it was; never his role in it. It was strangely gratifying to hear, who he was rather than where he was.

"Simon the Dancer attacked ships of any nation and made trading in the Mediterranean Sea increasingly difficult for everyone. Many therefore looked for ways to stop his attacks with bribes for safe passage or even employing him as a privateer in their navy. They commandeered his services because in his time, Zymen, or Simon as the English liked to call him, was one of the finest and deadliest of pirates."

"That's enough Murat."

"Ignore him Haarlem," I leaned closer to the blonde vampire who had a hard time holding his smile.

"The Turks nicknamed him the Dali-Capitan which means Devil-Captain. After three more years of pirating, he had become quite rich and lived in an opulent palace. The only pirate to have such ties to the coast. He became very rich very fast."

I couldn't help but turn to the vampire behind me who seemed to be contemplating murder as he looked at his smirking friend. "Didn't eat Arthur Owen Bentley, huh? *This* was your pretense of a human life?" Why did it feel like he'd lied to me? What the hell had I expected from a demon?

Scathing black eyes snapped at me. "Don't sound so betrayed, Brown. It wasn't personal."

"Oh drop it, will you Jack?" With an intolerant breath, I leveled my glare at him. "Your holier-than-thou attitude is not fooling anyone. You were a vampire. You weren't a saint and you certainly aren't now. I already know that. It would be a lot less tedious for all of us if you would just let it go. I know what and who you are. You have nothing to prove to me. Besides, you're not exactly doing a prime job of it with your confused mood swings. When you decide on what you want me to believe you are – a monster or a man, you let me know."

I smacked the half-empty mug of coffee on the trolley and walked to the balcony doors.

"Personally?" Pausing on the threshold, I turned back to him, the two starkly different vampires watching me guardedly. "I like the combination of both; because that's what you are. And your story will not be complete without either."

I was halfway into the room before he called out to me. "Wait."

I sighed. Always delaying till the last possible moment. Turning back to the balcony I watched him with tolerant resolve. When he seemed to struggle with the rest of his words, I raised an eyebrow.

Rolling his eyes, the man growled low under his breath. "Get your ass back out here Brown, the story's not finished."

I couldn't help it.

Laughing like a jacked-up hyena, I walked back into the night and stood between the two vampires as if death didn't flank me from all corners.

It was easier to be around him since Algiers. There was a lighter side of him then. As if he had less to prove to me, and more to tell me. Of course, our growing camaraderie and understanding didn't lessen his arrogance.

He threw back his head and laughed.

Like a belly-aching, roaring laugh that echoed off the walls for long mocking minutes.

I didn't think it was possible for a vampire with no breath in his lungs. Jerk.

"You think this is funny Jack?"

"Maybe not entirely funny," he paused to snicker some more as he leaned against the window in the study, the moon casting silver glows around him as usual, "but it is very entertaining. Little Miss Brown, tussling with another one of her moral dilemmas."

Did I mention that sometimes, I really hated this guy? "So you abandoned Haarlem in his mission and let *him* live?"

"I didn't let anyone do anything." Sipping the last of his blood, his grin was feral. Oddly becoming on him. "He failed to kill Hitler in forty-four because Hitler wasn't meant to die."

I snatched the empty wineglass from him as he sat there twirling it. Hoping to keep my hands busy unless I gave in to the need to strangle him. "The damned monster was responsible for the deaths of 43 million people, including the systematic genocide of an estimated six million Jews as well as various other groups of people. Haarlem had a chance to stop the Holocaust but you didn't lift a damn finger for some misplaced belief in destiny?" Furious with his twisted reasoning I walked to the decanter and poured him another glass.

Rolling his eyes, Jack plunked down in his favorite chair. "Come now Brown, you can't really buy into that tawdry, guilt-ridden melodrama he was spouting!"

"Oh right!" I nearly smacked the glass against his chest, but he caught it in time before it spilled on his black silk shirt. "I forget I'm talking to the only guilt-free man in the western hemisphere."

"Not true." With a tiny knowing smile, he gently wrestled my fingers off. "Guilt is just something I abandoned in the eighteenth century."

Shaking my head at his complacency I couldn't believe this was the same brooding man I'd walked in on that night six weeks ago. "I can't believe you! You could have prevented it all!"

"Oh come on!" His calm humor melted into a scowl as he took a hefty sip, tongue sliding over his elongating fangs and like most nights, it only registered, and didn't unsettle. "It entirely too arrogant to imagine that one man can alter the course of history."

"You cannot talk of arrogance." Leaning over him as he had over me on more than one occasion, I braced my hands on the arms of his chair and met his eyes dead on. "And you cannot deny that killing him would have saved thousands if not millions of lives."

His mouth twisted into an amused sneer. "Yes, maybe Germany would have won the war if they'd killed him in forty-three like Rommel wanted." He bent forward, his cold nose nearly brushing mine. I would probably go cross-eyed but there was no way I was backing down. "History makes men sweetheart. Men don't make history."

"Bah!" I shoved myself away and threw up my hands in defeat. "I don't care for your philosophical mumbo jumbo."

"It's not philosophical Brown. It's what I've been saying since the beginning. I'm talking about the time." He came out of his chair emphatically, following me in the wake of my pacing. "For the Germans; you have to understand that the time was right, the zeitgeist. If it hadn't been a little painter from Austria, it could have been anyone! A shopkeeper, or a gardener. Hitler himself wasn't much of a leader. He failed sixth grade for crying out loud."

I stopped pacing long enough to turn and glower at him. "Are you making a point anytime soon?"

"My point is," he smiled indulgently, hands holding my shoulders, one also dangling the wineglass of blood over my nice new sweater he gave me for Christmas, "it doesn't matter. The time needed a Fuhrer."

"You really are an arrogant pain in the ass sometimes."

Snickering he downed the glass in one gulp and shrugged. "You're just sporting a little tunnel vision, Precious. Killing is killing. No one knows it better than I do."

"Why? Because you're a vampire?"

"Are you claiming the ends justify the means?" He snorted. "If that's your argument Brown, it's not very original."

"I'm only saying that without him, the world would be a better place!"

"Hmmm," he contemplated that and for a second I thought I'd finally won an argument before he continued, "that's what he thought, didn't he; about the Jews? What was his name, Adolf, something or the other?"

I picked up the cushion and smacked him with it.

Adam bringing me my evening tea was just in time to see it and crashed into an end table.

I suppose it was shocking.

I'd made friends with the vampire.

He hadn't been kidding when he said he was nocturnal. And it didn't help that by keeping his hours I was already falling asleep during my breakfast. This naturally meant that at nearly two in the morning, I was awake and wandering into the kitchen alone.

With my head poked into the refrigerator, I reached for the bottle of milk before I saw the neat rows of thick congealing red liquid at the bottom in unmarked jars. Despite how long I'd been used to it, it still turned my stomach.

I couldn't help but murmur to myself, "My god is that..."

"Yes is it."

With a shriek, I spun around in fright, the glass bottle slipping from my fingers.

One dark hand caught the bottle and the other wrapped around my upper arm before I went sprawling into the refrigerator.

White teeth flashed at me in the pallid light. "A tad skittish aren't you?"

I would have answered but I was otherwise occupied.

Pressed intimately close to the unsettling cold heat of his body, I stared up into his eyes stupidly while he set me rightly on my feet and kicked the refrigerator door shut. When I hadn't spoken or looked away from his face, the black eyes flickered with the endless amusement that I seemed to be to him before maneuvering me towards one of the stools that lined the huge black marble counter islanded in the middle of the kitchen. Setting me down firmly on the little round seat, his mouth twitched as he set the milk bottle in front of me. "Cookies?"

I remember nodding numbly as he walked over to one of the cabinets and reached up for the box of chocolate chip cookies.

And I changed everything when I looked at his ass.

Contrary to popular belief, I'm not an idiot. I know when I stare at a man's ass. I know when I want him. And I know why.

Just so the record is straight, I had been in conversation with this enigmatic vampire for nearly two months, traveled with him, ate with him, argued with him and had completely made peace with the fact that he drank blood to survive and possessed various superhuman powers that could snap me like a toothpick. But I'd never seen so much of him before.

Clad only in simple white cotton drawstring pajamas that hung agonizingly low on his narrow hips, he was not the same black-garbed vampire I sat in the study with.

This was a deliciously structured African night god carved out of sinful black chocolate.

Holy shit!

Shaking myself out of my suddenly traitorous train of thought, I mourned the sudden quirk of his eyebrow when I realize he could probably hear the change in my skittering heartbeat. I had to remind myself that this man appealed to me on an intellectual level. Of course, it didn't help that he was absolutely yummy to look at and the fact that I'd finally gotten around the whole concept of 'monster' and sexless corpse to mouth-watering and blunt want. The sudden realization that he was beautiful and I had finally fallen (and not just in front of the refrigerator or my living room) sent me stumbling away from the stool in horror.

He stood there for a moment in the stark light of the kitchen, head tilted to the side curiously, black eyes silently questioning as I put some distance between us.

Then he stiffened.

I could tell he read the naked fear in the stiffness of my muscles and the gasping breaths I was drawing, but I could also see that the reason eluded him. Grateful once that his in-human powers didn't extend to mind reading I tried to rein in some control over my screaming pulse and erratic hormones. Maybe I was premenstrual. That was all, I reassured myself. A natural reaction to the flawless chest, dark scintillating skin stretched over natural, lean muscle and perfectly proportioned bone structure. As soon as my hormones returned to their simple state of homeostasis in my blood, I'd be normal again, and he'd be a walking corpse again. Yes, I told myself. It was only a matter of time.

It couldn't be more than chemicals. Could it?

"Brown?"

"Emily!" I suddenly snapped furiously with his serenity.

Caught off guard by my biting tone, he carefully placed the box of cookies on the counter and stood back. Face a mask of caution he held my gaze firmly as if I was a skittish deer. "Tell me what's wrong."

"I need tomorrow off."

Confused at my request, he asked his favorite question. "Why?"

"I just do." It was irrational and childish to blame him for my epiphany but the truth was that I couldn't afford to fall for anyone right now, least of all a know-it-all, elitist vampire to whom I was a mere annoyance and a necessity. "I'll compensate on Sunday."

There was a flash of misplaced hurt in his onyx eyes before his brow darkened at me with brusque disappointment, his usually husky voice clipped. "You're not a prisoner here, Brown. You can go as you please. In fact, if this is becoming unpleasant for you, I'll pay you now and you can go away."

The sharp stab of pain reminded me that I needed to be clear. "Please don't misunderstand, I'm not quitting."

"Maybe you should."

It was suddenly hard to breathe as I blinked at him in shock. "Do you want me to?"

He shrugged indifferently. "Leave your notes behind."

Thunderstruck, I stared at him. "Dammit Jack, I'm not quitting!" Despite the discomforted blood singing in my veins and the need to run compelling me away, I took a step towards him. "I'm asking for a day off! Just a day off!"

His knowing eyes cut back to mine sharply. "Why?" My heart skipped a beat before climbing up onto a roller coaster and his eyes narrowed. "There." He pointed an accusing finger at my chest. "Why is it doing that?"

"I don't know," I lied.

"You realize Brown, that by now I know every hitch in your breath and every beat of your heart. It's not easy to deceive me."

I looked up at him sharply, my heart thudding low at the implication. But I there was no implication. He was a vampire. Hearts were just another way to read me like people read faces. For him it was intrinsic. Not intimate like it was to a human.

The telltale heart!

"I just need some fresh air, Jack."

His arm lifted with precision. "The balcony is that way."

Fisting my hands to keep from hitting him, I glowered. "Jack, I just need some space."

"Why?"

"Argh!" Running a frustrating hand through my hair, I turned my back to him and tried to calm my breathing. It was like talking to a brick wall. How could two people or one person and one non-person have such a meaningful conversation but not be able to communicate coherently? Damn human hormones! "It's so hard to talk to you sometimes!"

"Just today apparently."

And then I really wanted to hit him. The compulsion was teeth jarring. Rubbing my temples, I tried to calm down. "God, please. Not right now. I just need a day off to gather my thoughts; I'm not quitting. I want to finish this book."

"I'll pay you in full."

My fury exploded as I took an impulsive step towards him, my teeth bared at him in a snarl.

The cocky eyebrow that usually was sexy on him was another log in my fiery temper.

It must have been quite a picture I presented standing there in my baby blue pajamas and bedraggled hair trying to pretend to mirror a certain vampire, but it was involuntary. I had already risen up to his level, my nose nearly touching his as I hissed at him. "I am not leaving!"

"You can if you want to."

And just like that the fire was smothered in my veins. Suddenly I was too tired.

I blame lack of sleep. I blame my unreliable female hormones because as I'd stepped up to him to do some serious bodily damage, I was now slumping against him, my hot forehead resting against his chest as I groaned in defeat. "I would have thought that besides our professional relationship, I had come to be your friend," I whispered almost too softly for anyone to hear, but I knew he heard me just fine. "I don't want to leave."

"Wolves don't make friends with little girls. They eat them," he pointed out in his usual morbidly philosophical way.

"I make friends with whomever I please." But where my voice should have held promise, it only sounded defeated. I couldn't miss that he didn't even bother to touch me as I stood there with my head leaning against him. He might as well have been made of marble and here I was trembling like a little girl. How amusing it must be to him. But I knew that he wouldn't allow me to chicken out of an explanation. So for his sake, I tried.

"I'm not as worldly or smart as you to keep this impersonal Jack. I enjoy your company. I always have. And I'm only asking for time off now because I just realized I'm very close to losing something else."

"Your sanity?"

"My dignity, to begin with." As I wanted to hedge, but I couldn't.

I allowed him a moment to wallow in his victory before I grabbed the earth under his feet firmly – and yanked. "But also, my heart."

I had expected the reaction, but it didn't hurt any less.

Like I'd burnt him, he took a wide step away from me, his beautiful face twisted like I'd socked him for a heartbreaking few seconds.

Then he seemed to compose himself.

With a deep breath, I looked away from him. It almost hurt to see his disappointment. He'd think it was tawdry, the human, falling for the vampire; Typical.

"I'm sure it's not new to you, but I hope in my case you'll believe me when I say that it's my problem. I will handle it, Jack. You don't need to worry."

"What isn't new to me?" He barked.

With a wince, I hoisted myself up on the stool and sat there as I opened the box of cookies dejectedly. "Women falling in love with you. Five hundred years of it." I peered at the cookie, glaring at the way it was brown and delicious like him. I had a feeling this had been creeping up on me for a while. How the hell did I miss it? "Anyway, I hadn't consciously decided to go down this road with anyone much less you, but I blame your shirtless state and the good lighting in this kitchen. Until last night I thought the Nile was just a river." I laughed drily at the joke. "So imagine my surprise when my heart dances the flamenco. Epiphanies can be a real pain. But you already knew that. Telltale heart." I bit moodily into the cookie and delighted in the flare of sweet chocolate on my tongue. It was like slow torture. How appropriate.

When he didn't speak, I lifted my eyes warily. "I just needed a day off to compose myself before what happened here...happened. But since it's too late now – I'll see you tomorrow. Same time." Picking up the box of cookies, I smiled weakly at him. "Mind if I take the cookies to bed?"

He only looked back, his face devoid of all feeling.

I feared my flinch was a little too obvious so I tucked the box of chocolate chip cookies firmly under my arm and saluted him. Then turning on my heel I marched out of the kitchen to drown my sorrows in chocolate.

If he wanted to fire me, I'd have to figure it out in the morning.

I'd probably fallen asleep in the cookie crumbs because everything around me was a rich brown.

"Mmmm, Jack."

"Stop hugging the damned pillow."

I frowned. Pillows were not supposed to talk. Cracking one eye open I squinted up in the darkness. Oh, bother, it was just Jack. Burying my face in the pillow I hugged it tightly. Just Jack.

"Get up, Brown."

I wanted to flip him off, but that would require me to forfeit my hold on the fluffy Jack.

"Emily?"

My name brought me crashing back to earth.

"Ahhh!" Head snapping up I rubbed my eyes to clear the sleep. That couldn't be him. Could it? "Wha..." Blinking in the darkness, I faintly made out the familiar shape silver-lined with moonlight. The silver light bounced off his perfectly shaped bald head. It couldn't be anyone else but him. "Jack?"

"You sleep like a rock."

With a groan, I touched my aching head before blindly reaching for the little clock on my bedside. "Jack," I whined, "it's four in the morning. I went to bed like two hours ago."

"Get up."

Frowning up at him, my eyes finally adjusted to the dark, I saw the harsh light of his eyes. "What? Why?"

"I have to show you something."

"Now?" I peered down at the clock again. "Can't this wait?"

"Would I be here if it could?"

Sitting up straighter I realized that he was right. He wouldn't be here. Why was he here? I took in his determined countenance in confusion. Then to my abject shock, he stood up and pulled my closet open, rifling through my belongings. "Hey, what are you doing?" Before I could climb out after him, my thick long coat hit me in the face.

"Put that on. It'll be cold."

Wrenching it off my head, I glowered up at him. "No. Not until you tell me where we're going."

Muscular arms crossing across his chest, he regarded me with a deliberate challenge. "Are you coming out or am I coming in?"

My jaw dropped at his insinuation as I tried to tell him off, and then realized that having Jackson Black in my bed might not be a bad idea. Narrowing one eye at him, I gave him a smile, which I hoped was coy rather than hopeful. "Will the results be the same either way?"

"If you mean my dragging you out by the scruff of your neck?" His onyx gaze burned. "Possibly."

Wrinkling my nose at his inability to play fair, I grumbled about fossilized old men.

Jack took a step forward menacingly and I went tumbling out of my little bed. "Okay! Okay, I'm up." Marveling at the odiously capricious man, I shoved my hands through the coat and had barely stepped into my old pumps before he grabbed my arm and proceeded to drag me out.

"Hey!" I struggled in his firm grip. "I resent being handled like a sack of flour!"

"Sacks of flour get thrown over the shoulder." He paused at the front door and raised an eyebrow. "Is that what you would like?"

Huddling in my warm coat, my eyes darted away from him. "Um…no."

The elevator ride was eerily silent. The silence brought back the horror I'd experienced in his kitchen not two hours ago. There was no other reason for this midnight escapade. He was trying to let me off easy.

Or he could just be leading me to an indiscriminate spot so he could suck me dry.

Either way, the silence wasn't heartening. I wondered if I should ask him where we were going, but I figured he could hear the nervous hitch in my heartbeat. He would have offered information if he had wanted to.

Then I noticed something odd. We were going up.

When the elevator opened to the last landing, I shivered half out of dread and more out of the sudden chill that blasted me.

Without looking back at me, Jack walked out onto the building's roof. Like the rest of the old building, the roof was as ornate with white plaster carvings now graying in the constant onslaught of the weather. Rubbing some feeling back into my arms, I saw Jack pause besides the railing. I gazed at his strong back in the thin black sweater, the sleek non-wrinkle black pants and bare toes. My, but the man had nice toes.

"Brown?"

Startled out of my fantasy I met those inscrutable black eyes as he held one hand out to me in a rather dramatic fashion. "Come."

What the hell was I? A dog?

"Wait." Staying rooted to my spot, I held up my hands as if to pause whatever he was leading up to. "Look, I'm willing to go wherever it is that people go to at four in the morning in their pajamas, but I need to know what you're planning." He turned to face me. "If this is about what happened in the kitchen, I told you already that it's no big deal. I can handle this. And if this is about the Benefit, well YOU should have told me about the black-and-white theme." He took a step closer to me and my heartbeat went careening off balance. Christ, he looked like a black panther. A very sexy, extremely ticked-off, Black Panther. "Unless this is about something completely different," I provided with a nervous swallow. He was getting closer. "In which case, I would appreciate it if you would tell me what it is that went wrong so that I can__" My breath and words choked in my throat when he stood there a few centimeters away, gazing down at me like I was insane.

"Brown?" He leaned down and my eyes widened as his sweet breath wafted across my mouth, lips parting to welcome it into my lungs. But he merely offered me a slanted look before scooping me up in my arms. "Shut up."

And my world tipped off its axis.

Clinging to the wide span of his shoulders, I buried my face into the crook of his neck as the wind threatened to take me away from the solid feel of him. Because nothing around me was solid except for him. I'd only kept my eyes open until he'd made the first leap from the roof before landing perfectly on another some forty feet away.

I'd always known he wasn't normal, but the blunt display of his inhumanity was like a metal-layered fist in my gut. But even with the absolute dread flooding my system, I realized that it wasn't him I was afraid of. What frightened me was the idea of falling fifty floors to my death without a parachute in sight, but his hold never faltered.

With one arm wrapped under my shoulders and the other under my knees, he carried me effortlessly across the Chicago rooftops.

And then the mad jumping and stomach-flipping landings stopped instantly. Although I was pretty sure my stomach or my heart, one of the other, had been left on that last roof. The fact that I felt more than heard the soft rumble of laughter in his chest meant that there was probably no room to even insert a spatula between us.

"You can let go now."

Unable to surrender my death grip on his shoulders, I shook my head spasmodically, again palpably feeling his impatience. "We're here," he added helpfully before dropping my legs and prying my arms away from his shoulders.

I will hate myself for it all my life, but my knees buckled and slid down the length of his body before falling flat on my face, staring up at his startled face. "Brown?" Squatting down beside me, he frowned before grabbing my shoulders and sitting me up.

"And you had problems with my driving," I spit out nastily.

Mouth quirking at the corners, he slowly straightened to his full height, his hands holding my arms firmly this time. "I figured I should protest for propriety's sake."

"Good job."

"Anytime." Steadying me experimentally, he stepped away to look into my face. "I forgot you human women had weak dispositions."

"Hey buddy, my disposition was perfectly sound when I left it on that last rollercoaster loop." I poked him in the chest, making sure to keep my weight equally balanced on both feet. "Let it come back to me and I'll be just fine."

He grinned wickedly and I realized that the death-defying trip was probably deliberate. Maybe he'd meant to rattle me because it worked. Grabbing my hand, he led me down a metal staircase. "Watch your step."

Keeping one hand firmly on the rail, I finally looked around only to blink in alarm. "A printing press?"

"The Chicago Times."

Eyes slingshot back to him, I stared in horror. Oh dear god, he'd brought me here to leave me. He was going to fire me and leave me as a 'good morning' gift for Mac so they could laugh about it like old friends later. Or maybe he intended to leave me bleeding on his desk as a reminder.

Pausing in our descent, he frowned up at me. "What the hell are you thinking?"

Gulping down the hysteria, I held his eyes anxiously. "Why?"

"Because your heart is doing that caged bird thing." His eyes hardened. "If I was going to eat you, Brown, you'd be good and digested by now."

I felt bad suddenly. It was true. He'd been nothing but tolerant of me so far. But that didn't really stop the spiraling fear in my belly. That meant he was going to leave me behind.

Rolling his eyes at my incessantly erratic heartbeat, he turned back and proceeded to drag me down the stairs and through the huge presses. "Have you heard of the Newsies?"

"I saw the Disney movie."

"They got it pretty accurate actually."

"I only watched it because I had this huge crush on Christian Bale." His feet smoked to a halt and I collided with his hard back. "Awo!" I held my nose; eyes squeezed shut against the sudden flash of colors. "You broke my nose."

Snorting exasperatingly, he batted my hands away and pinched my nose lightly between his fingers before sighing. "It's fine," he muttered grumpily. "Now will you kindly stop interrupting?"

Grumbling about overgrown musclemen, I let him lead me around to a printing press and positioned me in front of the dark silent giant. With his hands on my shoulders, he held me. "Stay," he commanded and then left me there in the semi-dark.

"Woof," I mumbled under my breath, but the crash behind me was proof that he probably heard me.

For a few nail-biting minutes, I looked around me in panic. What if he did leave? What if I stood there waiting like an idiot forever and he never came back?

And then like a match was struck, light erupted around me. Blinded momentarily I held one arm up over my eyes before slowly opening them as the giants began to groan and come to life.

Gaze slowly sliding up over the huge rollers, I watched the papers moving with lightning speed, pictures blurring all around me as I stood there in the middle of the huge press facilities that I'd never really seen before. I knew that Chicago Times had a huge setup, but I didn't know how big. Like a little kid on a field trip, I drank in the sheer expanse of the facility in awe.

It was only when my eyes made one complete pass over the entire scene before me that I saw him standing there beside me. Like a dark, beautiful Greek statue he stood there staring down into the press in front of me, his face unreadable.

My brow wrinkled. "Jack?"

With a sigh, he turned his head and looked down at me. "They've already run the story, but I wanted to see what you thought of it."

Both eyebrows hiking up, I waited patiently for him to make sense, but when he offered no other explanation, I blinked. "What story?"

Shaking his head at my apparent stupidity, he reached forward and picked up a copy of the newspaper that the press had just deposited in a neatly bound pile. Snapping the front page open, he thrust it at me with enough force to make me jump back, but I caught it in time to see the picture glaring up at me.

The blood drained from my face when I caught the headline above it. 'JACKSON BLACK'S LADY IN RED!'

"Oh my god!"

I stared in horror at a perfect shot of Jack twirling me around the dance floor, his mouth parted slightly against my temple, one hand splayed against my lower back, the other holding my hand close to his heart while I draped over him with a horribly lovesick smile on my face.

I looked positively scandalous. Like a groupie! Of course, he felt compelled I saw it. This is what he'd been seeing and here I thought I was handling being in love with him so carefully.

But more than that I stared at the odd fit we seemed to make. Besides his sinful dark good looks, impeccable shave and cut, I was a trim, pale woman with tumbling mahogany curls pinned on her head in a knee-length red dress that stood out like a beacon in its surroundings.

It was then that I realized I was the only color in the picture and even though I paled in comparison to his good looks, I was no cockroach.

"Do you believe me now?"

Slowly I lifted my stunned brown eyes up to him. "They think I'm your..."

"When I make an appearance at a Benefit for the first time in seven years with a stunning woman in a red dress, I'm bound to make the front page."

I wondered about the stunning part. "But I'm just a..."

"You're never just anything, Brown." He shook his head sadly. "But I've never understood how you can be so damned clueless."

Staggering under the sudden onslaught of too much information, I wobbled on my feet, the newspaper held uselessly beside me. "I don't understand. You knew this would happen?"

"I anticipated it."

"But then why did you let me go with you?"

Running a frustrated hand over his smooth skull, the vampire with all the answers turned away, troubled. "I should have told you to turn around and go back to your damned room. I should have told you that in the red little number, you were begging to be eaten."

Mouth gaping at the knowledge that he had known, I stood there rooted to the spot. "Why didn't you say anything?"

"Because I didn't want to!" He snapped, whipping around to glower at me. The black onyx of his eyes was flashing with hellfire. "Because you smiled that wide smile at me like I'd given you the goddamn world. Because I didn't have it in me to make you go back and change when you looked..."

My mouth ran dry when he paused, his face tormented. Heart fluttering madly, I looked back at him. Unblinking. "Looked what?"

Throwing up his hands he began to pace. "This is insane!"

"Looked what, Jackson?"

"Brilliant!" He growled, only there was no menace in this voice this time. Only defeat. "You were the brightest and the most beautiful thing I'd seen in a long time and trust me sweetheart; I've been around for a while."

"I don't understand."

His hands caught my shoulders and shook me. "That's it, Brown. You don't understand. THIS is what I am!" His snarl completely changed his face, the fangs flashing at me with wicked intent. The bones in his face became more prominent, eyes glowing gold. "This is what I'm used to! I should have known there was something wrong with you the moment you wanted to touch me while I was primed to suck you dry! I should have known something must have been disconnected in your head because when you saw the monster, I didn't hear your damned heart jump in fear like I know it should. Like it does when I tell you to go home!" He shook me again, nearly rattling my teeth and making me gasp. "I came into your house that day to remind you of what I was but the thought of someone else being with you; I reacted before I knew what I was doing. Taking you to Algiers was a stupid thing to do. I should never have introduced you to Murat! Everything I did then was deliberate and you have the audacity to stand there in front of a five-hundred-year-old man like a damned martyr and say that you've lost your heart to the monster and you'll handle it? You can't handle anything, Brown. You never could!"

I winced when his fingers bit into my arms. "I never asked you for anything."

"No." He bit out as if it pained him to say it. "You said you understood how I must be used to women declaring their undying love to me after living five hundred years, but you were wrong!" He hissed, eyes holding mine captive, the heat flaring under my skin as I felt panic and fear and longing crash into each other before filling every crevice of my being. "I can live five hundred years or five thousand, but all I've ever gotten from a woman is fear, lust, and blood! I'm the perfect predator. My prey desires me the utmost. But never love. It's an uneasy alliance until the end."

"The end?"

"Until I kill you. And trust me when I say this sweetheart, if you stay with me I WILL kill you. It's only a matter of time."

"Oh."

"Oh!?" He snarled, leaning close enough to show me the golden flecks growing richer in color. To see the muscle, pulse spasmodically in his temple. "After all of that, all you can say is 'oh'? Damn you, Brown. Does self-preservation mean anything to you?"

I whimpered softly. "I'm sorry if you're not scary enough! How the hell am I supposed to downshift to terror when you look like that!"

"I don't want you to fear me, Brown," he scowled and jerked away from me, putting considerable distance between us. "Fear I can deal with, but you, I cannot deal with."

"What are you doing?" I whispered in escalating panic. "Is this some pathetic prelude to you firing me for my own good?"

"It's my book. I decide when it's done. And I say it's done." He looked down his nose at me, imperiously. Like I was a worm he'd just discovered.

"You can't do that!"

He cocked an eyebrow. "Can't I?"

Stepping up to him, I glared up at him pointedly. "Listen to me you pompous ass, if my heart is suffering palpitations in your presence it's my problem. Why the hell are you making such a big deal about this?"

"I'm a vampire!" He thundered.

Wincing at the near-deafening roar of his voice, I held up a hand, the other wrapping the coat tighter around me. "No need to shout. I know you're a vampire."

"Do you, Brown? Do you really?"

I couldn't help the defeated sigh. "If it makes you feel any better, I don't care."

His eyes hardened. "No, it doesn't make me feel any better," he spat distastefully.

And then my breath froze in his lungs as he leaned down with blunt speed. I could tell just by the hiss of his breath against my jugular that it was meant to be a warning. "Do you know what your blood smells like to me now that you've said it's mine?"

Smothering the tremble I tried to keep from jerking away or worse leaning into him as he continued his intimidation games. "Should I get the violins going?"

Cold, confident fingers slipped into my coat and I couldn't help the gasp of breath, my own confidence going up in smoke when those chilled digits slid up to press against the unsteady thumping of my heart. Various curses choked in my throat as he purred against my skin.

"Do you know what it sings to me?"

Swallowing against the sudden dryness of my throat, I licked my lips. "I'm partial to Queen."

The cold heat was gone in the blink of an eye, leaving my skin flushing. A few feet away the onyx eyes blazed with fury. "You are the stupidest girl I've ever met."

"It's a human trait," I retorted as my breath slowly and steadily became normal again. I wanted to slap him for that conceited display of prowess. It didn't help that his mere proximity made me weak in the knees. If he did decide to eat me, I had a feeling I wouldn't so much as move a muscle. I didn't like the lack of control over the situation. But he'd caught me off guard before. Now I had a better idea of what he was leading up to. "For the record, if this is really is an attempt to safeguard the stupid naïve girl, then I suggest you give it a rest. You should have thought of that when you didn't let me leave."

"I!?" He stepped back as if I'd socked him, aghast.

And my anger returned. "Yes you, you pompous arrogant leech! You've had plenty of time to send me away." He blinked at the violent outburst but I was on a roll. "Don't play the gentleman with me."

"When have I ever been anything but?"

"Please! If you really wanted me gone, you should have never called me back the first night we met."

"You cannot be immature enough to think that I expected to declare my undying love to you."

And even though the thought hadn't crossed my mind, his words stabbed just the same. "Well, I never expected to declare my undying love to you either. Mr. Black; yet here we are." I spread my arms around as if I had nothing to hide. "To tell you the truth, I was perfectly fine being your employee until you decided to personalize our association. You're right. It is your fault. Do you really think I'm that childish or naïve to think that you couldn't find a date at the last minute?"

He didn't even have to flinch, but the light in his eyes was a testament that I'd hit the nail on the head.

"You know contrary to popular belief," I spat at him venomously; "I am not that naïve and neither am I stupid. I knew what you were doing that night. When I walked out in that inappropriately red dress; I saw you. If I looked like you'd given me the world, then you stood there and smiled at me as if that was exactly what you had planned to do in the first place! Before that night, I had nothing but scholarly interest in you. YOU changed everything."

"Please," he snorted, face twisting cruelly, "you said my shirtless state in the kitchen made you realize you were in love with me. What are you; sixteen!?"

"No I'm twenty-six, but then who's counting?" Crossing my arms, I held his gaze unblinkingly. "You had my heart when you took me to the benefit, but in the kitchen, I was dangerously close to jumping your seriously ancient undead bones." An eyebrow shot up. Maybe my maddened rage was making me hallucinate. But I could have sworn, for just a moment, I felt his eyes snuck a hungry glance over my tightly strung frame. "Now," I spoke confidently and his eyes narrowed. "I might want you like I want breath, but I'm not a little girl. If the wolf is no need to be had, the wolf can go to hell. I'm a professional woman. I can finish my job, despite what my heart or my hormones are screaming. So spare me the heroic rejection for my own good. I am old enough to know what I want. I don't need a sexy but morally screwed-up old vampire to give me a lesson in right and wrong. So if we're done humiliating me, I'd like to go home please." With that, I walked past him and up the metal stairs.

He followed. I could hear the soft footfalls of his bare feet.

Those damn chocolate brown toes had done it for me. Walking purposefully to the edge of the building, I stared down at the brightening street and sighed. It would be daylight soon. If we didn't leave soon, someone was liable to see a grown man hopping across the roofs.

Then something occurred to me.

Glancing down at my feet, I noticed they stood a few inches away from the edge, and the ten-floor drop. "I have a question."

"I don't have time."

"Just one."

There was an exasperated grunt. "Fine."

"If the wolf doesn't feel anything for the child, why is he trying to protect her from himself?"

"He's not; the child is delusional."

I turned rather gracefully, even for me. I met those unfaltering black eyes and squared my jaw. "So if I fell down this ledge, you wouldn't catch me."

Everything about him went still. Which is saying a lot considering the man can be a corpse when he wants to. "I would save anyone who'd be insane enough to fly without wings. I'm a good Samaritan."

I wanted to smile, but I had a feeling it would be sad for him. "Even if it meant exposing yourself to the world?"

This time I saw those black eyes surge. The vampire tilted his head mockingly. "In that case, happy landing."

And then to my horror, he turned and started walking away.

Maybe my heart broke. When with each painful heave of it in my chest, I watched him walk further away.

Maybe he didn't hear the hitch in my breath, or maybe he didn't care as I took that final step back.

Maybe it was deliberate. Maybe I'd forgotten where I was. Maybe I'd lost my mind.

But suddenly I was weightless.

And then flying.

I guess death was very simple. Everything was silent for the first few seconds, the wind tearing at my skin, laying me bare to my wants and desires. The mad longing; those few seconds I wondered if God remembered me. I wondered if I believed in Him. If He believed in me.

THUMP.

I watched my reflection in the window of the building, one hand lifting up as I passed the tenth floor. If I touched my reflection maybe I could save myself. Maybe I'd signed over my life to him when I'd agreed to stay.

THUMP.

My heartbeat was suddenly too loud, too intrusive as I passed the ninth floor.

The eighth-floor window said I was going to die.

THUMP. THUMP.

And then I realized that my heart wasn't beating like a wild bird in a cage.

I was holding my breath.

Head tipping back I realized it was the sound of bare feet hitting concrete. The dark blur dove off the ledge above me, spread-eagle, and then sharpened like a bullet.

Sixth floor.

The shuddering breath rang through my ears like a deafening wave in the ocean. A tsunami. Save me, it pleaded.

My eyes sliding shut, I swallowed and held my arms out to him in silent surrender.

I had barely passed the fourth floor when arms like bands of steel wrapped around my back, knees bending, forcing my legs around his waist.

And I clung to life. The fine earthy smell of him filled my senses, breathing life back into my veins and I took my first shuddering breath.

CRACK.

Hard, inhuman flesh collided against the asphalt.

The earth stood still.

As the early morning traffic in downtown Chicago came to a screaming, screeching halt, my savior held me tight and jumped back up into the air.

Smiling idiotically into his neck as the curses whispered furiously in my ear, I realized the headlines would change tomorrow.

He swung through my bedroom window.

Shielding me in the safety of his arms, he drove through the glass, cutting and skewering himself sadistically before tossing me on the bed. Scratch less.

Suddenly scared for him I opened my mouth to stop him, but he climbed back onto the shattered window frame, the fathomless black eyes deadly. "Pack your bags and get out," he grated out, his voice rough with barely contained rage and then he disappeared.

I wondered if it was worth having him belong to me if he didn't stay.

"You realize that this was not part of the deal."

It was late in the afternoon when I stood in front of my boss. Behind the old brown desk, he leaned back in his swivel chair, making it squeak in protest. Calculating blue eyes, glowered at me, even though his mouth was caught in a stiff little smile. "But exceptions can be made."

In other words, Jack had called him and demanded a favor.

"That's really sweet of you Mac," I spoke softly but clearly, "but entirely unnecessary." I held out the white unmarked envelope. "My formal resignation. You can adjust my annual leave to my notice period. I'm sure you won't have a problem with that."

For a moment, his hawk-like eyes watched me with interest, wondering if he could somehow use this to make money. When he realized I wasn't budging he took the white envelope and shrugged. "Goodbye."

I left everything behind.

Self-preservation had already kicked in.

The flying man would have to face the presses alone.

"Mac, there's a call for you on line two."

Grumbling around the cigarette in his mouth, he typed the last few words of the letter he'd use to extort money from the crooked senator. "Kill it, Cheryl, I'm busy!"

"It's Mr. Black, sir," she offered pointedly.

The steady beat of the keys on his keyboard stilled and Sean McKenzie blinked started at the intercom as if it was his secretary herself. "Jack?"

"Yes, sir."

Of course, who else could intimidate his icy secretary for interrupting him? Unwillingly, and with much delay, he picked up his extension. "Mac."

"I have the Memoirs you wanted."

Maybe this day wasn't a waste after all. Sitting up higher in his chair, the editor grinned widely. "That's my boy. Finished them yourself? I always did say you would have been better off writing it."

"I could never find the right words."

"And you can now?"

"Apparently."

"Insignificant! You've finally written the most accurate account of a vampire's life through all the major historical events. It'll be an instant hit! You'll be bigger than Dan Brown!"

"I don't want my name mentioned in the authorship."

The Editor of the Chicago Times blinked in surprise. "What? What the hell do you mean you don't want your name on it? Who the hell else could have written it?"

"I want it done under the name Emily Brown. "At the stunned silence, the philanthropist sighed. "It's my book. I choose who gets credit for it at CT."

Leaning back in his chair, Mac took a deep drag on his cigarette. "That's fine, Jackie boy. But you realize that you can't give credit to someone who isn't CT."

"What?"

"Miss Brown, no longer works here."

"You fired her!?" The voice thundered and Sean held it away from his ear with a wince.

"Relax bro. I said I wouldn't, didn't I? She quit."

"And you let her!?"

Rolling his eyes, he stubbed out his cigarette. "Come on Jackie, you know I don't have time to play nursemaid to B-grade writers."

"If she was a B-grade writer, why the hell did you send her to me?"

"Because I wanted to help the kid out," the bald-faced lie rolled off his silver tongue with a grin.

"Then help yourself out, Mac. If you don't find her in the next two hours, I'm going to turn you into a human straw."

At the potent threat, Sean sat up straighter and frowned. "You haven't killed anyone for more than a century."

"I can change my mind. Find her, Mac," the vampire warned, "or I will have to rethink my diet plan."

The line went dead and Sean McKenzie stared at the receiver.

Shit.

Adam watched the man pacing in the study. He'd seen his master drifting through his days, retreating back into himself. He felt guilty for resenting the chaos that the woman had brought with her. Because for those few weeks, her light had touched the darkness in the vampire's eyes, he'd seen the human. He'd never seen Jackson smile as much, or smirk as much when the woman dared to disagree with his historical notions. He'd never seen Jackson snarl and growl in frustrated anger, in helpless abandon. Emotions that he'd never allowed himself to feel. Not until little Miss Emily.

"Dammit, Adam!" The pacing man ran a weary hand over his smooth scalp, a nervous habit that he probably mimicked since the days he had hair. Adam's mouth twitched at the inward joke, but Jackson was shaking his head. "I never should have let her go. I never should have trusted that swine of a newspaperman to hold his end of the deal."

"I believe he said he didn't fire her."

"Of course, he didn't fire her. The moment Brown thought that it was a favor I called in, she ran."

"You should have left her alone when that was what you decided."

Spinning on his heel, Jackson glared at his assistant. "You're not really helping here Adam."

Used to the brooding sessions after the two hundred years he'd spent by this vampire's side, Adam tried not to roll his eyes. "What would you have me do Master Black?"

"Help me find her."

Picking up the keys from the table, Adam tossed the ones to the Bentley at Jackson. "Shall I take the south side?"

And the two men walked out looking for a needle in a roomful of haystacks.

"See the marketplace
In old Algiers
Send me photographs and souvenirs
Just remember
When a dream appears
You belong to me."

To outsiders, the Kasbah appears to be a confusing labyrinth of lanes and dead-end alleys flanked by picturesque houses; however if one loses oneself there, it is enough to go down again towards the sea to reposition oneself. It took me days with my nose in the map to be able to find my way through the serpentine walkways. As much as Haarlem insisted to accompany me, I had a feeling Algiers wouldn't really speak with me unless

I was alone.

It was there, standing in the Place des Martyrs gazing up at the monument, its eternal flame amidst the three palm leaves, when my story came to me. I could understand why Renoir had wanted to paint the Garden of test with its exotic plants it could make anyone want to create something. I started writing the first two chapters there. And then it was as easy as sin to go through the old city on my bicycle until I returned with legs aching and soul empty, poured onto my pages. Haarlem said I was drowning.

I wasn't sure if he was entirely wrong.

I was mostly too tired to argue and too preoccupied to wonder about the whys and hows of my escape to Algiers.

It was an escape. Because I knew that this was the last place Jackson would look for me – if he ever did.

"He is a stupid man."

Sighing I straightened from where I was scribbling in my notebook as we sat in the little café beside the busy street. In the darkening evening, I met the pale vampire's eyes irately. "What are you doing here Haarlem?"

"I came to see you dying."

With a roll of my eyes, I picked up my teacup and took a sip only to wince. My tea had long before gone cold. "Don't be so damned melodramatic."

"You might as well be dying My Dear. I've never seen such melancholy. So the idiot turned you out. It's not the end of the world."

I wished I could explain this to him. "Haarlem, I didn't come to you so you could psychoanalyze me."

"No," he crossed his arms and dropped into the small wicker chair. "You came to me so that I could hide you. But you cannot hide forever Emily."

I smiled faintly at the name. "Is it just wrong that my own name seems foreign to me?"

The cold hand touched mine and I flinched. Cold hands should all be the same. They should.

"Emily?"

Sliding my hand gently out from under his, I looked into the bustling streets as people went about their business, the call of the hawkers. "Stop saying my name. I know what you want to know."

"I already know."

Tired of his questions and innuendoes already I leaned back in my chair and frowned at him, my lip curling sullenly. "You said you didn't have a problem hiding me."

"Yes," he glared pointedly. "I said I would hide you, but only until you caught your bearing."

"Sick of me?"

He gasped as if I'd stabbed him and I instantly felt guilty.

With a wince, I leaned forward and palmed his hand. "I didn't mean that." Trying to find the right words, I took a deep breath. "I just haven't caught my bearing yet."

"And you will not. My Dear, do you know what it means to love a vampire?"

"Not you too."

His hand caught might firmly before I could pull away. "No Emily, he should have explained better. Instead of trying to scare you away, he should have explained what that would mean."

My blink of confusion was enough for him to sigh. "We will speak over some dinner." He motioned for the waiter and ordered sandwiches for the both of us. "And this time you will eat everything or I will not tell you."

My curiosity getting the better of me, I left the heartbreak in the little notebook for the moment.

I'd been living with it for weeks. It wouldn't matter if I listen to another vampire story for a few hours.

But the truth was, I was hungry for it, as always.

"If I know Zymen, and I do know him; he probably told you he wanted your blood."

"He said he would have to kill me."

Haarlem nodded his eyes cautiously on mine. "Yes. Eventually." When I didn't wretch or tremble in fear he sighed. "He is right about one thing though; you've no sense of self-preservation."

"Ask me if I feel the same way about you sucking me dry."

The mere curl of my lip was answering enough for him and he chuckled. "Uncanny. You must really love him."

"Can we please not relive my insanity?"

Noting the hysterical lilt in my voice he smiled reassuringly. "He is a fool. Not many of us find a mate." I was startled at the word. It seemed primal and medieval, but then I had a feeling the significance was of just such origin. He began with lackluster facts, not as apt at capturing my imagination as Jackson was, but he spoke simply. "For a vampire, it is unheard of to find a mate in a human, simply because no vampire has the power to resist temptation. The ones who aren't turned, are killed; sometimes without deliberation. If it is love, then mostly by accident."

"You mean if I stay human…"

"He will go mad with it and eventually eat you."

"But that's if he loves me as well and I think we've already established…"

"YOU have established, sweetheart" Haarlem glared. "Do you suppose he brings all his secretaries to Algiers?"

I bristled. "I am not his secretary!"

"Precisely. But you cannot be foolish enough to think that he hasn't had women in his life." I didn't particularly like the idea. The golden vampire chuckled at my distasteful expression. "Five hundred years is a long time and Zymen isn't exactly tough to look at."

"Jackson, if you don't mind."

"Whatever," he rolled his eyes at my preference. "My point being that he has had his choice of human morsels."

I glared at him. "You know if I was depressed before, this conversation is making me suicidal."

"He cares for you, Emily!" He exclaimed, frustrated. "I've never met his women."

"What about the blonde he wagered the Palace for?"

Haarlem rolled his eyes, exasperated. He wasn't used to my logic. "My Dear, I wagered it back to him for YOU!"

My mouth dropped open almost comically. "Haarlem!"

"The ruddy pirate wouldn't budge!" He waved a hand dismissing the train of thought. "What I mean is, that he's wanted his home back for centuries; do you really think he would have passed up the opportunity to reacquire it? For the price of a pretty human?"

"You bet on ME!?"

The blue eyes sparked with irritation. "Didn't I say he wouldn't agree?"

"And I thought you were my friend!" I rose to gather my things.

"Sit down you crazed dame!" He grabbed one of my shoulders firmly and smacked me back into the chair forcefully. "I swear I don't understand women at all sometimes and I have a new one in my bed every night."

Crossing my arms, I glowered at him. "Yeah, I know you do."

His mouth quirked. "You are missing the point, Belle."

"That's because you're not making any."

He sighed and held my gaze plainly. "He is mad about you. Hell, I could see it the moment you both walked into my home."

I frowned at his logic and what he was alluding to. "That makes no sense, he threw me out. In fact, every time he thought I was leaving, he stood gallantly out of the way so I could go."

"He wouldn't bother trying to protect you if he didn't."

"How is throwing me out protecting me!?"

"I can wager anything he's looking for you right now. And you know it."

"I know no such thing," I grunted and crossed my arms defensively as the waiter placed our food on the table.

"Really, My Dear? Then why would you need to hide?"

The French fry stopped in midair and I slowly raised my eyes to his smug smirk.

"You are hiding because you know he's looking for you and you want him to suffer for the heartache he's caused you. Personally, I think it's fitting. That bastard has had it easy for way too long."

My silence gave him more courage.

"You know he loves you and you want him to admit it. The woman in you would not have it any other way. You need him to say it. To say he desires you. That he loves you. That he would kill for you. Even if the life he was taking would be yours. Even if it would tear him to ribbons to do it, breaking every rule he's made for himself. You want him on his arrogant knees so that you can be sure. After five hundred years, you have to be the one woman he has to fight for because you know him well enough to know that's the only way you'll keep him." My blood caught fire, and he grinned at the sudden rush of breath through my nose. "Because you like the combination of vampire and man; neither alone will be enough for you, Emily."

Throwing the fry back onto the plate, I wrenched my bag off the floor and stuffed my notebook into it. Blinded with rage and guilt, I couldn't form the words to scream at him. My breath wouldn't calm enough to allow it.

I could hear the pounding footfalls, but I took off in a run. Harder and faster than I ever had.

"Stop running Emily!"

I wanted to tell him to drop dead. I wanted to tell him he was delusional.

But my throat closed around the words and my vision blurred. Hot scalding heat building there until I stepped off the curb.

"Emily, stop!"

I didn't hear the screeching tires until it was too late.

"You can't kill him, Master Black."

Sprawled in his favorite chair, he glared into the night beyond his window. "It's been three weeks Adam," he grated out between clenched teeth, his grip nearly shattering the wine glass in his hand. "The man can't find a girl in three weeks! He's completely useless!"

"But not worth breaking the rules for," Adam sighed at the tightly strung man. "Especially since you haven't had much luck either."

"She couldn't have vanished!"

It was painful to see him in the state he was in. Adam realized it would have been better had the woman never come at all. His master was worse off now than when she'd first come. "Master..."

"No." The hand lifted up in the darkness, quaking in its restraint. "Leave me right now Adam,"

"But Master..."

"I said LEAVE!" The vampire roared, ochre eyes unforgiving.

The assistant only sighed. "Cell phone."

It was then that Jack finally realized that the ringing in his ears wasn't because of the copious amounts of alcohol mixing with the blood but rather the little black cube trilling softly. It was only when he saw the flash of the name that he picked it up and flipped it open. "What's wrong?"

"Where are you?" Haarlem's voice was carefully apathetic.

"What's happened?" Something was wrong. Haarlem wouldn't bother calling long distance otherwise.

"Come home Zymen."

If Jackson's heart still beat, it would have stopped. "Tell me."

His friend was silent for a moment. "It's Emily. There's been an accident. She's been hurt."

Adam darted forward to grab the falling goblet of blood before it hit the floor. His Master's eyes slammed shut as if something had physically struck him. Hard.

On shaky legs, he rose. Jackson was torn between screaming in fury that Emily had been in Algiers without his knowledge and nearly mute with the notion of her being hurt. "What do you mean she'd been hurt?"

Adam stilled at the shuttered question.

Haarlem sighed. "She's in the City hospital. There was a car. She looked okay, but I'm waiting to hear from the doctors. You should come."

"Keys." The phone rattled onto the table as the vampire strode to his desk to fish out his passport and wallet. "Where are my keys?"

Adam picked up the fallen phone. "Master Haarlem?"

"Adam, don't let him drive."

"I won't." Hanging up, Adam helped gather the essentials before he called ahead to the airport to prep the jet.

For a man who said eternity was overrated, the trip was endless. He didn't speak. He didn't bother.

There was nothing to be said.

He'd thrown her out and she'd gone to his home. He should have guessed it. He should have known how much she had liked it there. Maybe he'd foolishly thought there was nothing between her and Haarlem.

The thought cut into his heart. It was ironic that he should feel its presence now.

When he'd wanted her to be away from him, he should have specified that it applied to all vampires, but as always Miss Emily Brown made her own rules. He wanted to hate her for her betrayal. Maybe she didn't love him, but the idea of him. But he knew it was unlikely.

Emily Brown had been in love with him. Exactly, as he'd seen the evidence, in their picture from the benefit. It had caught her without pretense and her tough girl shell. He hadn't believed her until he'd seen the picture his PR office had faxed to him. He never should have taken her to the press. It had spiraled out of his control from there. It had come apart at the seams when she'd taken the step off the ledge. He knew that she wouldn't stop as long as he stayed.

A muscle worked in his jaw.

He'd been all kinds of fool with her.

And now she was hurt. Maybe dying.

When he stepped into the hospital, finding Haarlem was easy enough. Keeping from tearing his head off was another issue altogether.

The blonde vampire reared back as the fist connected with his jaw. With a grunt, he held his aching jaw while he held one hand up before another blow came for him. "She's alive!" He watched the nearly fully morphed vampire and smiled weakly at the nurse that stared in horror. "Distraught husband."

Upon realizing that his audience was about to have a heart attack and consoled that Haarlem said she was fine, he calmed. "Where is she?"

Moaning at the bruise that was slowly forming there, Haarlem pointed to the door behind him. "They gave her sedatives, she'd hardly coherent, but she's awake for now."

Jackson didn't stick around to see him eye the nurse pathetically before he was happily tended to. But all he could see was Emily. She was white against the white of the hospital bed.

He wanted to go back and throttle Haarlem. She didn't look fine to him. She smelled sterile; her heart was slower than he would have liked; her skin pale, her lips dry. Gone was the rosy hue of her creamy complexion. Gone were the rich highlights in her hair that now hung limply over one shoulder. Gone was the woman who laughed and fought him at every turn.

Almost as if she could feel his eyes, her head turned and he met the startling hazel of her eyes. She squinted at him lethargically. "Jackson?"

Swallowing the need to hit something, he walked to her side and touched her hand, the only part of her that hadn't begun to bruise. The left cheekbone was already yellowing, a bandage secured around her forehead where he could smell the blood that had begun to dry. Under the ugly hospital gown were more bandages and even more bruises, even though he couldn't see them. He knew exactly where she was bleeding. And as much as the sight of her cut into his soul, the smell of her fresh blood shot his nerves to hell.

For a moment he didn't say anything, just squeezed her hand gently, more for his own reassurance, than hers. "I'm here."

Her tongue darted out to lick her dry lips and she swallowed thickly. "I'm sorry."

He held the dry laugh. It was his fault she was here and she was asking for his forgiveness. "What grave sin have you committed now?"

Her mouth tilted up at the corners. "Tell me what time it is and I'll count."

He couldn't help but smile at the quirk. "You know there are other ways to give me a heart attack. You didn't have to almost kill yourself."

"Showing up naked?"

"That's one." He chuckled low under his breath, pulling his hand and stuffing it in his pocket before she realized how badly it was shaking. "You're making jokes, so I'm assuming there's no permanent damage."

"Why don't you make sure?" She offered him a heartbreakingly hopeful smile and Jack had to physically restrain himself from gathering her in his arms. He didn't trust himself to hold her. Not because she was bleeding. He was afraid he'd hold her too tightly. He was afraid he wouldn't be able to let go.

"You're in no shape to hold up your end of this offer."

She grimaced in what he hoped was disappointment but he could see the pain etched in every hitch of her heartbeat. "I told him not to call you until the doctors' confirmed something."

"I would have come anyway."

Her eyes seemed to brighten at that. "I know you would have," she whispered weakly, eyes sliding shut.

"I was worried." It was a grossly understated fact. "I couldn't...I wasn't..." He struggled with his words.

"My usually eloquent vampire suddenly at a loss for words?"

He shuddered visibly at her possessive pronoun. Allowing himself to palpably express his struggle while her eyes were shut, a soft drug-induced smile on her parched lips. He wondered if she would even remember this conversation. "I'm trying to wrap my head around the idea of you being hurt. It is...unthinkable," he admitted softly.

"Nothing's broken," she provided helpfully, cracking one eye open. "No permanent damage like you said."

Maybe he flinched. Maybe he blinked. It didn't matter, her eyes opened slowly and her breath hitched for an instant. "I see. How permanent?"

Black eyes darting away, he shrugged noncommittally.

He never wanted her anywhere near a hospital with angry purple bruises marrying her perfect skin in the paper-thin ugly gown. He didn't want her hurt in any way. And now he would always remember that she could bruise. That there was a possibility she could die. It was easier, knowing she was somewhere living her life. Easier than living with the prospect of her death.

It infuriated him that the picture of her pale sickly form would stay with him for eternity. It would plague him as no memory had plagued him.

"Jack?"

He couldn't contain the growl. "Damn, you Brown. Why couldn't you have waited?"

Her lips tipped up at the corners. "I did. Just wasn't counting on this." Her eyes slid sideways to the glass of water and he lifted it to her lips. He didn't miss that she couldn't drink much. "Now tell me."

"How would you like it?" He whispered gently, hand sliding over her brow.

"Between the eyes, thank you."

He sighed. "Always Brave."

"Stop hedging," her request morphed into a moan as the ECG gave a lurch. His hand fastened on hers tightly, her eyes opening despite the pain he could see in them. "Never mind," she winced as he helped her settle. "Just tell me you love me and I'll go in peace."

He couldn't shake the bone-deep terror he'd felt when he'd received the call in his office. Staring down at her, he grabbed her shoulders carefully but firmly. "Have you lost your mind, Brown?"

"I love you; I must have." She chuckled through the painful tremors that coursed through her body.

"Damn you, Emily! You're not going to die."

When the wave of pain subsided for a moment she fell back against the mattress with gasping breath. "Oh. Could have fooled me." With a groan, her hazy brown eyes opened into his. "Better ideas?"

"None you would like."

"Try me."

"I don't even know if it is much better than dying."

She seemed to darken in color. Almost sad now. "Jack, let it go." Her eyes slid shut with a sigh. "Just stay with me for now." She lifted a trembling hand to him.

"No." Taking a step back, he let out an upset breath through his nose and she saw the painful indecision on his beautiful face. "Of all the times I thought to give you eternity, this isn't what I had in mind."

Her hand dropped back to the bed and she went still, her chest heaving with each beep of the machine. "Was that a proposal?"

With a snarl, the vampire morphed, his fangs elongating, the bones in his face rippling in his frustration. "Don't romanticize it, Brown! Do you even realize what this would mean?"

I knew what he had to do to save me.

Fate's twisted hand had brought us to this crossroads deliberately.

Pledging my heart to him had meant that one day he would have to kill me. He would have to kill me to keep me. And I was all kinds of twisted that I wasn't afraid of dying, I was afraid for him. He would have to break his vows.

The vampire had been brought to his arrogant knees.

Haarlem's words haunted me. They would haunt me every waking breath and even in sleep.

With my insides burning, and my senses swimming with painkillers, I took a steadying breath before speaking.

"Haarlem was right. I needed you to come find me. I needed to see that you'd go through the trouble for me. That you'd want me enough to break your damn rules." His eyes darkened but I plunged on. "He was right about it all. But you're here, Jack. That's enough for me."

"Well, it is NOT enough for me!" He thundered.

"Sir, I'm afraid I will have to ask you to leave."

Whipping around, the vampire snarled viciously at the nurse, sending her screeching out of the room.

With a moan, I tried to sit up. "Oh god, stop! This is insane!"

And then he was beside me in a single stride.

"You should have cried."

Unsure if I hear him correctly, I gaped up at him. "What?"

Eyes burning, he leaned down, nose nearly level with mine. "If you had, I would have stayed."

"You wanted me to cry!?" I stared at him incredulously.

"No." Then he frowned. "Maybe. Belle cries at the end of the movie."

Mouth still agape, I couldn't help bristling at his illogical complaint. "Because the Beast turns into a real boy!"

With a derisive snort, he walked to the hospital room door and bolted it. "You're mixing your fairytales, Brown." I stare with grotesque fascination as he shrugged out of his wrinkled designer jacket and rolled up the sleeve of one arm. "But you're right about one thing. I do love you." My breath left me in a shuttered gasp. Knowing it deep down and hearing the words were two very different things. "If you'd cried on my shoulder that night and begged me rather than go jumping off buildings, I would have stayed. But you're a smart woman, Brown. If I had stayed then, I would have blamed you for trapping me." His eyes cut through me like steel, breaking past all inhibitions, all pretenses.

The genuine fear heightened the beeping of the machine, but he didn't stop as he climbed up on the narrow bed, straddling my limp body. "The thought didn't even cross my mind," I whispered, eyes memorizing each detail of his face. Such a nice old face.

"I know, Brown; which is what makes it all the more tragic." He hissed against my mouth and my eyes slid shut. "I cannot blame anyone for where we are today besides myself. Clever witch."

He leaned in and for a moment I thought he was going to kiss me. I froze, choking as my heart beat franticly against my ribcage in a bid for freedom. As if it could sense what was to come. Instead, he tilted his head at the last instant, bringing his mouth close enough to my cheek so that I could feel his lips there. I felt a slight wet flick of warmth as he just barely pushed his tongue past his lips and touched my cheek with it and I lost my breath.

He tasted my tears, I realized with a jolt. Tears I didn't even know I'd shed. He tasted the evidence of my feelings for him. It was not a human gesture, but it was alarmingly intimate. I felt bare all of a sudden and then my heart went very still as if it was being stroked in a fashion it liked.

And like the time I was falling down the ten-floor building, I trembled. "Save me." My eyes squeezed tight and I couldn't suppress the shiver.

He trailed his mouth down, lingering at my jawline. The fangs harmlessly scraped against the skin there and like a silent answer my head tilted and I bared my throat. "Jackson…"

He made a soft, anxious sound, pressed his lips to the screaming pulse, licking there as if he could taste it and then sank the fangs into my jugular.

EPILOGUE

"You are the most aggravating, spoiled, contemptible man I have ever met."

Lounging in his favorite chair, the man in question took a casual sip from his crystal goblet and smirked. "That's exactly what the Russians said."

Hands on my hips, I growled low in my chest, hating him for the knots he'd effectively tied me in. Again. "The Czar was celebrating victories in battle while the people rose up in revolt. That's like children dying in the war and the president having a party!"

Licking his fangs the vampire wrapped one hand around my wrist and dragged me into his lap easily. "No Em. That was Iraq."

"Sneaky bastard," I hissed, feeling his hand – his soft, warm hand – slide under my blouse to rest against the skin of my lower back and pull me flush against him.

"Hmm," was his only response. His breath was hot against my lips. I could feel myself begin to tremble as they brushed lightly over mine, like a feather. He rubbed his nose against mine and made a strange sort of purring sound and trailing light kisses along my jaw. "Nothing changes, My Dear Emily," he said, moving his mouth against my ear and my bones turned to mercury. "Not war. It's only the weapons that change."

Tilting my head back to his ministrations I sighed in happy defeat. "I should break something over your egotistical head, My Dear Jack."

"I'm still recovering from that last concussion you gave me," he chuckled against my throat and I shivered. "I've heard if you fall asleep with a concussion you never wake up."

"One can only hope."

Black eyes glinting with mischief, he nuzzled his nose against mine. "You're too kind, Emily My Love. Now please be quiet so I can kiss you."

"Brown," I murmured huskily against his mouth, nails teasing against the nape of his neck. "Call me, Brown."

"Shut up, Brown."

With a sad sigh, Adam rolled the tea trolley back out of the study as I shrieked with helpless laughter.

THE END

ABOUT THE AUTHOR
(In my husband, Javed Lodhi's words, because, come on!
Who better to say nice things about me?)

A technologist by profession, Fatima is a gifted writer. Besides 'The Ink Weave,' she has authored numerous other novels and short stories. All of which we are pushing her to publish.

She is a regular and popular writer of countless fan-fiction. She also contributes to 'Letters of the Editor' in local newspapers with her biting wit and humorous critique of social injustice. Apart from being a writer, she is a quirky, loving mother, a natural artist, a singer and an entrepreneur.

She has proven herself in more ways than she knows.

Find her work at:

https://fatimanatasha.wixsite.com/authorartist

www.ingramcontent.com/pod-product-compliance
Lightning Source LLC
Chambersburg PA
CBHW061231170626
46809CB00007B/2628